CONTINUUM

By

Mary Marshall

To find other book titles by this author or to find out more about the
author go to www.TheParanormalMD.com

Dedication

This book is dedicated with love to Alexandra and Vivian. Both of you are a constant source of happiness and inspiration to me. I am very thankful for you being part of my life.

Acknowledgment

I'd like to give thanks to those who helped me execute this book. I appreciate those who have in some capacity helped with editing and graphics. This book would not have seen the light of day if not for their help. Pam Hermon, Frank Heiberger, Stephan Szabo, and Karen Madsen, thank you for your work in helping with the copyediting and other suggestions. Thank you Jay Bachochin of ChumBuckets Studios for listening, seeing my vision, and creating this book cover.

Also a big thank you to all those who not only believed in me and this book, but supported and encouraged me through the years to keep writing.

Preface

Between my love of theoretical science, quantum physics in particular, and my fascination with the human condition, this time travel story came to be.

As an educator who teaches paranormal studies courses at various colleges and institutions, I deal directly with the investigation and research of the paranormal, including: ghosts, ufology, and cryptozoology. I educate others on what I've learned, the possibilities, and facts. The scientific notion of time travel, wormholes, portals, and other dimensions speaks to me.

The human mind and condition is a source of fascination to me. I have often wondered how people of a certain age get to be the way they are. What happened to them and what occurred in their lives that formed them into the very being they have become?

Continuum sets out to address all these aspects and more through this revealing and entertaining story. I hope you will enjoy reading *Continuum*.

CHAPTER ONE

"Thank God It's Friday. It's 7:20 a.m. at an already warm temperature of 73 degrees," the announcer declared, his voice blaring from the car radio. "The high temperature today is expected to reach 100 degrees. Looks like it's going to be another record breaker for 1992. That's all for now. I'll be reporting again at 8:00. Have a nice morning."

"Thanks, Jack," The DJ returned. "Now, let's start the day with an oldie but a goody." Just as he finished his sentence, the song, *We Are the World*, began. Kate reached over and turned off the radio.

"Look at this traffic." Kate mumbled to herself in dismay. She found herself once again trapped in the morning rush of traffic on Lake Shore Drive. I've got to find an alternate route to get downtown to work. She grasped the steering wheeling tightly trying to hold in her frustration. The heat built up inside the car and Kate began to perspire. "I hate this car! Something is always breaking down. This time it's the stupid air conditioner."

Chicago in August is not where Kate wanted to be. It was hot and uncomfortable, with an unappealing locker room odor. The beaches are overcrowded with its visitors leaving behind trash to scatter in the wind aimlessly. Although the cool lake breeze was always welcomed by the beachgoers, the water is often dirty and fishy smelling.

Kate tried to temporarily escape the moment and began to daydream. Instead of pleasant thoughts, her mind drifted to subjects more disheartening. Her two-year marriage which ended in divorce came to mind first. She thought Jeremy Taylor, a handsome lawyer, was the perfect mate for her, until Jeremy decided another woman was better suited for him.

A busty brunette with eyes like a cat – or was that claws, Kate thought. My marriage to him, and his affair with her was a hard lesson to learn; but one I learned well. Bitch! Bastard! Oh, well, live and learn, and never, ever, forget.

Then there was Daniel Wolski. Their relationship had been an on again, off again, sort of relationship. One that they had recently and completely, ended.

Daniel was an attractive man, always keeping his appearance neat. One of the things that Kate admired about him, besides his good looks, which included a dimpled chin, was his humor. Daniel's wit and sometimes offbeat view of the world and himself was irresistible. What he lacked in finesse, he made up with charm. His golden blonde hair and blue eyes were matched by those of Kate, with his skin color even more fair than hers.

Their involvement with each other was more of a comfortable friendship than a romantic love affair. The sex was good, but the relationship as a whole lacked substance and passion. They parted from each other on good terms, each accepting the fact they were not meant to be with each other. Harboring no ill feelings, they both went their separate ways.

BEEP! The car horn startled Kate. She turned and yelled, "Hey, shove it! Where the hell do you expect me to go? There are five thousand cars bumper to bumper in front of me, jerk!"

Glancing at her wrist watch, she felt she was becoming nauseated, which she thought was from the heat and all of the exhaust fumes from the cars in traffic. Realizing the time, she became more upset. She knew she would never make it to work by 8 o'clock and would be late, which seemed to be happening more often lately.

The downtown office building at which she worked stood sixty-five stories high. The building's interior was as unimpressive as the exterior, and the mortar and yellow brick had been crumbling for years. The white and gray walls inside lacked a good painting, and were worn and drab, as was the general appearance of the interior.

Walking in a hurry, she was pleasantly surprised to see Joe holding the elevator doors open for her.

"Hi, Joe! Can you push number 16 for me, please? Looks like they still have you cleaning up this dump, huh?"

"Yeah, well, not too much longer 'til I can retire."

"Probably doesn't seem soon enough, does it?"

"To tell the truth, some days, no, it don't."

Joe was the type of person who worked hard his whole life, without really complaining. He always had a kind word for others and was always there when you needed him. Kate thought how terrible it is that these types of people are usually those we give the least recognition to, barely exchanging words with them as we hurry on our way to matters that seem more important at the time.

"Take it easy, Joe," Kate said over her shoulder as she stepped off the elevator.

"Where have you been Kate Taylor? You're twenty minutes late! Mr. Frank has been asking to see you. I've tried to stall him, but I think he knows you weren't really here. You better get your tail in his office right now, otherwise you're going to be in serious trouble."

"Spare me the dramatics, okay? And thanks for trying to cover for me."

Kate dreaded her meetings with Mr. Frank, an overzealous high-strung sort of man.

"Kate, we have problems, big problems," he ranted as he paced the gray carpeted floor. "We've lost hundreds of thousands of dollars in profit sharing and pension funds. The records are all screwed up. As trust administrator, you have the responsibility of overseeing the people who handle those accounts. In other words, your accounts," he said with his voice raising.

3

Getting lost in thoughts as he spoke them, Mr. Frank began picking lint off of a couple of anti-acid tablets he had pulled out of his pocket.

Mr. Frank's clothing always appeared slightly disheveled. He wore the same three outdated polyester suits week after week. His incessant habit of rubbing his hands together annoyed Kate to no end.

"Alright, alright! I'll take care of it. We had something similar to this happen about four years ago due to a glitch in the computer system. Just keep—"

"—Well, if I recall. . . , " Mr. Frank interrupted.

Oh, no! Kate thought as she slumped down into a black leather chair. When he begins with, "Well, if I recall...," I'm in for a ten minute story. Pretending to listen, she let her mind drift.

Mr. Frank's wife had recently had an interior designer decorate his office at her husband's expense. The walls were a trendy mauve and on the walls, joined at the ceiling flowery wallpaper bordered. Only one picture, a print with its obscure design and colors, hung on the wall directly behind his desk.

As Mr. Frank continued to babble on, Kate stopped herself from glancing around the room. Although disinterested, she didn't want to be rude, and she tried to look attentive. She knitted her eyebrows together, slightly squinting her blue eyes to in a thoughtful and interested manner despite allowing her thoughts to wander.

I wonder if Sarah and Jim would let me retreat at their cabin in Wooster Lake. I can use the two weeks of vacation time I have coming. Then I can get out and away from this lousy rat race, Kate thought.

Being unhappy had become a way of life for Kate. Nothing seemed to matter to her any longer. She was completely uninterested and frustrated with her work. Her personal life wasn't any more satisfying. Already married and divorced once, she longed to have a man in her life that would always be there for her. Someone unlike her first husband whom she could never rely on. She wanted romance, and love, and children of her own someday.

Kate thought how wonderful that would—

"Don't you agree Kate?" Mr. Frank asked, abruptly interrupting her daydreaming.

"Well, Mr. Frank, I don't want to be impertinent in my response to you, but I really should get back to work now if you want me to address and resolve the problems at hand," she stated, hoping she wouldn't have to answer a question that she hadn't heard.

"Of course, you're right, of course. Yes, get right to it and fix those accounts, the computers, your staff, whatever the hell the problems are." Kate heard him say as she hurriedly left his office.

Kate didn't have a private office of her own. She shared one large office room with many employees. Most of the others were seated behind desks much like her own. Thin opaque plastic partitions that were situated around their desks served as walls, seeming to encase them in miniature cubicles.

Upon reaching her desk, Kate sat down in her chair and slipped off her white, two and half inch heeled shoes. Shoving her shoe to the side with her foot, Kate reached over to pick up her phone that was ringing.

"Is Kate Taylor in?" the woman on the phone questioned.

"Hi, Mom. What's wrong? Why are you calling me at work?"

"Nothing really, it's just . . .," Her 62 year old Mother, Leala, couldn't finish her sentence as she began to weep quietly.

"Oh, Mom! We've been through this before," Kate responded empathetically, her voice softening to console her Mother. "You know that selling the house is the best thing to do. Ever since

Daddy died, it's been almost impossible for you, with all your health problems, to keep up with all the work that house requires. The grass mowing, snow shoveling, not to mention all the repairs that old place needs to have done. It's falling apart, and neither you, nor me, have the knowledge or money to fix it."

"I know. I know. I just have so many memories and emotional attachments to this old house," Leala said with a whimper.

"I do, too, but you know Dad wouldn't want either of us to struggle over the maintenance and care of the house. Besides, your sister, Aunt Vera, has been asking you for a year to come and live with her. She has plenty of room, and her son, John, maintains the place nicely for her. He's always over there fixing something. Living there, you wouldn't have to worry about the things you do now, like the roof leaking, or the storm windows missing, or the water heater needing to be replaced."

"Your Aunt Vera is a pain in the ass," she retorted with irritation in her voice.

"Mom!" Kate was shocked by her Mother's choice of words.

"Well, for twenty years she wanted nothing to do with me or your Father. We would call her repeatedly with little or no response from her. You don't remember – as a matter of fact, you weren't even born yet – but there are terrible things she did. After my brother Terrance died in that accident, she didn't even come to his funeral. My Mother was so devastated by his death and Vera's actions. Not only had my Mother lost a son, but her own daughter didn't even acknowledge her own Mother's grief or her brother's death.

"Maybe she couldn't cope with her own grief and was unable to deal with the whole situation."

"Hogwash! She was just too busy with her own life and preoccupations. Did you know that your Father and I paid for all of the funeral expenses, too?"

6

"Mom, wasn't Vera's husband in Korea at the time?"

"Yes, so what?"

"Maybe she feared Uncle Al's death and was worried that he would not return home, and that affected her reaction to Terrance's death."

"Even if that were true, where was she six months later when her Mother became ill? I was left to care for our Mother. Your Father and I had very little money then, and the hospital bills were expensive. Did she offer one cent to help pay for those bills?"

"Mom, that was years ago, people change. I realize that was a difficult time for you and she wasn't there to help. Whatever her reasons were then, good or bad, she is there for you now. In the past fifteen years, since her husband died, she has more than proven her love and concern for you and the family. She has been loyal and caring. I don't know what she was like, or what made her change, but she has, and that's all that should matter. Now, she wants you to come and live with her so that you two can become even closer as sisters."

"Probably because she knows what a rat she was and wants to make amends with her conscious before it's too late. Me living with her would just ease her conscious, wouldn't it? It's just a gesture of . . ."

"Hey, now you're being unfair and sarcastic. It's entirely possible her intentions are honorable."

"You're right. I'm just being – I love her. She sometimes just gets on my nerves and rubs me the wrong way."

"And maybe you're just looking for an excuse not to move."

"You think you're pretty smart, don't you?" she questioned in jest with a smile on her face, knowing her daughter was probably right on the mark.

CHAPTER TWO

An entire workweek had passed and again it was Friday. On this particular Friday, the time seemed to move swiftly. Kate's anticipation of leaving the next morning on vacation preoccupied her mind most of the day. Her clothes were packed for her trip and she studied the map to find the route she had to take to get to the cabin.

Sitting at her desk, she watched the clock across the room on the wall, waiting for the workday to end. Making mental notes on any last minute preparation she may have overlooked previously, she tried to wait patiently and worked very little.

Kate told no one, except, of course, Jim and Sara, where she was vacationing. The "escape" made her feel more comfortable for reasons she couldn't explain.

Kate sat almost idly for the last ten minutes of her work day. When 4:30 arrived, she quickly gathered her belongings and left for home, not even bidding a goodbye or farewell to others in the office.

Getting in her car, Kate headed for Lake Shore Drive. The traffic was bumper to bumper, as was usual for the time of the day. She lazily sat back in the driver's seat and turned on the car radio to listen to the day's news. She switched channels several times. Most of the news stations were reporting about the possibility of a new treatment and cure for AIDS, an outbreak of polio in the southern states, and terrorist attacks upon American citizens. Finally, she decided she didn't really want to hear the news at all and turned on an all-music station.

An hour and forty-five minutes passed before she reached home. Perspiring from the hot temperature, Kate peeled her clothes off her body as soon as she got inside of her apartment.

She felt it urgent that she take a shower and wash her hair. Stepping in the shower, she turned on the water. She relished in the clean, tingling sensation the spraying water gave to her skin and body. Turning the showerhead, she adjusted its control to massage.

The warm water beat down from the showerhead upon her perspiring body. Letting her head drop forward, she placed her neck and shoulders in the path of the jetting water. She allowed it to pulsate against her, soothing her tense and aching muscles. Soon her muscles began to release the tensions of the day.

Rrring...Rinng.

By the time she had gotten to the phone, it had stopped ringing. "God, I hate when that happens!" she exclaimed. Thinking to herself, she began to recall how many times before now that she had ran for the phone, and then, when she picked up the receiver, no one was on the other end. Well, at least I've got an answering machine now. If someone had something really important to say or wants me to call them, they can leave a message on the recorder.

She tippy-toed her way back to the bathroom to properly dry off. She saw all the little puddles of water she had made on the floor and grunted, "Look at the mess I've made!"

After she dried off and dressed, she wiped the floor dry. While she started to make something for dinner, she listened to the messages left on the answering machine: "Hi, this is your cousin Sue. I just wanted to find out if you're coming to Nancy's baby shower? You never responded, like I asked on the bottom of your invite. I need to know how many people I need to – beeeep." The machine had cut off the rest of the message.

"...This is Sara. Hello, I'm not home right now (laugh). I'm calling to wish you well on your trip tomorrow. See you when you get back. Beep, beep, beep."

Kate smiled at the message left by Sara and intentionally ignored the message left by Sue.

Sue was a first cousin on her Father's side of the family. She rarely ever spoke to Sue or her sister Nancy, except on occasions like a wedding or a funeral. Years ago, her Mother had a huge, irreconcilable argument with their Mother, Jeanette. Kate never knew what it was about, but her Mother and Jeanette stopped speaking with each other. Since that time, the family's relationship has been distant and strained. Kate personally has no qualms with her Aunt Jeanette, but has always disliked her daughters. Indifferent to the estranged relationship the two families had, Kate, long ago, decided to have as little to do with them as possible.

Kate turned on the TV to watch one of her favorite shows while she ate. Although St. Elsewhere, a medical show, was first televised ten years earlier, she could now watch it in reruns. After she finished, she readied herself for bed, intentionally setting the alarm clock an hour later than usual.

Lying in bed she felt the need to pray, a thought that was usually a distant one. In the past few years Kate had lost any connection with God she once had. She kept telling herself that she ought to pray more, or go to church, or read the Bible, but she never did. Something else always seemed to be more important. She knew she believed in God, but she had serious doubts. She knew that God was there, and someday, she would have to confront Him.

Our Father, who art in heaven, she began to recite in her mind. Becoming increasingly weary, she fell into a sleep halfway through the prayer, as she had many times before. Her thoughts drifted into a dream-like state.

The next morning arrived, designated by the sun shining low in the east of the sky. Kate was awakened by the blaring buzzing coming from her alarm clock. Startled, she jumped out of bed and shut it off. Still drowsy, she climbed back into bed. She lay in bed a while longer, even though she was awake. Stretching her limbs, she began to slowly bring life to her body, allowing a small groan to escape from her lips.

After she had finished her morning coffee, she became nauseated. Soon she found herself vomiting in the washroom with her head over the toilet bowl.

Not today she thought. I can't handle this.

Considering she hadn't eaten anything since the night before, it didn't take long to empty her stomach. Although she had stopped vomiting, she continued to feel sick to her stomach. She swallowed a couple doses of Pepto-Bismol and rested on the couch for about half an hour.

Her rest was interrupted by a phone call.

"Hi, Mom, what's up?"

"I know you're going on vacation today, but I wanted to tell you that I've decided to sell the house and move."

"Really? What made you decide? I thought you were so against it." The tone of her voice became high pitched and louder.

"Well, I just weighed the pros and the cons of my situation and decided it would be better to sell and move."

"I'm really glad to hear this. I think you're doing the right thing, but why right now? I mean, you are going to have to deal with real estate people and movers, and all. You knew I would be going out of town and wouldn't be here."

"Kate, you're only going for two weeks. What do you think is going to happen while you're gone? Besides, I'm not an idiot! I am capable of taking care of myself and tending to some tasks without you," her Mother answered with sarcasm in her voice.

"Yes, I know that. Don't get defensive on me now. It's just you know you sometimes get confused about matters. I don't want anybody taking advantage of you," Kate pleaded to her Mother's sensibility and understanding.

"What is that supposed to mean? You think I'm an incapable, senile, old lady, don't you?" she responded with anger.

"Mom...," Kate dragged out her name, feeling frustrated and dismayed. "You know I don't think you're incompetent. I didn't

11

mean that the way it sounded. I love you and I worry about you. I'm sorry if I hurt your feelings."

Momentary silence reigned between them on the phone. Finally, Leala broke the silence. "I love you too, and I know you love me. I'll wait until you return home before I do anything about the house. It would be nice to have you here to help make the decisions." Her anger had given way to a calmer judgment of the situation. "Not to change the subject, but you still haven't told me where you are going."

"I know I haven't, and I don't intend to either. Remember, I told you I wanted to keep it a secret."

"That's stupid and irresponsible. What if you get in an accident or something? Who's going to even know if you're dead?"

"First of all, someone does know where I'm going to be. So, if something happens to me, I promise you'll be the first one to know it. Second of all, I just feel better for some unexplainable reason, not telling anyone. It's sort of like escaping from reality for awhile, hiding out."

"Hiding out! From what? From who? I'll tell you one thing Kate, it's a sad day when a girl can't even tell her Mother where she's vacationing."

"Don't try and make me feel guilty, it won't work. I've got to get going now, Mom. I'll talk to you when I get back, I love you and don't forget that."

"I love you too, you independent, bullheaded daughter of mine," she said affectionately. "You just be careful and watch out for yourself. I worry about you when you go away. You're driving aren't you?" she questioned with anxiety.

"Yes, I'm driving."

"Okay, I know you want to get going. I'll see you soon."

"I love you! See you later. Bye," Kate reassured her Mother in a pacifying tone of voice.

Kate and her Mother had a loving, but difficult relationship. Her Mother had a bad habit of complaining and worrying about everything, especially about matters in which Kate was involved. Kate had always been a worrier, too, even though she hated to admit it. She had also become cynical and pessimistic through the years. Slightly rebellious since birth, her nature was to be a loner, yet a very loving, compassionate person. Kate's Mother seemed to know how to bring out the best and worst in Kate. Kate seemed to have the same effect on her Mother. It had not always been like this, it had just intensified when Kate became an adult.

Kate hung up the phone, sat back, and thought for a little while.

"Katie," she recalled her Mother saying to her, "I always want you to remember this...Whenever you're away from me, wherever you might go in your lifetime, I will somehow, someway be there for you." This memory was a pleasant one to take with her as Kate left the house to start her trip.

CHAPTER THREE

Kate arrived at the cabin safely, as the trip had been uneventful. Finding the cabin among the trees had proven to be more difficult than she had anticipated. The cabin was set farther back into the woods than she had thought it would be. After turning off of a paved, main highway, she had to drive on a poorly cleared dirt road. Although the cabin was only a couple minutes from the highway, the area beyond was quiet and rustic.

Upon reaching the cabin, she brought her belongings into the house and took a look around the outside of the cabin. Beautiful maple trees surrounded the immediate area. Just beyond them towered some oak trees. Nestled next to them stood a couple of fir trees and evergreens flourished all around. She saw that some rabbits had made a home nearby and she got pleasure from the idea of seeing them at a closer range. Various types of birds were flying above her in the sky, but she was not familiar with the names of their species. Feeling confident that she would become better acquainted with everything later, she went inside the cabin to get cleaned up.

She had stopped at a grocery store and bought some food before she had arrived at the cabin. Kate had also brought some food and other supplies from home with her, deciding it would be best to clear out her refrigerator at home before she left for vacation.

The cabin was modest, but had most of the conveniences of home. She stocked the shelves and the refrigerator with food. The house was completed with indoor plumbing, shower, tub and toilet. The kitchen sink was equipped with a garbage disposal and water purifying system. After completing a few tasks, she moved into the living room to relax.

The living room, along with the rest of the cabin, had a musty odor, like most seasonal cabins do. Kate was pleasantly surprised to see a window air conditioner in one of the front windows. Hoping that there would be an air conditioner in the bedroom, she went to take a look. Fortunately, there was one in there also.

Well, it looks as though I'm prepared for any hot day that may be in store for me. This place is a great getaway. I was a little concerned that this place might be too rustic or austere for me. I'm glad to see that my concerns weren't valid. Although, I do wish there was a television. I suppose that's okay, I shouldn't be viewing one anyway. I'm on a country retreat, a getaway. I'll have to suffer, and just listen to the radio.

Kate fixed a quick lunch, a sandwich and chips. She ate slowly as she sat on the front porch enjoying the view. When she had finished, she looked at her watch to see what time it was. To her dismay, less than an hour had passed. She thought that much more time had gone by than actually did. She began to wonder if time was going to continue to move as slowly for the rest of her trip. Boredom had already begun to set in.

With much time on her hands, she let her mind drift from one thought to another. Soon, most of her thoughts were self-centered. Slowly, she became consumed with thoughts of self-pity. Her depression became even more profound, making it difficult for her to complete even simple tasks.

By late afternoon, Kate's emotions were sinking low, as was the sun in the sky. She thought it best to call Sara and let her know that she had arrived and was doing fine, even though she knew that she was not fine. She didn't want to cause anyone worry. She drove into a nearby town and phoned Sara from a public pay phone.

"Hello, it's me, Kate."

"Did you get there without any trouble?" Sara asked.

"Yeah, it was fairly easy to find the place."

"Good, good. So, how do you like the cabin and the solitude?

"It's a little quieter than I anticipated, but I'm keeping busy," Kate lied.

"It does take a little getting used to. It's such a change from the bustle of the city."

"I don't want to keep you. I know you and Jim must be getting ready for dinner. I just wanted to call and tell you that I'm okay and don't worry. Would you do me a favor and call my Mom and let her know that I'm fine, but don't tell her where I am? If she knew I was up here all by myself she wouldn't sleep until I got back home. She's such a worrywart."

"Sure, no problem. Give me a call in a couple of days."

"Okay, I'll call you back in a few days or so."

"Promise me you'll call no later than Wednesday," Sara insisted.

"I'll call!"

"Promise, Kate Taylor! I don't know why I put up with you." Sara said in jest.

"I don't know why you put up with me either," Kate responded sadly. "You're a good friend and I don't deserve you. I promise I'll call. Talk to you later, bye." Kate hung up the phone feeling very despondent.

Kate immediately got back in her car and drove back to the cabin. She thought about Sara all the way home. The friendship between the two girls had started in grammar school. Through the years they had many differences, yet still remained friends. However, in the past few years they became more distant to each other on a personal level, no longer confiding in each other as they once did; no longer going out nearly as frequently as they once did. They seemed to go separate ways in their lives, ways that did not allow much time for the other. Sad as it seemed at times, Kate was glad to have Sara for a friend, even if it was not an especially close friendship. The two girls had a great sense of respect for each other. They shared a special bond that was formed as children. An understanding that endured in spite of change. Kate knew in her heart, despite of everything, Sara would be there for her and that they would remain friends for life.

When Kate arrived back at the cabin, she was not feeling very hungry. Kate went in the bedroom to unpack the jewelry she had brought. She had many expensive gold chains and diamond pendants that she had purchased for herself. Always fond of jewelry, she indulged in many shopping sprees and she usually came home with a piece of fine jewelry.

Kate usually wore at least two or three gold necklaces, a gold bracelet and a couple rings. She had one ring she always wore, a family heirloom, a large ruby surrounded by three small diamonds set in eighteen carat gold. Another ring she had was a large diamond with a matching band that was covered in diamonds. The matching set were her engagement and wedding rings, very expensive and beautiful, but they held many bad memories for her. She never wore them, but she could never bring herself to sell them either. She felt that if she were to get rid of them it would be denying a part of her life that was important to her.

For memories' sake, she found herself putting the wedding rings on her finger for the first time in a couple of years. She waved her hand slowly in front of her trying to catch the light in the diamonds. Sitting down on the bed, she admired the sparkles reflecting from the diamonds on the rings.

I think I'll leave it on for a while. No one is here to see that I'm wearing the rings that jerk, ex-husband of mine, gave me.

Playing with her jewelry a while longer, she laid out a few pieces of jewelry she intended on wearing the next day.

The hours had passed and the sky above had grown dark and silent. The sound of crickets echoed in the stillness of the night. Kate was astounded at the blackness outside of the window she looked through.

The darkness seems to have no end she thought. Leaning against the window, she strained her eyes trying to catch a glimpse of anything beyond the front porch. Failing in her attempt to see better, she moved away from the window, discouraged, even a bit frightened.

Wow, what a temperature change. It has gotten quite cool since the sun has gone down.

She reached for a sweater she had lying over the back of a chair, and put it on. Walking over to the fireplace, she started to make a fire inside the cinder blocks.

The fire quickly began to burn brightly and warmly. She gazed blankly into the flames at first. She moved closer so she could feel the heat of the fire across her face. Almost mesmerized by the fire's amber blaze, she stared at it for over an hour. In the distant corners of her mind, she contemplated ending her life. No more sorrows. No more uncertainties. No more pain. Yet, other thoughts of survival and pursuit clouded her thoughts of death.

Suddenly, she felt drained of energy and tired. In addition to feeling sleepy, she felt ill. Her stomach was queasy.

I better get to bed before I become really sick. I just can't seem to get better. Now, besides getting sick to my stomach and bloating all the time, I'm going to have my vacation ruined by it she thought.

Slowly, she put out the flames in the fireplace. When she was sure it was extinguished, she went to bed for the night.

The next morning brought the promise of a new day, but in Kate's mind it brought little hope. Rising out of bed, she showered and dressed herself. She went to the mirror wearing a pink tank top and pink striped shorts and applied makeup to her face. Soft shades of rose blush highlighted her cheeks and blended nicely with the lightly applied rose shaded lipstick she used. Never fond of eye shadow, she only used mascara to bring out the beauty of her almond-shaped, blue eyes.

Although her hair was clean and dry, she found trouble in controlling its feral appearance.

That's the last time I forget to take hair conditioner with me, she thought. My hair looks terrible.

Pulling a brush through her hair repeatedly, she was able to get some manageability to it. Grouping her hair into one hand, she put it into a ponytail at the back of her head.

So much for style, she thought. If I can't get my hair to do anything else, I'll just put it in a tail. At least it will be out of my way while I'm hiking through the woods today.

She grabbed the necklaces off the dresser and put them on, along with a set of pearl earrings, and a bracelet. She completely forgot to take off her wedding rings she had put on her finger the night before. For a moment longer, she admired the jewelry she had put on, and then left the cottage.

Kate didn't bother to lock the door on the cabin, and she left some of the windows open. She figured it was in a secluded area and that no one else was around to intrude.

I have to admit despite feeling miserably depressed, it is a beautiful looking day.

As Kate casually walked along, she carefully watched the path she chose to take. She wanted to become familiar with the area so she wouldn't get lost. Along the way she listened to the birds mellifluous voices singing. In spite of all the beauty around her, she became very melancholy.

She walked for at least an hour before becoming aware of how far she had traveled. Then, feeling a bit tired, she stopped and plopped herself down on the ground.

Clovers! I haven't looked for a four leaf clover in years.

Tucking her legs underneath her body, she leaned over and started searching through the clover patch.

The forest around her was vast and green. She almost felt like a part of her surroundings. She amused herself with thoughts of little leprechauns, like the leprechauns her Father used to tell her about when she was little.

"You see," he would say at the end of his stories, "God created all things great and wonderful. The Earth, the Heavens, and you, my little leprechaun." Followed with a toss in the air and a huge hug.

How she loved those stories. How she loved those hugs. She felt so safe and secure at those times. She only wished she could feel that way again. The tears in her eyes built, until they broke free and cascaded down her cheeks. With the back of her hand, she brushed back her tears. Her face was as moist as the morning dew that settled in the grass below. Kate's thoughts drifted.

"Katie-kins, are we feeling sorry for ourselves again?" her Mother's voice echoed through her mind.

"No, Mommy. It's just that my friend Timmy called me a name."

"What did he call you, Honey?" "Go ahead, this time it's okay to say it and tell me. What did he call you?"

"A brat!" Katie blurted out, bursting into more tears.

"Oh." Trying to conceal finding humor in the situation, Leala continued, "Now Katie, you and I know that what he said wasn't very nice, but you shouldn't let what people say bother you so. You know that you're not a brat, and I know that you're not a brat. That's all that should matter. Now stop feeling sorry for yourself and get on with the day."

"Okay, Mommy. I'll try."

"You're a big girl now. No need for all that crying," her Mother said gently, reaching down for a soothing hug of reassurance.

The sun, brightly visible through the trees, was rising higher in the sky. It must be almost 10:00 now Kate thought as she pulled herself up from the ground, brushing off the wet blades of grass stuck to her bottom and backside. While glancing down, she noticed something slightly shining from within the clover patch. She leaned over to get a closer look. Reaching down, she wiggled her long fingers through the clovers trying to retrieve it. The sun's light reflected off the object and gave it a dull glimmer.

How interesting. Half a heart shaped locket, and although broken, the chain is still attached. I wonder if the other half of the heart is lying on the ground too. Searching to no avail, Kate stood up and admired what she had found.

I wonder who it belonged to she thought. What a shame for someone to have lost it. It looks very tarnished and old. I bet this locket has been lying here for a very long time. I can barely read the inscription here on the inside of this half of the heart.

She read out loud, "Tis wise to learn. Tis Godlike to create."

Turning the gold piece over, she saw the letter "S" inscribed upon it. I'm sure this locket meant a lot to someone she thought. Whoever thought of that inscription and whoever received it must have had a very special relationship.

She decided to keep it, secretly wishing it would bring her good luck. She tucked it into pocket and continued her stroll through the woods.

Along the way, she began to fantasize. She imagined the locket belonged to a couple of lovers. The two faceless lovers were doomed by some unforeseen tragedy. The locket she had found was all that was left of their long lost romance.

Like the lovers Kate fantasized about, her romances never lasted either. She had given up on the promise of ever finding a suitable mate with whom she could share her life. Her previous relationships with men had all ended in failure. She had become so disillusioned about finding a mate that she no longer allowed herself to believe that she would ever marry again. She became withdrawn from any social events involving single, unmarried people. Pretending to herself, and others, that she no longer cared took a toll on her emotionally.

I just don't understand life anymore she thought to herself. What are we born for anyway? What is the purpose? We're born, and then we die. Between the two, we go through hell trying to succeed at something, with expectations of falling in love and raising a family - none of which is promised. There is crime up the whazoo, sickness, suffering, and a whole lot of confusion. If we're lucky, maybe, just maybe, some good things will happen to us. Sometimes, I think God figures he has to throw in a couple of good things just to pacify us until we get to Heaven. I don't know if all of it is worth it just so we can die and go to Heaven. It's kind of a long time to wait and a lot of misery to survive, until we can finally get some peace and happiness.

A little deeper into the woods, Kate noticed two deer in the distance. As she tried to quietly creep closer, the deer saw her and stood still, their eyes filled with fright. Kate tried not to make any noises as she drew closer, but without warning, a twig cracked under the weight of her foot. Instantly, the deer fled from her sight.

That figures she thought. That's the story of my life. Look, but don't touch. Get real close, but not quite close enough.

Loneliness had become a too familiar feeling. As she looked through the winding branches of the trees, she felt great sadness. Her entire life had been lived only for the convenient use of other people. She rarely received any recognition for her accomplishments and achievements, and any small gestures she may have put forth were overlooked and long forgotten. The entire meaning of her life had become a trite and punishing ritual in which she was to exist every day until her death.

Understanding that much more substance of nature lay beneath what the eye saw, she admired nature for its simplistic and beautiful appearance. Nature and its growth was a complicated, long, and diligent process that became strong and forceful through the grace of God. Yet, in what should have been a peaceful and harmonious moment with nature, she began to cry. She then felt even more distant in her connection with the world.

Tossing her head back in anguish, she sobbed, dwelling on her own inadequacies.

Kate let her body slide down the trunk of the tree to the ground. Resting her back against the base of the tree, she sat sobbing. Without even realizing it, she slowly drifted into sleep.

When Kate awoke, she had no idea what time it was. She felt and heard her stomach rumble from hunger. Although she felt physically rested, she still felt emotionally drained.

Standing up, she headed back in the direction of the cabin. While walking, Kate tried not to think of anything that she would find disturbing. She tried to focus her attention to more positive matters. She occasionally stopped to look for unusual looking flowers and to pick them. She watched the birds fly to and fro from tree to tree, and tried to enjoy the forest around her.

As she walked, the weather and the sky above had begun to change. Kate, preoccupied, didn't notice. She continued to examine the greenery surrounding her.

Within minutes, the sky in the distance was gray and drab. Clusters of clouds moved wildly, encircling each other in a dance.

Kate was admiring the strength of the towering trees when it occurred to her that all the birds that had been singing and flying above were gone. They were nowhere in sight. Suddenly, she felt a cold, chilling wind swoosh across her body, causing her to notice how quickly and suddenly the weather was changing. The clouds in the sky above her began to rumble. Covering the sun in their path. It was almost as if the sky seemed to be enclosing its surroundings, pushing relentlessly in and downward. Lightning shot sharply across the darkening sky, while the roaring of the wind grew louder.

"Is this a tornado?" she spoke aloud to herself.

Never having actually seen one in person, she was as curious as she was frightened. Kate stayed a little longer, unconcerned for her own safety.

How peculiar this storm is coming out of nowhere with no particular direction she thought.

With the storm's increasing intensity, Kate became concerned about its impact on the cabin. She decided she should leave and go try to secure the cabin.

The sky was black. Everything around seemed to furiously whip at her. Forcing her way against the strong wind, Kate was hurled backwards and knocked off her feet. The trees began to sway and bend fiercely. She wondered if she would ever make it back to the cabin. Kate tried to stand up and gain leverage on the ground, but because of the impact of the howling wind, she could not keep her balance. Terrified, she kept trying. She started to feel as if it was a contest between her and the forces around her, a contest she intended to win. Determined, she moved toward the cabin. Just then, a limb from a maple tree snapped, fell, and struck her, knocking Kate unconscious.

CHAPTER FOUR

"Dear, dear," a kindly old woman, wearing a cotton floral designed dress, gently spoke. "We're going to take you to the hospital. You just keep calm. It'll take a little while to get into the city. We're going to a hospital in Chicago. Wooster Lake doesn't have a hospital, and the nearest and best hospitals are in Chicago."

Kate, barely conscious, found herself in the back seat of a large car. An elderly, grey haired man sat behind an awkwardly proportioned steering wheel. He never turned his head to look back at his wife or Kate. Except for occasional glances in the rear view mirror, he watched the road ahead, diligently driving the car.

Trying to speak, Kate mumbled barely audible words, "Where am I? The storm and the tree . . . What . . . ?"

"Now, now, Dear. Please try and save your energy. You've got a nasty bump on your head. Good thing George and I found you when we did. Poor thing. We found you lying on the side of the road."

"Something hit me on my head. I think it was a tree branch, and it knocked me unconscious. When I woke up, I tried to get back to the cabin, but I couldn't find it. I felt so dizzy. I could barely stand. Then I saw a dirt road and thought that I could maybe find help. That's the last thing I remember, until now."

"What were you doing out in those woods all by yourself?" Martha, the old woman, asked. Martha wore her salt and pepper colored hair in a tightly wound bun at the back of her head. Martha gently rubbed Kate's head, pushing Kate's hair back from her face, soothing Kate, who was in pain and seemed incoherent. Martha's hands, wrinkled with age, felt soft against Kate's forehead.

"George, do you know of a cabin in or near the north end of Wooster Lake?" Martha asked.

Looking thoughtful for a few seconds, George replied, "Can't say I do. I did hear though, that the state is going to start selling pieces of that property next spring."

Confused by the conversation, Kate forced herself to sit up.

"I don't think you should do that dear. No need to strain yourself. We're almost there," Martha said insistently.

Sitting up, despite the request, Kate asked, "Where are we going?"

"I told you, to the hospital," Martha answered, concerned for Kate, who seemed to be disoriented.

Kate looked around the car. The interior was oversized and bulky. On the outside, the chrome shined brightly, reflecting the sun's rays. Looking farther back on the car, Kate saw a wing tailed rear end.

"Cool," Kate said, finding the car extraordinary in its condition and appearance.

"Here, put on my sweater." Martha wrapped the sweater around Kate's shoulders.

"Where did you get such an excellent car like this? Have you had it a long time?"

"Well, we bought it a few years ago. Took a lot of our savings, I might add."

"Must have, an antique car like this would cost a fortune."

Baffled, Martha met her eyes with George's eyes in the rear view mirror.

"Are we almost there?" Martha questioned in urgency.

"Just about."

"Now how are you feeling?" Martha asked Kate.

"Terrible. My head hurts and I feel so dizzy."

Kate leaned forward and gazed out the window. None of her surroundings looked familiar, yet she did recognize some of the buildings they passed. Feeling uneasy, Kate began to wonder if she was being taken to Chicago.

Maybe these people are crazy and they are kidnapping me. No, that's nonsense she thought.

Within minutes, the eerie feeling Kate had earlier was all too quickly becoming a reality. The strange appearance of her surroundings took on some meaning. All the cars that she passed looked as old as the one she was in. The clothes that the pedestrians were wearing were as odd as Martha's.

Kate tried to put what she was seeing into perspective, but only became more boggled about what was happening. Passing a large billboard, Kate read its advertisement:

Paramount Pictures Presents
Cary Grant and Grace Kelly in
To Catch a Thief.
A sure winner as this year's best picture
Copyright MCIV, [1955]

The fresh glazing over the sign looked shiny and new. The bigger than life-sized faces of Cary and Grace mesmerized Kate for a moment.

Becoming frightened, Kate began to believe she was in a different time, a year other than 1992. She had seen girls wearing hoop skirts and gas station attendants wearing uniforms. Many streets had no street lights, only an occasional lamp lined the road. There were even sections of the road that were still unpaved, exposing brick paths to travel on.

What the hell is happening to me? This is impossible, Kate thought. *I know I'm not delirious and no one has dreams this vivid.*

Filled with anxiety, she called out and insisted that George turn the car radio on. Obliging her, George leaned over and turned on the radio.

The radio announcer's voice began, "Takes six minutes, last six months. Vista car wax—turbo whipped as only Simoniz can make it." The voice coming from the radio swiftly changed. The unmistakably gentle, soft, yet perky voice of a woman continued the next commercial advertisement. "No squeeze! No ooze! No cap to lose! Ipana Tooth Paste, now only 88 cents at a store near you."

What?! Kate thought, as the regular announcer continued.

"It's time now for a quick review of the day's top stories. President Eisenhower and Vice President Nixon have once again stunned the public with their decision on . . . "

Kate's head swooned as her thoughts raced to justify what she had heard. "Eisenhower, Nixon, Vice President?" As much as she wanted to, Kate could no longer deny her present reality. It was indeed 1955 as she had read on the poster they passed minutes before.

But how? How is this possible? She thought. *What would cause something like this to happen?* Too many questions and too many fears began to surface, overwhelming her instantly. The pain in her head increased as she fell back into the seat.

Martha kept calling for George to hurry to the hospital as she tried to comfort the ailing Kate. Without warning, Kate collapsed into Martha's arms. Her head lay limp on Martha's lap.

CHAPTER FIVE

The cool and sterile smell of antiseptic filled the hospital room in which Kate lay. Its obtrusive odor permeated Kate's nose, stimulated her senses, and brought her out of her deep sleep. The stiff and scratchy feeling of the sheets against her skin felt offensive as she turned and it irritated her skin.

Awakening in foreign surroundings, Kate deduced where she was. It was obvious that she was in a hospital, yet it appeared a bit odd. The white metal cabinet that stood at the side of her bed looked out of date, as did the metal bowl that rested on top of it.

"Hello, and how are we feeling? Better, I hope. You just looked terrible when they brought you in here."

The nurse, a stout woman, looked worn, yet devoted and concerned. Her hair, rolled at the front towards the back of her head, looked neat and attractive, complementing the nurse's round face.

Despite her pain and weakness, Kate sat up in bed to question the nurse.

"I don't want to sound like an idiot, but who exactly brought me here to this hospital?"

"Oh, my," the nurse gasped, "You don't know? You don't remember? You just lie down now. That bump on your head may be worse than we anticipated. I'm going to find your Doctor and have him take another look at you."

"I'm sure it's only temporary," Kate assured the nurse and herself. "You see, I don't think I knew the people. However, I do recall something about a car—no, a storm. Yeah, that's it, a storm, but my memory is so unclear." Her face twisted with frustration.

"Now don't you worry yourself. I'm sure it will all come back to you soon. I really must go and get the Doctor now. I'm sure he will want to reexamine you, just to make sure your condition hasn't worsened." Stopping herself from speaking, her face became flustered as did her speech. "Oh my, I didn't mean to frighten you. I didn't mean for you to think—you just relax. Sometimes my mouth is moving before I send my thoughts to it. You just never mind me."

Appearing more shaken than Kate, Nurse Wessley left the room to search for the Doctor.

Almost amused at the nurse's bumbled attempt to comfort her, Kate fell into a deep slumber.

While Kate slept, all the chaos common to a hospital continued. The nurses and Doctors rushed in and out of the patients' rooms with urgency. The orderlies washed and buffed the hallway floors with a swift pace.

The hospital's halls appeared ordinary. Square tiles covered the walls, and the ceilings were white and higher than necessary. However, beyond those walls, in the rooms of the patients, things from years past made their presence known. White metal tin pans were used as washbasins. The beds were much less comfortable for the patients, particularly those with disabling conditions. There were no automatic position adjustors for the beds, ones that provide for several different positions. There only was a hand crank at the foot of the bed, capable of two positions, and it was placed in such a place that only the nurse could reach it.

There was no television. Some rooms contained three, four, even five beds. Most of those rooms were cramped, because they were built and sized for only two beds.

The hospital room lighting was dim. Mostly only lit with one 50-watt bulb. None of the rooms afforded any personal hygiene accessories such as tissues, toothpaste, or toothbrushes. They did provide soap and towels. Any other items wanted were to be brought to the hospital by the patients, their families, or friends.

When Kate awoke, the pain in her head had eased some. She found Nurse Wessley standing alongside of her bed.

"I'll be right back," the nurse stated. "I was told that as soon as you were awake, I was to call the Doctor and let him know." Scurrying out of the room, she left no time for Kate to ask her any questions.

During the nurse's absence, Kate became fearful of her own bewilderment. She began to recollect what she had seen and heard before waking up in the hospital. Was she accurately recalling what happened? If she was, something very wrong and unexplainable was happening to her.

Kate's own curiosity got the better of her. She got up out of bed and went searching for some answers to her questions. Although her head was aching, she left the hospital room and went walking in the halls.

A newspaper she thought. I've got to find a newspaper or magazine. I have to prove to myself that I was, or am, delirious.

Hesitantly, she made her way off the floor, hiding from the hospital staff. Soon she found herself on the main floor.

Adding to her fear that she wasn't crazy, she noticed how different and outdated the hospital appeared. The people that she passed in the halls looked odd to her. Yet she wasn't able or ready to evaluate the reason. Upon reaching a more central area of the main floor, her heart began racing and the pain in her head throbbed.

"Oh my God!" she exclaimed out loud. Her eyes widened, as she looked around her at the flow of people coming and going from her view.

Most of the men dressed in three-piece suits with narrow lapels. Wide brimmed hats and slicked back hair seemed to be the sporting style, except for a few younger men that wore their hair longer in the fashion named a D.A. or ducktail.

The womens' appearances varied more than the men. Some wore large, layered skirts, while others dressed in sleeker, tighter pencil skirts. Both were worn at mid-calf length. The fabrics varied, but wool and cotton dominated.

The women in the halls wore their hair short and cropped. Teasing of the hair seemed popular, as did a stiff and firm hair wave. The younger girls chose ponytails, some with scarves wrapped around the tail, while tiny sections of the hair curled toward the face at the sides of their head.

The women carried straw or leather handbags of various shapes, round, square and tubular. The most extravagant looking purse was a large triangular purse with fake jewels covering it. They wore three-inch high-heeled stiletto shoes or loafers. Some of the girls wore saddle shoes.

Kate rushed up to a nearby newspaper stand situated in the lobby. Her eyes widened and her heart pounded as she read the headlines of a local paper: "New young rock idol, nicknamed The Pelvis is told, 'Go home! Elvis Presley' . . ."

For a moment, she couldn't believe her eyes. She continued to look at other publications that were being sold. William Holden and Grace Kelly's pictures seemed to be on many of the magazine covers. While a publication called, *Movie Star News* states: "*The Honeymooners*, 'The Great One,' Gleason signs for 78 episodes but decides to stop after 39." Her eyes made one final stop, at the date on the newspaper: August 23, 1955.

CHAPTER SIX

To Kate the impossibility of the situation felt like punch to the gut. Her chin quivered as her eyes filled with tears. Stepping back from the stand, she almost tripped over her own feet. Fear and loneliness swelled up inside her as she clutched her arms around herself feeling insane. Without warning, her body began to tremble and her legs became weak. Her mouth moved slightly, as if trying to speak, but it was unable to form words.

Within seconds, all that Kate knew as real and sane was dismissed from her. The place in which she stood was foreign and surreal. She could not justify a single thing she was being exposed to, nor was she capable of understanding it.

Without even knowing why, she headed back to her hospital room. Her body no longer took commands from her brain and reacted to the stress of the moment on its own. Her arms fell limp to her sides and her legs dragged beneath her as she walked through the hall to the stairwell. Sliding her shoulder along the wall, she slowly reached the stairs.

Once in the stairwell, her anxieties built, until she verbally exploded. She was yelling and screaming. Her will forced against her body, and she ran up the stairs, not stopping until she reached the fourth floor.

By the time she reached the fourth floor, she had exhausted herself. She no longer yelled, but quietly stood leaning against the door trying to catch her breath. Unable to calm herself any further, she began to hyperventilate. Her heart felt as though it was going to pound through her chest and she felt faint. Her sight became narrowed and dim as the door she reached for faded before her eyes.

She somehow managed to open the door and enter into the hall before collapsing to the floor.

A nurse had almost immediately spotted Kate lying on the floor unconscious. Before rushing to Kate's side, she summoned the help of two orderlies standing nearby. With their assistance, they carried Kate back to her room.

"Jerold, try and contact Dr. Hill, her physician. Ask him what he wants us to do with her." The tall, large-boned nurse hovered over Kate trying to connect an oxygen mask over Kate's face; but her long, red painted fingernails were constantly getting entwined with the elastic band attached to the mask.

Within minutes Dr. Hill came to Kate's room.

"Boy, this one has sure been trouble," he snidely commented to one of the nurses. "She has a mild concussion, but that gives no reason for the type of behavior she has been displaying. I was just told by a staff member that they saw her crying and yelling irrationally in the stairwell. I don't know, maybe I should run a few more tests. Maybe I'm overlooking something. Maybe it is also time I consider bringing the police in on this too. Maybe she isn't even who she says she is. One thing is for sure, I simply cannot have her running through the halls causing havoc."

Nurse Wessley, who was also in the room, quickly interrupted with a comment, "She wasn't causing trouble. I'm sure she just couldn't find her way back to her room. This is a large hospital. She probably just went for a walk and fainted." Nurse Wessley was a compassionate type who liked Kate and felt it necessary to speak in Kate's defense.

"All that may be true, but she was told to stay in bed until I instructed her otherwise for health reasons. I think for her own safety, we should confine her to her bed, until I've had a chance to talk with her and evaluate the situation. I believe it will be in her best interest."

"Do you really think that is necessary, Doctor?" Nurse Wessley asked in dismay.

"I think after twenty years practicing medicine, I'm perfectly capable of making a decision without having to justify it to a nurse," he responded curtly, looking directly into Nurse Wessley's eyes. Expecting no response to his remark, he hastily left the room.

"Well, you heard what he said. Let's get on with it," the tall nurse, Anna Berris, retorted.

Nurse Berris had been a registered nurse for thirty-two years. She had little compassion for the patients she attended to. Her face appeared hard and emotionless. As she performed her daily duties, she never fraternized with the other nurses, seeming to have little patience with them or their attitudes about work or the patients.

Feeling remorse, Nurse Wessley quietly obeyed her superiors and restrained Kate to her hospital bed.

Upon leaving the room, Nurse Wessley thought about how frightened Kate will be when she wake up. "I must make an effort to try and be here when she wakes. At least I can be of some comfort to her."

During the night, Nurse Wessley slipped back into Kate's room and untied her. She believed the restraints weren't necessary, and she was willing to take the risk of disciplinary actions or losing her job.

Kate had stayed asleep the rest of that day and night and didn't wake up until the next morning. Opening her eyes, she looked around the room and realized the previous day was not a dream, but very real.

She knew for the first time that she was no longer in the year 1992. Even though she did not understand how it was possible, she knew she wasn't crazy. She now clearly remembered everything that had happened to her since she went on vacation. Still unsure what to do about her situation, she calmly tried to think.

Should I try and explain what has happened to me? Will anyone believe me if I do? They'll probably think that I'm a lunatic. Still, I have to try and help myself out of this mess. I have to get some answers.

She decided that it would be better not to try and convince the staff she was from another time. She did not understand it herself, so how could she explain it to someone else? Besides, they wouldn't believe her, and she didn't blame them. She decided it would be better to go along with whatever they wanted until she could be released from the hospital. In the meantime, she was going to try and keep some sort of perspective on the situation and try to get some answers.

Suddenly feeling very alone in her decision and surroundings, she turned over on her side and cried. Her tears ran off the sides of her temples and onto the pillow she was resting her head upon. Soon the pillowcase was wet with signs of her fear and loneliness. Her mouth drooped in sadness and her chin quivered. Trying to comfort herself, she brought her legs, bent at the knee, up to her chest. Wrapping her arms around her legs, she hugged them tightly against her body. Rocking herself like a baby, she stayed cradled for a while, crying quietly into the pillow.

While she was lying there, Kate thought not only of her present situation, but also of her family and home, wishing desperately that she could be with them now. Beginning to feel childlike, she continued to lie curled up, finding the position soothing.

What am I going to do? She questioned in a sad and frightened way. God, I wish there was someone I could talk to. Someone who might understand and care. Her voice trailed off as a quiet whimper replaced her words.

In the hall, a young woman with auburn hair and brown eyes happened to be passing by Kate's room. The sorrowful noises coming from Kate quickly caught her attention. The woman's compassion drew her into the room.

"Are you alright? Do you want me to call a Doctor or get you something?" Her voice sounded sympathetic and sincere.

Kate, wallowing in her own self-pity, didn't even look up at her visitor. She instead, buried her face into the pillow.

"Are you in pain? Is there something I can do for you?" she asked again, her voice pleading for a response. "Maybe I should just leave. I'm sorry if I've intruded. I was just passing by, and you sounded as if you needed help."

Kate burst into a laugh, startling the other woman with her response. "Do I need help!" Kate sarcastically responded. Looking the other woman directly in the face, she continued to talk. "I need more help than you, or anyone else, can possibly give me."

Insulted and a bit frightened by Kate's attitude, her visitor began to leave the room.

"Wait! I'm sorry! Please don't leave. I don't know why I acted like that. I don't usually treat people like that. To be honest, I don't know much of anything for certain these days." Kate's face softened and her voice mellowed.

"No, no, it was my fault for inviting myself into your room so unexpectedly. Let's start all over . . . Hi, my name is Leala."

Although Kate couldn't explain it, she felt as though she recognized Leala. It seemed impossible, considering she was now existing in the year 1955, but Kate was sure she knew that face.

"I'm sorry, what did you say your name is? I've got a bad bump on my head, and I'm a little dazed at times."

"Leala, Leala Tierney."

Kate's face turned white, losing its color. Her eyes and mouth hung open in shock. Unable to speak, she looked at Leala in a horrified way. Momentarily closing her eyes, she tried to justify the presence of the woman standing in front of her.

"Are you going to faint? Oh my word, I better get a Doctor." Worried about Kate, Leala hurried out of the room to get help.

Kate fell back into a somewhat sitting position onto the bed. Her mouth quickly tried to release her thoughts into words, before Leala left, to no avail. Leala had turned into the hall before Kate could utter a word.

"Leala!" Kate called out after her, hoping Leala would hear and respond. Receiving no immediate reply, Kate's eyes looked down on the floor with sadness as her lips mumbled the truth. "Mom."

The woman with whom she had been speaking was in fact her own Mother at the youthful age of 26. Kate thought how odd it was to see her Mother even younger than herself.

Leala's face, smooth and supple looking, was framed by a beautiful mane of auburn hair that fell in a soft curl around her shoulders.

This has to be more than a coincidence. Obviously, I came into this time and met my Mother for a reason. A reason that remains a mystery to me.

Soon, two nurses urgently entered the room. Nurse Berris's face apparently flushed from rushing to get to the room.

"Now, what seems to be the problem?" Nurse Berris retorted harshly.

Standing in the doorway, Leala looked in. She had followed the nurses and came back to the room to check on Kate.

Kate had recovered quickly from the shock of seeing her Mother. She knew she had to become more adept at calming herself and facing reality, even though it was a reality that seemed an impossibility. She knew that for her own survival, she was going to have to adjust more readily than she ever had to before in life.

"You don't have to be so curt. I just felt terribly dizzy. I'm better now, except for this nauseous feeling that doesn't seem to go away." Putting her hand on her stomach, Kate rubbed it gently.

"You're sure that's all it was?" asked Nurse Wessley.

"Positive."

Leala stepped into the room and spoke to the nurses, "I'm sorry if I caused any trouble. She suddenly looked awfully ill and I just thought—"

Kate interrupted Leala, "And it was a kind thought. It's nice to know people who will go out of their way for you. Thank you very much for your concern."

Blushing, Leala responded, "It's the only right thing to do. I'm glad I was here to help you."

"Well, ladies, I wish I could stay and chit-chat, but I have work to do," Nurse Berris said. Motioning Nurse Wessley to follow, she walked out of the room. Nurse Wessley spoke not a word, but looked back at Kate and Leala and shrugged her shoulders as she left.

Kate spoke first, her eyes gleaming with joy at getting the chance to be alone with Leala. "It looks like it's just the two of us now," she started. "I'm glad you came back to see me. Let's start all over again. My name is Kate Taylor."

"I don't mean to get personal, but what are you in here for?"

"I was in an accident in the woods. A tree branch broke off and fell, striking me on the head."

"How terrible. Is it still painful?"

"A little." Kate looked long and hard at Leala. She felt that it was astonishing that this moment could happen, and was happening. She wanted to cherish this meeting and study every detail about her Mother's face.

Her intense staring made Leala uncomfortable, but she continued to converse with little hesitation, finding herself interested in knowing Kate better.

"Are you married?"

"Umm, no, not anymore." As soon as Kate said that, she regretted it, feeling that it would have been better to have replied with a simple no. However, she was making up her past history as she went along and that thought crossed her mind first.

Leala was curious as to why Kate was no longer married, but felt it would be impolite to question that subject any further.

"What part of town do you live in?" Leala asked.

"I live on the northwest side."

"So do I. What a coincidence. Do you live with family or by yourself?"

Kate realized that she had made an error in stating where she lived. How was she going to explain that she has no family nearby? She knew she couldn't give her address, because she didn't really live there. At least not in 1955, she didn't. She wasn't even sure if her apartment building was in existence in 1955. Taking a few seconds to think, she quickly thought about what she would say next.

"Actually, I'm temporarily staying in a motel. I'm originally from Canada. That's where my family lives at the present time."

Kate found it a little exciting, even a bit mentally cathartic, to make up a whole new life for herself. Making up a past made her feel in control of her present situation.

Leala's face lit up with excitement. "How exciting. I've always wanted to go to a different country, but my husband's work keeps us close to home. He does construction on houses."

In an instant, Kate's heart raced. Thoughts of her Father, who had been dead for years, filled her mind. She wanted to ask many questions about her Father but didn't dare. Instead, she used self-control and refrained from asking any direct questions. She feared it would appear strange if she did.

"What is your husband's name?" she innocently asked.

"Kean. Can you tell he's Irish? Kean Tierney. You can't get any more Irish than he is," Leala chuckled.

"What are you here for? Is some family member or friend a patient?"

"Oh no. I came to the hospital for a pregnancy test. I have a friend that usually works on this floor, so I was stopping by to visit her. Unfortunately, she's not working today. I was leaving when I passed by your room and, well, you know the rest."

"A pregnancy test?" Kate thought.

"Are you pregnant?" Kate asked.

"I don't know yet. I just had the test taken this morning. It will take a few days for them to run the test, and then I will find out. I'm so nervous and anxious for the results I can barely contain myself. You see, Kean and I have wanted a baby for a long time. I've been with child twice before, but each time I miscarried. I guess God didn't think it was time for us to have a child yet."

"I hope you are pregnant," Kate sympathized with Leala.

"I pray I'm with child too. I'm especially praying that if I am, God will let me keep the baby. I don't think I could go through another loss again. To be honest, I don't think Kean could handle another tragedy either." Leala's eyes filled with tears that she held back from falling onto her cheeks.

Kate knew Leala was pregnant but couldn't tell her that as fact. Kate had figured out the date and the date she was born. It was

41

obvious by deduction; her Mother was pregnant with her. Kate was Leala and Kean's only child. Although it seemed impossible that she was there talking with her Mom, and her Mom was pregnant with her at the same point in time, it was happening.

"When are you going to be released from the hospital?" Leala asked, changing the subject.

"I'm not sure. The Doctor told me I should be well enough to leave in a couple of days. Basically, he said that he has one test he hasn't gotten the results from. When he gets the results, he'll probably send me home." Kate secretly became very nervous at the thought of being released. She knew she had no home to go to. She had no money or even a change of clothes. Where would she go, and how would she eat?

Looking at her wristwatch, Leala saw it was getting to be time for her to leave. "I have to be getting home now. It's been a pleasure talking with you."

"The pleasure has been all mine," Kate answered earnestly.

"When you get out of the hospital, give me a call. Maybe we can get together for lunch or something." Leala took a blank piece of paper from her purse and wrote down her phone number and address.

"That would be great. I'm new in town, and I don't know anyone. It would be nice to have a friend to show me around and talk with. Especially someone like you," Kate smiled.

"Thank you. How sweet of you to say that. Then it is definitely a date. When you are released, you get in touch with me. I'll be waiting for your call." Leala handed Kate the paper with her address and telephone number.

"I'll be looking forward to it. Thanks again for everything."

Kate became sad and frightened as Leala left the room. Leala, her Mother, had given her some sense of security even if it was a false sense of belonging.

Kate sat back on her bed and began to think of ways she could survive on the outside of the hospital. She was no longer in control of her life and destiny, and she knew it. Her existence, as it was, had become a fight for survival in a strange and different, old world. A past world she knew very little about.

What am I going to do for money? Even if I get a job, I won't receive a paycheck for a couple of weeks. Besides, what type of job am I qualified for in this day and age? I'm an expert with DOS computers. All my accounting and bookkeeping work was always done with the aid of a computer. A lot of good that does me here in this period of time. Computers as I know them don't even exist yet, at least not the convenient and efficient ones of the '90's used regularly in the workplace.

Sighing out loud, Kate repeatedly asked herself the same questions over and over again: I need money. Where can I get some money? How can I get some money?

Almost as if she were answering Kate, Nurse Wessley brought in Kate's personal belongings.

"Hi, Kate. I brought you your things. Sorry it has taken so long for you to get them back. We took them from you when you were brought into the hospital. It was a matter of hospital policy. Since you were unconscious and needed treatment, we had to remove your clothing and all your jewelry. Don't worry though, we kept your valuables in the hospital safe."

Kate knew she was wearing jewelry, but couldn't remember exactly what pieces they were.

Nurse Wessley handed Kate one plastic bag with her clothes in it and another with jewelry in it. "You may notice an additional item of clothing among your belongings. I noticed you came in here wearing swimwear. I thought you may want something more to

43

cover up when leaving here. Since you know no one in town who can bring you different clothes to leave in, I took it upon myself to slip in one of my older dresses for you to leave here in.. If you don't mind me saying so, what lovely and, if you don't mind me saying so, expensive jewelry. At the risk of being pretentious, I have to ask, is it real?"

Kate took the bag and emptied its contents in her lap. "Yes, it's all real."

Kate looked over the jewelry to see what was there. She was surprised to see her wedding rings among the contents.

I must have forgotten to take these wedding rings off, she thought to herself, I'm sure glad now that I forgot to take them off. She also was relieved to see the ruby family heirloom ring. She placed that one on her finger with hope she would not have to resort to having to sell that ring in order to survive. All the rest of the jewelry should be worth plenty of money if I try and pawn them. Probably not as much as was originally paid for them, but according to 1955 standards, it should equal out to be the same value.

Nurse Wessley couldn't help but admire the gold and diamonds. She had never owned so much valuable jewelry.

Kate put down the wedding rings and fingered through the gold chains in her lap. These should do well for money too, she thought. Immediately her attention was drawn to an unfamiliar item at the bottom. Picking it up, she commented, "This isn't mine."

It was the gold shaped, broken heart she found in the woods. She temporarily forgot about finding it in the woods and putting it in her pocket before the accident and her travel through time.

"It must be. Are you sure? I can't imagine how it would have gotten into this bag if it weren't. They're usually very careful about these things downstairs," Nurse Wessley said, her face looking puzzled. "To be honest, I don't recall . . . Oh, wait a minute, yes, this is mine. I found this in the grass right before I had the accident. I just forgot about it."

44

"I thought so. I didn't think they would make a mistake like that," she replied confidently.

"Thank you for bringing me this. I don't know what I would do without it." Kate understood that statement held more truth than Nurse Wessley could know.

"Well, duty calls," the nurse said in a jestful way.

"Thanks again," Kate called out as Nurse Wessley left the room.

Kate looked up toward the heavens and silently thanked God for his perfect timing in receiving her jewelry back.

Who said it doesn't pay to love shopping, especially for non-essentials like diamonds and gold? She smiled, relaxing for the first time that day. At least I'll have some money to look forward to when I get out of here. Not to mention the things it can get me, like a temporary place to live and food to eat.

Kate got up out of the bed and sat in a chair that was tucked in a corner of the room. From the chair she looked out a window situated nearby. She watched the people walking on the sidewalk and admired the old-fashioned cars that drove by. The most distinguished car that passed by was a brand new '56 Thunderbird, just out on the market as a preview of the cars of the next year. One of the ugliest cars she spotted was a 1950 Ford wagon, a family car.

Just think, she thought to herself as she looked at the pedestrians, they haven't even heard of the Edsel yet.

Kate closed her eyes to rest. The strain of everything that had happened to her was taking its toll on her physically. Although she had tried to rest her body and mind, she found it impossible to stop her mind from working overtime.

She still had so many questions and very few answers. She contemplated where she might be able to find some answers about her travel through time. How can I go about researching time travel, or at least what is theorized about it? A couple of possibilities came to mind. One was the library, the other a college or university. The second of the two seemed to offer a more feasible chance of getting some information. It makes sense that a teaching facility would have some answers.

Early the next morning, Dr. Hill visited Kate.

"Good morning, Kate. How are you feeling this morning?" Dr. Hill asked with a forced cheerfulness.

"Much better. When do you think I will be able to get out of this place? Did you get the results back from that test you took?"

"As a matter of fact, I did; but before I explain the results, I'd like to discuss something with you first."

Kate instantly became worried, anticipating the worst. She sat up straight in bed and stiffened her body and began wringing her hands together.

"Since you've been a patient here at the hospital, you've exhibited some unusual behavior. Taking into consideration, the state of your health, I still found your behavior too irrational and hysterical at times. So, I find it my duty to suggest outpatient mental therapy, and/or counseling for you. I might also add that I think you will find it very beneficial."

"What? You're the one with a screw loose. I realize that I might have acted a little strangely at times, but give me a break. I had a tree fall on my head. What did you expect?" Her face contorted with anger.

"See, you're showing me how irrational you can be right now."

Kate calmed down and stared directly into the Doctor's eyes. "Tell me Doctor, how would you react if someone just told you that you were a nutcase? Of course I'm a little upset. Any normal person would be."

"Miss Taylor, like I said before, it is only a suggestion. However, I did take the liberty of making an appointment for you."

Kate threw her arms and hands up in disbelief of his impertinence. "How dare you!" she interrupted.

"Please, let me finish what I was saying. If you should decide not to go and see this psychiatrist, just give him a call and cancel the appointment. There is one more reason for me wanting you to go for counseling, and that has to do with the results of the test I took. I feel it necessary for you to have help."

"Please stop dragging this out, just tell me what's wrong with me," she pleaded.

"You are going to have a baby."

As the words came out of the Doctor's mouth, Kate sat there motionless and her face was expressionless. She had clearly heard and understood the Doctor, but found herself unable to respond.

The Doctor continued to speak, rushing his thoughts and words.

"I know that at first this may sound wonderful, but you must realize how difficult it will be raising a child completely on your own. According to the records you helped fill out, you are no longer married. I urge you to contact your ex-husband and let him know you are carrying his child. I'm sure that any honorable man will take responsibility for his part in this . . . matter." He hesitated. "Furthermore, you will need some financial assistance in raising this baby. At least he may provide you with some support."

At a slow and steady pace, Kate absorbed the information being spoken to her. She was becoming used to the many surprises life seemed to be bombarding her with. She was more able to endure the stress and keep her composure. Although she was taken off her guard by the latest news she received, she was able to think rationally. "Doctor, why do you treat me like I'm a child? I'm not incompetent. I do have a brain and . . ."

The Doctor stopped her in mid-sentence by interrupting her with his own words, "I don't mean to degrade you in any way, but you must admit your situation is a difficult one at best. It's not easy for a woman in this day and age to raise a child alone. It's just not socially accepted, and I'm sure you will find many people who are morally opposed to divorce and a child who'll be a bastard."

"That's it! Get out! Get out now!" she yelled, pointing to the door. She was so angry that her fact became flushed. "No one has the right to say something like that to me, no one, or to call an innocent, unborn child such a vile name. You better sign my release from this hospital right now, or I'll put you through a living hell."

Unable to contain herself, she got out of bed and grabbed her clothes out of the cubby closet in the room.

The Doctor appeared flustered by Kate's reaction, which further demonstrated his ignorance of women. Without saying another word, the Doctor left the room abruptly with every intention of signing a release form for Kate. He concluded that it would be a relief to rid himself of this mad woman.

Kate dressed quickly in the dress Nurse Wessley had so kindly given her and gathered the few belongings she had. Still livid, she hustled through the hospital corridors. She immediately left the fourth floor, and the confinement of the hospital, behind her.

CHAPTER SEVEN

In her fury, Kate had not allowed herself time to plan ahead. She didn't expect to be leaving the hospital immediately and had no course of action planned. However, one of her strengths was being able to adapt easily to new situations. She had always been an intelligent girl, using logic as a tool for her survival.

Kate walked for hours, weighing the pros and cons of her situation. Rather than feeling lost and frightened, as she first did, she began to feel elated. The thought of having a chance to start her life over again intrigued her, and the thought of having a baby delighted her.

I've always been missing something in my life. Maybe that something was a child. I always felt like part of me was never complete, like I was never whole.

Kate took one last look at her jewelry.

I guess it's time to say goodbye to some of this jewelry. I just can't bear to get rid of my family heirloom ring. Maybe I won't have to. All the other gold and diamonds should be worth more than enough to support me for a while, at least until I can get a job.

Placing the broken heart locket between her forefinger and thumb, she took a closer look at it.

No one is going to want to buy this broken thing she thought.

Deciding to keep the locket, she kept it separate from the jewelry she was going to sell. She put the ruby ring heirloom on her right hand finger again. She had always cherished the ring and felt great comfort having it back where it belonged.

On her sixteenth birthday, Kate received that ruby as a gift from her Mother. Her Mother seemed to have a fondness and attachment to the ring at the time and told her it had belonged to her grandMother. She repeatedly stressed the love and affection the ring reminded her of. She often said the ring held fond memories of yesteryear passed. From the moment she received it, Kate felt a peculiar attachment to the ring. She felt honored to have it. She rarely removed it from her finger.

Kate searched the streets for a place to sell her jewelry. She asked many pedestrians if they knew of a pawnshop. Most of the men laughed at her and said nothing. Most of the women seemed appalled at her inquiry, stating that they had no idea where such a place might be. Finally, by accident, she saw a flashing window sign, "Ernie's." Under the store's name was a written sign that read, "We buy and sell. Most items available or wanted for cash."

Instantly, she went into the store, feeling relieved she had found a place to sell her jewelry.

Once inside, she looked around at its contemptible atmosphere. The store was a small sized room. She assumed that beyond her view there must have been a back room for storage. There were two counters, but a cash register wasn't on either of them. She didn't see any jewelry displayed in the glass cases below the counters and wondered if she could sell her jewelry there.

Suddenly, the man behind the counter spoke. "Is there something you need?" His voice was gruff from years of chain smoking cigarettes and cigars.

The man behind the counter wore a short sleeve white shirt that was badly soiled. He was overweight with a large protruding stomach that sagged over his belt. His thinning hair was oiled with hair tonic, but he didn't bother to comb it in a neat fashion. Instead, it appeared messy, with strands of hair sticking out from his head. His face was worn with creases and wrinkles that seemed more noticeable because of the cigarette he clenched between his teeth. The incessant smoke from his cigarette seemed to irritate his eyes. He squinted to look past the cloud of smoke encircling his face.

"I said, do you need something?"

Kate turned toward the man who had startled her. "I think so. I have some jewelry that I would like to sell. I need to get top price for it." Although she was a bit hesitant about being there, she felt confident about bargaining for a good deal.

"Listen, lady, everybody wants top dollar. Let me see what you got first," he said, gesturing for her to put the jewelry on the counter for him to see.

He took a few minutes to examine all the pieces she had placed on the counter.

"I must say, this stuff looks like really good quality. Are you sure this stuff ain't stolen?" Tilting his head down, as he looked at Kate.

Insulted, Kate became nervous at his accusation. She was worried that he might interpret her nervousness for guilt. "Positive! Where would I get things like these? Do I look like a crook to you?"

"No, you don't, but how do I know that you don't have a boyfriend standing outside waiting for you. He might be the thief."

"Give me a break," she said in disbelief. "The jewelry isn't stolen. I bought it myself. Besides, even if I hadn't, you can't tell me that this type of business survives only on non-stolen merchandise. More than half the stuff in here is probably stolen."

"Well, if it is stolen, I surely don't know about it," he said sheepishly.

Kate didn't wish to continue with the subject any further. "Do you want the jewelry or not?" she abruptly questioned.

Surprisingly, the man responded well to her rudeness. He seemed quite comfortable with her tone of voice and changed attitude. He writes his offer onto a piece of paper and slides it across the counter over to Kate

"No way! You know it's worth a hellava lot more than that." Kate's face appeared stern and serious. Her eyebrows furrowed.

"Hey, I gotta sell this stuff and make some kinda profit. What do you think this is, a charity?"

"You know very well you are going to make a good buck off this stuff, so don't try and fool me," she insisted.

"Take it or leave it lady," he stated sharply, sure that Kate's gender would give in to such pressure.

"I guess I'll have to leave it." Kate gathered her jewelry, turned away, and slowly started to leave. She tried to keep a poker face, as if to convince him that she knew she would get a better offer elsewhere.

The moment seemed to drag on for Kate, who was really unsure if she was doing the right thing. She desperately needed that money but was willing to gamble for a larger sum. She only hoped that her ploy would work and convince the man to give her more money.

"Alright, alright, I'll give you what you want for the stuff."

Kate was relieved and thrilled. She wasn't a gambling sort of person by nature, but this time it worked. She quickly took the money and left the establishment, sighing and smiling as the door closed behind her.

Kate stopped at a nearby café and ate a late lunch. She asked her waitress, who had a pleasant personality, if she knew of a good, but reasonable, hotel. The waitress suggested the Belmont Manor.

Kate went directly to the motel and checked into a room on the second floor.

The hotel was clean but in need of a few obvious repairs. The dark green carpet was very worn in areas, almost exposing the wood floors beneath. The lofty ceiling needed to be painted, and some new furniture would have nicely spruced up the appearance of the place. Yet, the atmosphere was still pleasant and the staff courteous.

As Kate lied in bed late that night, she couldn't sleep, thinking about her Mother's pregnancy and her own pregnancy. She wanted to share the news of her pregnancy with her Mother. She thought about how strange it was going to be to tell her the news.

I can't believe I'm actually pregnant with Daniel's child. I wish I could tell him even though we are not lovers anymore. I wonder if he'd be pleased or if he'd be upset and view the baby as an intrusion on his independent, carefree lifestyle.

Kate got out of bed and paced the floor.

This whole situation is completely weird. I'm pregnant and my Mother is pregnant with me. I just don't understand how this can be happening. I'm living through all this and I haven't even been born yet.

The time fled, and it was well into the wee hours of the night. The temperature dropped, and it became cool outside. Kate had had the window open but was forced to shut it, because she was getting chilled. Finding herself once again getting in bed and lying down, she still could not sleep.

The meeting with her Mother stayed on her mind. At first when she saw her Mom, she was shocked. However, very soon afterwards, she felt as though she wanted to embrace Leala in her arms, to touch her and hug her, almost as if to make sure she was real and not an illusion.

A couple of days had passed before Kate had settled some matters that needed her attention. She had gone shopping and purchased some new clothes, shoes, and other personal items. Deciding what to buy was an experience she would not forget. She was unfamiliar with the styles of the year and found the clothes sizes fit differently than in her era. She had to try on many different clothes even though she only wanted one outfit.

With matters well in hand, she felt it was time to visit her Mother. She called Leala to set time to meet her for lunch.

Leala was thrilled to hear from Kate and wanted to meet with her that very day. They decided that a picnic lunch in the park would be nice, considering that it was so warm and sunny day.

When Kate reached Grant Park, she went to the particular place, where they had agreed to meet at noon. She only brought an apple and a sandwich, which she bought from a delicatessen around the corner from the motel.

"Hi!" Leala's voice brought Kate's attention to her arrival.

"Hi," Kate yelled across the green, grassy park. Leala sped up her walking pace to greet Kate more properly.

"This was just a marvelous idea to come here today. We couldn't have had a nicer day for a picnic. Isn't it just lovely out here?" Leala stated enthusiastically. Tilting her head back, she looked up at the clear blue sky. "Do you feel that refreshing breeze coming from over the lake?" She flipped her hanging hair back off her shoulder.

Kate looked at Leala and felt that her enthusiasm was contagious. She suddenly felt very relaxed and at ease being there with someone who was a stranger, yet someone she had known for years. Leala seemed so fresh and full of life, so young and vibrant.

"I'm glad we were able to get together today. I've been looking forward to it," Kate said smiling.

"Me too. I think it was more than chance that we met."

Kate's eyes grew large. What could her Mother be talking about?

Leala continued, "My best friend for years just moved away to another state and I've been kind of feeling lonely lately. Then, by coincidence, I meet you. You're new in town and tell me you don't know anyone and probably need a friend . . . Well, all I can say is, I think it was more than just chance. Do you believe in God?" Leala seemed a natural at chattering.

Kate had never known her Mother to be so charmingly chatty. She seemed to just keep prattling on, changing the subject from one thing to the next. Finally, Kate realized there might be more to her Mother's excited behavior than she thought. I bet she just found out that she's pregnant. I knew that her and Dad had wanted a baby so desperately. I'm sure that must be why she is prattling so. She is excited and is finding it difficult to contain her emotions.

Kate asked, "Did you get the results from your pregnancy test?"

"Yes . . ."

"Are you or aren't you?" Kate asked, knowing the answer already.

"I'm going to have a baby!" Her face expressed great joy.

"Congratulations! You deserve to be happy." Kate was thrilled for her Mother.

"Thank you for your support. I haven't even told Kean yet. I plan on telling him when he gets home from work today. I know he'll be overjoyed."

Kate, for the first time in her life, felt extremely secure about herself. She was able to see, firsthand, just how much she meant to her Mother. She had taken their love for granted over the years, but now she could see how much joy she had been able to give them by just being born.

Their conversation continued for hours. They became well acquainted with each other by the end of the afternoon.

"You know, Kate, I've been thinking. You mentioned earlier that you are in need of a more permanent place to live. It just so happens that my neighbor will be moving this weekend to another apartment elsewhere. I was wondering if you might be interested in taking a look at the apartment next to mine? The rent is reasonable, and the place is clean. What do you think?"

"That sounds like a good idea. Are you sure I won't be imposing on your privacy?" Kate asked, hoping that her Mother would not feel that way.

"Don't be silly. It would be nice having a friend nearby, especially in my condition. I don't anticipate any problems, unless of course, you don't feel comfortable living so close to me?"

Kate was amused about the possibilities the situation presented. If this had been 1992 and she were talking to her Mother at home, she would definitely have had reservations about living so close to her Mother. She knew that she would in fact probably hate the idea of her Mom living right next to her. But, here in 1955, things were different. The idea of living next to Leala was thrilling and comforting. She anticipated their new friendship would thrive and blossom.

"Oh, no, I don't. I don't expect there to be any problems. I'm sure things will work out fine."

"That is, if I actually stay here long enough in this time to move into the apartment," she thought. "I don't know what may, or can, or will happen, from this day to the next. Am I here to stay permanently in 1955?"

"Then it's settled," Leala said. "As soon as my neighbor moves all her things out this weekend, I'll call you. I'll even let my landlord know that I know someone who is interested in renting the apartment. I'm sure he'll be relieved that he doesn't have to come over and show the place himself." Leala glanced at her watch.

Kate had not yet told Leala that she, herself was pregnant. Now, she thought, was the time to make the announcement.

"Leala, I have something I have to tell you. I'm not sure if it will change your opinion of me, but . . . ." Her voice trailed off as she remembered what Dr. Hill had told her about some people's reaction to issues like this.

"Kaaatte . . . What's wrong? What is it?" Leala's face looked worried.

"I'm pregnant, too," Kate blurted out, waiting for a bad reaction to her statement.

"How wonderful! Why are you so upset? Do you not want the baby?"

"No, it's not that. I definitely want the baby. I was just afraid that you would lose respect for me or be disappointed. Dr. Hill told me that being unmarried and being pregnant was just not acceptable, and that—"

"Oh, what does that dumb Doctor know anyway? It's not your fault that you conceived a baby before you got divorced or—" Leala blushed, realizing the baby might be fathered by someone other than Kate's ex-husband.

Kate sheepishly let Leala believe she was married at the time the baby was conceived. *I guess that's true. It's not my fault that my husband left me for another woman.* Kate had lied, but felt it was a necessary one to tell.

"It's true that some people are old-fashioned and narrow-minded in their thinking, but don't worry about it. It's usually the men who have the most trouble with issues that deal with women like this. However, you will find that women are much more accepting and supportive. We just don't tell our husbands everything." Leala smiled.

"You know, I have to tell you again, I'm really very glad we met and became friends. I'm going to need a friend to help me get through all this change." Kate was referring not only to her pregnancy, but to the whole new lifestyle she was being forced to deal with.

"This might sound a little queer, but I've never felt as comfortable so quickly in any of the other friendships I've had. I'm really glad we have become friends too," Leala said affectionately.

"Look at the sky. It's getting dark. What time is it?"

"Oh my goodness! It's getting late. Kean is going to kill me if I don't get home and have his dinner ready to serve for him when he gets home. As a matter of fact, he's probably home right now wondering where I am, and where his dinner is. I didn't realize it was so late. I've got to get going." Her voice sounded panicky.

Leala quickly stood up and gathered her things.

"I'll call you soon," Leala called back over her shoulder as she rushed toward her home.

CHAPTER EIGHT

Kate took advantage of the couple of days until she was to meet again with her Mother and see the vacant apartment. She watched and studied people and read as many newspapers and magazines as she could, hoping to better acquaint herself with the new world she was living in.

I find it difficult to understand the intentional ignorance so many people have. They seem to purposely bury their heads in the sand, so that they won't see anything bad that is going on in the world, or more specifically, their country.

Before Kate knew it, the week had passed and it was almost Saturday. I hope Leala hasn't forgotten to call me.

Kate was feeling insecure again. Leala was the only person Kate could rely on, besides herself, and Kate was feeling rather vulnerable.

The day was still early and Kate thought about going to the university.

I don't want to miss Leala's call, but I really need to get some answers and maybe some help about my travel through time. I really like it here, and I love being able to see my Mom so young. I'm thrilled to have the chance to experience 1955, but I don't belong here and my baby doesn't belong here. I want to go back home and raise my baby there. I need to consider not only myself now. I have another unborn life to think about now, too. I wish I knew how I got here in the first place and why? I didn't think time travel was even possible. I'm sure nobody does. I wonder if there have been other people who have traveled through time. I suppose there could be. Who, except them, would know? Just like me, I'm sure they wouldn't tell anybody for the same reasons I haven't told anyone.

Deciding to go to the university, Kate left a message with the motel receptionist.

"If a Leala Tierney calls, tell her I will be back later and that I will return her call,"

Kate flagged down a taxicab and went to the University of Illinois in Chicago.

Once she reached the university and went inside, Kate stood in awe of the building's size.

Kate had lived in Chicago her whole life, but had never seen the inside of University of Illinois before. She had been like many other people who never see much of the city in which they live, always caught up in the daily routine of things and never taking time to stop and look around them.

Kate didn't know where to begin her search. However, with the assistance of other people, her search was narrowed down. She was told the name of one particular professor who might be able to help her find answers to her questions. His name was Professor Stephen Adler and he taught classes on campus. He had a good reputation for his patience with his students and his ability to enlighten them with new ideas of multiple dimensions, special theory of relativity, and his own theories regarding quantum physics.

Stephen Adler was a fine teacher. He enjoyed opening up and expanding his students' minds to all sorts of possibilities, making them think in ways they hadn't before. Using some of his own research and theories, along with Einstein's, Planck's and Bose's, he saw the tremendous possibilities of quantum mechanics.

As Kate opened the door to a classroom, she noticed there was a class in session. Trying to be as quiet as possible, she snuck in and sat at the back of the auditorium sized room and sat in one of the seats available. Kate sat there silently, watching, listening, and thinking.

So that's Professor Adler. He's much younger than I anticipated and he's very attractive with that dark brown hair and blue eyes.

"Summer's almost over and this is your last chance to pass this course. I know you can do it if you work as diligently as you have been." Looking at a large clock on the wall, Professor Adler finished what he was saying. "Our time is up now, but don't take the world around you for granted. There's more to it than we can explain . . . and a lot more to it than I'm sure any of you can explain. So study hard," he said to his students in a lighthearted and jestful way. His voice was deep and full in tone to match his 6'1 frame, yet he spoke softly and quietly.

The students scattered into the isles and out the classroom door.

Now's my chance to speak with him before his next class or before he leaves for an appointment. What do I say to him? Do I try to explain myself? How do I explain myself? I can't really tell him the truth.

Confused but determined, Kate approached Professor Adler with some apprehension. "Professor Adler, you don't know me, but I really need to talk to you."

Kate was interrupted. "I'm sorry, I really don't have the time for this right now. I don't mean to be rude, but I must get to my next class. His face expressed sincerity as he gathered his books and papers.

"I realize you are a very busy man, but I would very much like to have a few minutes of your time. If not now, maybe we can arrange a meeting soon?" Kate said hopefully.

"I suppose that can be arranged." Tilting his eyes to one side, he pondered for a few seconds. "I don't have my appointment book with me, but I believe next Monday morning would be a good time for me. Will that be a suitable day for you?" His dazzling blue eyes seemed to pierce Kate, sending a warm chill through her.

"That would be fine," Kate stuttered slightly, finding herself attracted to the Professor. "What time and where?"

"How about 10:30 in the morning in the cafeteria?" Stephan's eyes subtly wandered, admiring Kate's beauty.

"Then 10:30 it is. Thank you very much for making time to meet with me. I just didn't know of anyone else to talk to and you have such a marvelous reputation. Well, thank you." Kate's face blushed a rosy shade of pink.

"It's been a pleasure meeting you." Stephan smiled. "I've got to be going now. I'll see you on Monday." Finding himself unable to take his eyes off Kate, he slowly backed out of the room. Finally, he turned around a bit embarrassed, and left the classroom.

Wow! He is gorgeous! Kate thought to herself. Feeling a bit embarrassed by her intense attraction to him, she felt her face become warm.

I hope my cheeks aren't flushed. I don't want him to think that I want to meet with him on a personal level. However, that wouldn't be such a bad thing.

Stephan had also found himself attracted to Kate. He found her looks refreshing and different from other women he knew. It was a difference he could not explain but a pleasant and exciting one all the same.

Kate returned to the motel and stopped at the desk to see if any messages had been left.

Thank God! Kate thought. Leala had called and had left a message for Kate to call her back as soon as she arrived back at the motel.

Kate called Leala and made arrangements to meet her the next morning. After the phone call, she went directly to her room. She was feeling very tired and nauseated again. She lay down on her bed and fell fast asleep.

Without realizing it, Kate had slept until the next morning. I can't believe I slept that long, she told herself when she woke up and realized what time it was. Feeling very hungry, since she had missed dinner the night before, she wanted to get breakfast right away. As soon as she got dressed, she went out for breakfast and ate at a nearby Woolworth's.

Although Kate was becoming familiar with the new, old Chicago she was living in, there was much she wasn't comfortable with yet. She still wore her hair in the way she was accustomed, rather than the styles of the time. It hung straight at shoulder length and was feathered in layers at the top. It had less style than usual, because she didn't have any hair styling tools, especially ones of the type she was used to using. She had bought some new makeup too, but found difficulty in applying it. The powder was cakey, and she was used to powder blush not pasty rouge. She simply could not bear to wear the dark red shades of lipstick that was available, and the mascara was thick and heavy.

I wonder if I look unusual to other people, I mean, the way I wear my hair and makeup, even the way I dress? I'm probably not wearing some of the clothes in the fashion they were meant to be worn.

Even though Kate wondered about what others might be thinking, she didn't worry about it. She was more concerned about getting an apartment to live in and getting some kind of job. She knew that the money she had now wasn't going to last forever.

Kate sat in a small booth rather than at the counter. She didn't have to meet Leala for half an hour.

The time passed quickly and uneventfully. She paid her bill and left a tip on the table for the waitress. As Kate was leaving the restaurant, her waitress called out after her.

"Ma'am. . ..ma'am, I think you left some of your own money by mistake." The waitress couldn't believe that someone would leave such a large sum of money as a tip, especially on a bill amounting to so little. Her honest nature forced her to stop Kate and return some of the money she thought Kate had accidentally left behind.

Kate stopped and looked at the money in the waitress' hand. Without realizing it, Kate had tipped the waitress according to the standards of 1992 with a sum that would seem extraordinary in the year 1955. Pausing for a few seconds, she tried to decide whether to claim it as a mistake and take the money back or let the waitress just keep it.

"No, I didn't make a mistake. It's all yours." Kate felt it was only right to reward the waitress for her honesty, so she decided to let her keep it. She figured she could afford to make such an error and be generous this one time.

"Thank you, thank you very much and come again," the waitress said to the leaving Kate.

Kate strolled down the street. She felt like walking to Leala's apartment building. The address she was given wasn't that far from where she was, and she thought a walk would do her good.

I wonder if I'll get a chance to see my Father? What do I say to him? How do I react? I know I'm going to want to throw my arms around him and give him a big hug, but I can't. There is so much I want to say to him. I want to tell him I love him . . . . God, this is so weird. My Father's been dead for years. After all the times I wished I could have the chance to see and talk to him again. Now, I get the opportunity, and I can't say a damn thing I want to. It's just not fair.

Kate tried to divert her thoughts to her Mother. Things seem to be going nicely between them. After years of knowing her Mother, Kate was finally beginning to understand her. At long last, Kate and her Mother had become friends, having a mutual respect and love for each other.

It's so odd, Kate thought, that my Mom and I could become friends so quickly, so naturally. Why couldn't it have been like that before?

Kate arrived at what she hoped would be her new home. She found Leala gardening out in front.

"I'm here," Kate announced, trying to get Leala's attention.

"Hi. How are you? It is so good to see you," Leala greeted Kate while standing up. "Well here it is."

The apartment house stood in its finely crafted wood frame. Two separate apartments were adjacent to each other. Side by side, they provided shelter for the people making their home inside. Even though the craftsmanship was apparently well done, the building was old, and the structure was weakening. The grey paint looked weather beaten, and some of the wooden stairs were chipping.

"I know it doesn't look like much, but the landlord hasn't been in good health the past couple of years. Kean keeps asking if he could fix things up, but the landlord won't hear of it. The landlord insists that he will take care of things himself, which, of course, means the place will probably fall apart before he's well enough. He has enough money, this building is one of several he owns. I wish he would just pay someone else to fix things up, like Kean." Leala smiled sheepishly.

"I think it's wonderful. Yes, it's a little run down, but the place is full of character. May I see the inside now?" Kate started to make her way up the stairs to the solid oak front door.

"Oh yes, I'm sorry. Of course you can see the inside. Keep in mind, the other apartment for rent in this building is identical to mine. So, if you like mine, excluding any difference in decorating tastes, you'll like the apartment next to me."

Upon entering the apartment, Kate got an unusual and exciting feeling, a feeling that one might get when searching through their grandMother's attic or reminiscing through an old family album.

She thought beyond this is a picturesque view of how her Mother lived. How often does any child get to have a firsthand look at how and where their parents lived?

With hope of promised insight, Kate entered her parents' home. Her eyes bounced from one object to the next, trying to take it all in. Feeling like a child in a candy store, her hands reached out to touch and feel and grab the objects and things belonging to yesteryear.

The couch was short and was trimmed with hand-carved wood. The two cushioned chairs sat low to the ground, appearing slightly over stuffed. The boldly large floral patterns covering all three pieces of furniture seemed obtrusive to the eye. A large floor lamp stood in a corner of the room. Blue colored glass, in the shape of teardrops, dangled from twisted brass arms at the top. The lighting unit on the lamp consisted of five light bulbs arranged symmetrically around the top. The wall behind the couch was covered in striped wallpaper that looked dry and peeling. The bare wood floor that she stood upon was clean but dull. Apparently, no wax or sealer had been used to give it a shiny, lustrous finish.

The small and more intimate items lying about the apartment were more intriguing than the furniture to Kate.

Glancing over into the dining area, an entire display of old, intricately cut crystal shown through glass cabinet doors.

I've never seen those crystal pieces before Kate thought to herself. I wonder whatever happened to them by the time I came along?

Placed up against the other wall was a large wooden buffet. Lying on top were several pictures of unfinished needlepoint. Above them on the wall were scattered framed photographs of family members and other people. Some of the photos she recognized, others remained mysterious faces and places. Even though the pictures looked old in their style, the photographs themselves appeared clean, supple, and well defined. In the far left room hung a grotesquely painted, oil painting. Trying to see who would have put their name to such a work, she moved closer to examine it for a signature. She only saw two initials at the bottom, J.T. More and more questions began to build up in Kate's mind. Hopefully, she thought, they soon could and would be answered.

A pearl beaded rosary was lying on a small round table beneath the painting. The gold cross attached to it was tarnished. In a pearl frame next to the rosary was a picture of the Sacred Heart of Jesus and a candle. The candle was encased in a rose colored glass. The flame inside burned proud and bright.

How touching Kate thought. Here before her eyes was testimony to her Mother's devotion to God and her religion. The last time she remembered her Mother openly worshipping was in second grade at her communion. Why had Leala stopped practicing her faith as she got older? Especially since she seems so devoted now. I have much to learn about my Mother whom I've known for thirty-six years.

"I'll take it!" Kate's voice burst out in glee.

"Wait a minute, you haven't even seen the rest of the place. How do you know you're going to like it? How can you be sure if you haven't seen beyond the living room?"

"In the short time I've had to get to know you, I've learned that our tastes in things are the same. Besides, the rent is cheap and what could be better than living next to my new best friend?"

"So, you think you really know me. Just wait till you catch me in the morning, when my hair is a mess and I have no makeup on. That, combined with my tattered robe might give you second thoughts about living here and frighten you away," Leala joked, filling the room with a boisterous laugh.

The two girls continued to giggle as they browsed through the rest of the house, making plans and jokes as to what the near future may have in store for them as neighbors.

Kate's secret reason for wanting to live there would remain just that, a secret. She knew she could not tell Leala that they were really Mother and daughter or that Kate had really come from a time and place that was years into the future.

They would think I'm crazy. Sometimes I think I'm crazy. I just know that Kean and Leala wouldn't believe me, and if they did, they would commit me to a mental institution.

Although Kate was alone with her secret, she felt safe with caring friends and family nearby.

Much time had passed, it was nearly 4 in the afternoon.

"Don't you think I should try and call the landlord and secure the lease for this place?"

"Yes, definitely. Why don't you use my telephone and make the necessary arrangement with the landlord, Mr. Chasnowit. While you do that, I must start dinner. Kean will be home in an hour." Leala pointed to the phone and excused herself, moving into the kitchen.

In her phone conversation with Mr. Chasnowit, Kate had made an arrangement to meet with him the next day. There she would sign the lease and receive the keys to her new home.

After finishing her conversation with Mr. Chasnowit, she hung up the phone and sat on the couch. Suddenly, a different realization drifted into her thoughts. She knew very little about living life in 1955.

What type of appliances should she use? A better question was what types were available for use? Would she know how to use them? What is daily life really like in this time? So far, not only were most of the items common to this time, foreign to her, so were the many common household items, as were the clothing people wore and the people's style and manners. The surrounding area and streets sometimes looked so unfamiliar. The stores and buildings she remembered being there weren't or something different stood in their place. Becoming a bit unnerved at what type of life style she was about to confront, she stood up and started pacing.

"Oh, by the way," Leala shouted from the kitchen, "Don't forget to cancel that appointment with that psychiatrist, Dr. Bonner."

"That's right, I completely forgot about that stupid appointment."

"I don't know why they insisted you go and see him in the first place. It was perfectly obvious to me and Nurse Wessley that you were of sound mind. So what if you were a little confused and frightened. You just went through a traumatic experience with the tornado and injury to your skull. Plus, all that being complicated by you expecting a baby." Leala sighed. "Even though I realize you will have difficult times ahead of you, having no husband, I think it will be great. We can both waddle down the street together. Besides, if you need help I'll give it to you."

"I still can't believe I'm pregnant. It's just so scary to think that I'll be living in a new place on my own, with a baby," Kate confided. She walked into the kitchen to see if she could help Leala.

"I know what you mean. I mean, I'm not alone, but it's scary to be pregnant." Her eyes were almost tearing.

"Don't worry Leala. Everything is going to be alright this time. And it's okay to be scared. I would be, too. That's normal, but I'm positive that you're going to have a wonderful, healthy baby. Trust me, I have never been wrong about something like this before." Kate's heart went out to Leala, who had begun crying. Kate put her arms around Leala to comfort her.

"My heart keeps saying it will be alright, but my brain keeps giving me doubts," she said wiping her tears away.

"Listen, before you know it, you're going to be feeling that baby move and kick," Kate said, trying to console Leala, who didn't know what Kate knew about the baby she was carrying.

"I know you're probably right. I shouldn't worry as much as I do." Leala stopped crying and continued making dinner, trying to take her mind off it.

Leala turned and looked at Kate. "By the way, how far along are you?"

"According to what the Doctor said, I'm about 10 weeks. He said he couldn't be sure but he gave me a due date of March 13th."

"My due date is March 28th."

"I guess that means that I'll be getting fat first," she joked.

"Yes, but you get to deliver first." Leala was feeling more relaxed and playful.

"You never know, I might deliver late and you early. Hey, do you have a radio?" Kate asked, changing the subject.

"Yes, but I don't think we should turn it on. Kean will be home any minute and I don't think he'll—"

"Hi, Honey. I'm home." Kean's voice carried into the kitchen from the front door.

Kate suddenly felt a cold chill travel up her spine. Her hands became cold and numb. She swallowed hard, feeling as though she had something large swelling up in her throat. Turning pale, she stood stifled and silent awaiting for her Father to appear.

Kean entered the room. Glancing at Kate, he turned and gave Leala a kiss hello.

"How was your day?" Leala asked Kean. Her face lit up as he kissed her.

"Fine. What have you been doing with yourself all day?" he asked Leala inquisitively, looking over at Kate.

"Kean, I'd like to introduce you to a new friend of mine. Kean this is Kate. Kate this is Kean."

Kean smiled and nodded his head as he said Hi to Kate. For a moment, Kate felt time freeze.

I can't deal with this, Kate thought. My Dad looks so young and handsome, so full of life. I want so very much to yell, "Daddy, it's me, Katie. Don't you recognize me?"

Kate knew she had to gain control of the situation and realize that it wasn't her or Kean's fault that things were the way they were.

"Hi. It's very nice to meet you. I've heard so much about you that I feel I already know you," Kate managed to squeeze out between her clenched teeth and tight lips.

Kate was trying her best to keep control on what she said. She didn't want to say anything unusual or damaging to the relationships.

"I hope it's been all good and not bad." Kean's eyes flashed with laughter as he smiled.

"Oh, Kean, stop needling." Leala gently slapped him on the arm. "Of course it's been all good." Turning to look at Kate, she continued. "He's always joking. Just ignore him and he'll stop," she said with a chuckle.

Kean left the room without another word. He went to change from his work clothes into something more clean and comfortable. Leala and Kate continued to talk in the kitchen.

"I hate to ask you this, but it's almost dinner time, and—" Leala hesitated.

"I'm sorry, yes, yes, I'll get going now. I didn't mean to be inconsiderate."

"I know that, and I didn't want you to think that you were being inconsiderate. It's just that, well, to be honest, I don't have enough food to serve for all of us. I wasn't prepared for company for dinner," Leala said, feeling embarrassed by the situation.

"Don't worry, I completely understand. I've got to get going anyway. I'll talk to you soon," Kate said, getting ready to leave.

"I'll not only talk to you, I'll be seeing you real soon. Hopefully everything will go fine tomorrow and you'll be moving in next door in a couple of days." Opening the front door for Kate, Leala bid her goodbye.

Kate walked back to the hotel feeling a bit lonely. She settled into her hotel room, relaxed, and read until it was bedtime, not bothering to eat dinner.

The following morning, Kate met with the landlord, Mr. Chasnowit. Their meeting went well and Kate got a chance to see the apartment she wanted to rent. They agreed upon the price for the rent, and she received the keys to the apartment.

"Well, here I am. I've got my own apartment," she said aloud to herself. Mr. Chasnowit had gone home.

Kate felt that it was odd that after all these years of living on her own that she would feel the same way she did the first time she got her own apartment.

Now all I need is some furniture, like a bed, a couch, a table she thought. Where am I going to find some second hand furniture, especially on a Sunday? At least I already have a stove and refrigerator here. If I had to get those things, that would put a real dent into my finances. I suppose I better start looking for a place to buy some of the things I need. I wonder if Leala would know of a store I could go to.

Kate went over to Leala's home, but found no one there. Feeling a little discouraged, she walked to the corner to try and find a telephone book at the local store there.

I wonder, do they have telephone books in 1955? I feel so stupid. I don't even know if telephone books exist. I suppose they probably do have telephone books. How else would someone be able to locate a particular person? Do they have the yellow pages? I feel so stupid right now. Here? I know very lttle.

Kate suddenly felt ridiculous at not being able to answer a few simple questions.

"Excuse me. Do you happen to know where I might be able to find a secondhand furniture store?" Kate asked the woman behind the counter at the corner store.

"As a matter of fact, I do. My brother-in-law picks up and delivers for one on the weekends. I believe it's over on Clark and Fullerton. It's called Bell, Book & Broomstick. Let me call my sister and get the exact address for you."

Kate waited patiently for the woman to return from calling her sister.

"Here you are. All the information you need is written down on this piece of paper." The woman handed Kate a small scrap of paper.

"Thank you very much. You've been very helpful."

Kate started to leave the store but stopped suddenly. "Excuse me. I'm sorry to bother you again, but do you know if the store is open for business today?"

"Yes, it sure is." The woman smiled. "Hope you find what you need," the woman said to Kate.

Kate found the quaint little store she was looking for. She picked out several pieces of furniture that she knew she would need. The store was unable to deliver the furniture the very same day, but agreed to make a delivery the next day.

When Kate arrived at her new apartment, she wondered about where and what she would sleep on that night. She went over to Leala's home to ask if she had a cot that she might be able to use.

"As a matter of fact, I do," Leala replied, "It is rather uncomfortable, but it should do for the night. I also have a pillow and blanket you can use."

"Great. What would I do without you?" Kate smiled and gave Leala a hug.

Kate no longer felt that she was seeing Leala as her Mother in her younger years. Somehow the relationship between Leala and herself seemed to be detached from the fact that Leala was her Mother. Leala had simply become a new and wonderful friend that she cherished. Her Mother still lived at home in 1992, awaiting Kate's return.

While Leala looked for the blanket and got the pillow, Kate started to think. I wonder if time is passing the same in 1992. If it is, everyone must be wondering what happened to me. My poor Mother must be insane with worry. I wish I could go home now or at least let everyone know that I'm okay and doing fine. I wish I could tell them that I love them and . . . . What does that all matter now? I'm stuck here whether I like it or not. This is a nice place to visit, but I don't want to live here. I want to take my baby home and show everyone.

Kean entered the room, his pants soiled from the yard work he had been doing. "Where is Leala? Oh, forgive my manners, Kate. I'm sorry. Hi. How are you?" He said absentmindedly.

You always did get absorbed in your work Kate thought to herself as she watched Kean look around the room for something.

"Honey, have you seen my yard stick? I need to measure the flower box you want me to make, and I know you used it the other day," Kean called out after Leala.

"Why do you think I always know where everything is in the house? When I used it last, I put it back where you always keep it. If it's not there, then you must have used it last and put it somewhere else," Leala yelled from the other room.

"Well, it's not there."

"Then, obviously, it's somewhere else. Look for it. Your guess is as good as mine." Her voice sounded a little irritated.

"Obviously it's somewhere else. Thanks for the help," Kean mumbled under his breath.

"Kean, who painted that picture on the dining room wall over there?" Kate asked, pointing with her finger.

"That thing over there? My sister Jeanette painted that and gave it to us for a Christmas present last year. Isn't it the ugliest damn thing you ever saw?" he said shaking his head in a combination of disgust and laughter. "I told Leala she didn't have to put it up, but she insisted, believing that it would offend Jeanette if we didn't display it. I don't see what the big deal is. Jeanette never comes over here for a visit anyway. Maybe once, twice a year. Just put the darn thing up then," he said innocently, as he raised his eyebrows in a naïve wonder.

Leala came back into the room with two blankets and a pillow. "I had the darndest time trying to get these blankets out of the closet. It looks like an avalanche in there. I was trying to take these out of a storage bin and everything kept falling on my head from the shelves above. Here you are Kate." She extended her hand to give Kate the blankets and pillow.

"I didn't mean to put you through so much trouble. Sorry for the inconvenience."

"Not your fault." Her eyes shifted to look at Kean. "If some people would put things back where they belong, I wouldn't have had any problems at all."

Kate wanted to smile at Leala's quibbling, but didn't think that Leala would take kindly to it.

"Yes, dear," Kean mockingly replied to her tone of voice. Shaking his head in wonder, he started to leave the room.

"Did you try looking under the back porch stairs? Remember, you were working out there last weekend?" Leala's tone of voice softened, as she realized she had been unnecessarily curt.

"No, I didn't, but it is probably there." Kean hastily left the room, as if on a mission.

"Thanks for the bedding. I'll return it as soon as I buy some stuff of my own."

"I'll have Kean bring the cot over later. If you need any more stuff, if I have it, it's yours." Leala giggled at the unusual choice of words, "stuff," and her own use of it.

"I'll see you later." Kate turned to leave.

"Wait! I wanted to ask you if maybe next week you would want to go to a movie. The World Series is going to be televised next week. The Dodgers are playing the Yankees. Anyway, since we don't have a television yet, Kean will probably go to O'Leary's to watch it on the television there. He's a big Cubs and Dodgers fan."

"That sounds like a great idea. Just let me know a little in advance the exact time and such."

"Good, I hate to watch those stupid sports games. Besides, the men frown upon women butting in on their private time or domain, and I'd just be sitting home all by myself." Leala scrunched up her nose in aversion.

On those words, the two women said their goodbyes. Kate used the rest of the day to clean and organize some of the belongings she had shopped for on the way home from the furniture store, but she still needed more items for the apartment and herself. She intended to go shopping after she had met with Professor Adler the next day.

Later that evening, Kate felt physically drained and exhausted. She had been very busy in the past few days, and it had begun to catch up with her. Wearily, she made up the cot and went to sleep.

CHAPTER NINE

Monday morning arrived with the promise of a new day. Kate's hopes were high, and she felt confident that her meeting with Professor Adler would be enlightening. She quickly got dressed and left the apartment.

While strolling down the street on her way to a local restaurant, she spotted a help wanted sign in a small gift shop.

I wonder what they would pay a sales girl. I have more than enough experience working with numbers. I've completed financial reports and done transactions, transferring sums of money that would seem astronomical to people of this time. Unfortunately, I can't prove it. So, if I apply for a job, I'll have to lie and tell them this will be my first job and that I have no experience.

Kate realized she didn't know how much longer the money she had would last. What if I never get home? The cost of living here and the added expense of having a baby will completely break me financially. I have to get a job, just to be on the safe side. And the faster, the better. Very soon I will start looking like I'm pregnant, and no one will want to hire an unwed pregnant woman.

Kate decided to skip breakfast. She looked at her watch and figured she would have enough time to go and apply for the job and still be on time for her meeting with Professor Adler.

Upon entering the gift shop, Kate found it to be quite charming. It was small, but was furnished with a variety of lovely gifts. There was a wonderful selection of music boxes and figurines, and one wall had shelves of cards to choose form. A sparkling clean case displayed elegant pieces of imported crystal.

"Good morning! And welcome to Regal Harbor. How may I help you?" A middle aged gentleman with graying hair and a small mustache approached Kate.

"Actually, I'm here for the job. I'd like to apply for the job position you advertised available."

"Oh, very good. I didn't think I would have such a quick response. I just put the help wanted sign up earlier this morning. Do you have any qualifications or job references?" he asked in a tenor voice as he peered over a small sized pair of black-framed eyeglasses perched on the tip of his nose.

"To be honest, this would be my first job." Kate quickly rushed into her following statements. "You see, I'm divorced and, well, I'm a very hard worker. I'm very good with numbers and figures."

"Calm down and relax. I don't bite," the storeowner interrupted. "My name is Mr. Fletcher. What is your name?" He sensed Kate's nervousness.

"Kate Taylor."

"Very pleased to meet you, Kate Taylor. I think there are a few things I should tell you about this job. First, it's only part time. Second, it doesn't pay very much. I own a small business and I pay the best I can afford to. Are you still interested?"

"Yes, I am. I've always wanted to work in a small place like this. I like to deal with people on a one-to-one basis, something you aren't able to do in a large and impersonal business. As a matter of fact, part time hours would be ideal for me right now." Kate began to feel more self-assured and confident.

"Would you be able to start tomorrow?" He cocked his head to the side and smiled.

"Perfect! I'll be here first thing in the morning."

The rest of their conversation was kept brief. They discussed such details as the hours she would be working, her exact pay, and she supplied him with information to complete an actual job application.

After Kate left the store, she wondered what would happen if he checked up on the personal background information she had given him.

If there is a God, Mr. Fletcher won't check the information I gave him. Almost nothing I told him was true—my date of birth, the social security number I gave him was mine, but not until another twenty years or so from now.

Kate tried to not think negatively and tried to put it out of her mind. Her main concern now was meeting the professor.

Kate hailed a taxicab and arrived at the University at a quarter after ten. She entered the building and asked for directions to the cafeteria.

It figures it would be on the other side of campus she thought to herself as she began to walk there.

Moments after she entered the cafeteria, Professor Adler arrived.

Kate was taken quite aback by the professor's appearance. He was even more handsome than she remembered. His strong build and frame was very masculine, and his blue eyes were alluring.

I wonder why he isn't married? What's wrong with him? She light heartedly thought

Professor Adler caught a glimpse of Kate through a crowd of students walking past her. He motioned with his arms for her to come and join him.

"Hi, how are you doing today?" Kate asked pleasantly.

"Fine, thank you. I have to apologize though," he shyly announced.

"For what?" she asked curiously.

"It seems I've forgotten your name."

Kate laughed. "Our first meeting was so rushed; I don't think I ever told you my name. It's Kate Taylor."

"Gee, I knew my memory wasn't what it used to be, but I knew I would never forget the name of such an attractive woman like yourself." Unsure about how his frankness would be perceived, he lowered his eyes and nervously adjusted the saltshaker on the table unnecessarily.

"Thank you, Professor Adler." Kate smiled, feeling complimented but a bit awkward.

"Please, call me Stephan. I would feel silly if you didn't."

"Okay, Stephan, why don't we get some food before we continue our talk." Kate started to get up.

"Sounds like a very good idea to me, I'm famished." Quickly, Stephan stood up and went over to help Kate out of her seat.

Stephan was a man devoted to his work. He never married, because he could never find a woman who could accept the long hours he his career required. However, lately he had been feeling a void in his life. At first he attributed it to his ease in his schedule at work, but later realized he lacked someone to share his life with. He began to want more permanence in his personal life and started to value having a relationship with a woman more than he did his work. He dated rarely and always found it a little difficult to talk with a woman of interest to him, even though his boyish charm and his masculine flirtations were very effective and attractive to the opposite sex.

Once they were seated, Kate silently tried to organize her thoughts.

I can't be too direct and honest with my reasons. I'm sure he'll think I'm crazy or playing some sort of practical joke at his expense. I'll be direct with my questions, but let him believe it's just my curiosity getting the better of me. Maybe I should lead him to believe I'm doing research for a local newspaper article.

The conversation began like many do. The topics were superficial, with little importance, like the weather and such. The almost, expected rhetoric that occurs. The only source of stimulation was not in their words but in an unforeseen exchange of energy between them, a true magnetism, and an unbridled physical attraction they seemed to try and hide from one another.

Stephan tried to be casual but he couldn't stop himself from surveying Kate's lovely features. Trying to be as casual as possible, he surrendered to his own desires and allowed his eyes to pass over her full breasts before glancing away.

"I'm sure you did not want to meet with me to discuss the weather and current news events. What is it that you wanted to speak with me about?" he said, finishing the last forkful of food on his plate.

"Do you believe in time travel?" Kate stared into his eyes as if looking for an answer.

"In theory, I suppose it may be possible."

Kate interrupted him. "No, do *YOU* believe in time travel? Do you believe it is actually possible? If so, how might that be?" she intently inquired.

"Off the record, yes. My students have asked me that question many times, but never with as much sincere intensity as you. Why is it so important to you to know if I do?"

"I've been doing some research and—"

"I thought so. Research. It's always research." He almost seemed emotionally hurt by Kate's response. "That's the only way a man like me ever gets to meet a beautiful lady like yourself." He was disappointed that her reasoning for there wasn't more than for research purposes.

"What do you mean, you thought so? And, thank you, but you don't know the first thing about me." Her eyes flared with childlike dare.

Stephan was taken a bit off guard by Kate's feisty response, "Now who's jumping to conclusions? I never said that I thought—"

Kate's mouth widened into a smile as she burst into laughter. "Our first argument and we've barely known each other for 30 minutes." Kate recognized the silliness of the moment.

"I suppose you're right. I apologize if I said something that upset you." He smiled.

"What do you mean, if you said something?" she began again.

"Alright, alright, I said something. I admit it, I'm guilty." He playfully threw his hands up in the air in a surrendering motion.

"I'm sorry too," she said, feeling satisfied and deeply drawn to Stephan.

"Now, to get back to the original question. Yes, I believe in time travel, but I can only theorize on its possibilities. Is there anything in particular you want to know?"

"How does time work? I mean, what could make time change? I already know about the speed of light and velocity. What I don't understand is how a person can actually be transferred from one point back to another?"

"Time has no beginning and no end. It can go on for infinity. We scale time like a ruler, running as an ordered series of events in a straight line. Each line and marking on that ruler is a forth-coming year. With man's limited knowledge of quantum mechanics at this point in our study, it is possible that someday we may be able to change our velocity through time. As predicted, most theorist believe in multiple dimensions with the fourth dimension being time. Despite Einstein stating we can only travel forward in time though, and not backwards in our own timeline, many theorists believe this may not be true. The oddities and seemingly unpredictability of the quantum world that we are beginning to understand has yet to come into agreement with classical physics and general relativity. Personally, I think there is a hole in time, or tear so to say, in the fabric and frequency of what divides one dimension or possibly universe from one another. We are just starting to come to terms with something called the Einstein-Rosen Bridge which is a type of black hole that may act as a wormhole that could provide a passageway from one world or dimension into another."

"A black hole?" Thoughts of a time travel movie Kate had seen years earlier came to mind.

"Imagine you are walking along a ruler." He took a piece of paper out of his briefcase and folded it into a thin strip the size of a ruler. He used his pen to make several lines at the edges of the paper, trying to make it resemble a ruler.

"Please continue," Kate said with enthusiasm.

"Here's the ruler, the continuum of time. You're walking along and all of a sudden, something unforeseen happens, you fall in one of these holes here." He pointed with his finger to a place on the paper where you might see a binder hole in a ruler. "You are no longer in the continuum of time as we know it. You are possibly in another dimension or simply a void in space. Time may have no meaning or may be measured differently than we do in our dimension."

Kate leaned closer to Stephan. "Do you mean to say there may be several of these holes in our space that would lead us into another space and time?"

Cupping his chin in his hand, Stephan said, "In theory, it's very possible."

"How would you get back though this hole? Is it possible to get back through a hole in space?" Her eyebrows knitted together, and her heart began pounding faster. She hoped he would give her some insight and answers to her dilemma.

Demonstrating with his fake ruler and finger, he continued, "This space here on the other side of the hole is vast. To get back out exactly where you came from would be unlikely. Therefore, if you were not careful, you could accidentally come back through any one of these other holes or places in time."

"This all sounds so bizarre and science fiction-like." Kate paused for a moment to reflect upon what Stephan just said to her.

I can't believe that something like what happened to me can happen by accident. Some greater power, like God, has to have a part in it. Kate thought.

There was still more questions in Kate's mind that she kept to herself for now: What was the reason she had traveled into a different time? Was it just an accident? Or was there a more profound explanation for her being when she was now in time? Feeling enlightened, yet discouraged at the same time, she at least had some hope of returning home, into the year 1992.

"I hope I have helped answer some of your questions," Stephan replied sincerely.

"Definitely. You've been very helpful. I'm very happy to have had the chance to talk with you. You're a very interesting man."

"You're a very interesting lady. I'm truly glad that I've had the chance and good fortune to meet you," he said, his eyes smiling mischievously at Kate.

"I suppose I shouldn't take up any more of your time. I'm sure you are a busy man and must have a class to teach."

Kate didn't really want their meeting to end; she secretly hoped that Stephan would invite her out on a date. Maybe with time, she might actually be able to confide her secret with Stephan. He, if anyone, might actually believe her when she told him that she traveled through time. She might have found a confidante that won't think her insane when she tried to speak the truth. Still fearful of his rejection, she knew now wasn't the time to divulge anything and decided that it wasn't worth the risk just yet. She valued the possibility of a long-lasting friendship, maybe even romance, more than she did the truth.

"For a teacher, you may be surprised to find that I sometimes have difficulty with words. That is to say, may I call on you sometime in the near future?" His face blushed with embarrassment.

"I would like that very much. How about next Saturday?"

Stephan seemed surprised at Kate's boldness, but was not offended. He even felt a little relieved that she responded the way she did.

Kate found his awkwardness and blushing charming. She found his gentlemanly ways to be refreshing.

"Fine, good . . . . great. Do you like movies or, would you rather see a concert or something?"

"Whatever you decide is fine. I like everything, everything except hockey and basketball." Kate laughed but meant what she said.

"I promise no basketball." He chuckled in his deep and breathy voice.

"What do you think? Does 7 o'clock sound like a good time?" Kate realized she was probably being too forceful for a woman in this era, but she had no intentions of letting this guy slip through her fingers.

"7 o'clock is just perfect. Where should I pick you up?" He fumbled through his briefcase, looking for a pen to write with.

Stephan wrote down the information as Kate spoke it, being very careful to have it written accurately. Stephan looked at his watch and stood up quickly. His body unfolded into a tall and strong structure with broad shoulders. "I'm sorry to be rushing off in this manner, but I have a class to teach," he stated apologetically.

"I understand perfectly. Please don't apologize."

"I will give you a call later this week to finalize our plans. I'm really looking forward to getting to know you better. I have a feeling there is more to you than meets the eye. You intrigue me, Kate Taylor." He looked long and hard into Kate's eyes.

"As you me." Kate paused with a flirtatious look. "Unfortunately, I don't have a phone yet. The phone company said it would take a week to ten days before it can be installed and hooked up, so I'll have to call you."

Stephan helped Kate out of her chair in a mannerly fashion, and they bid their final farewells to each other.

The days of the week passed quickly, and the week's end was at present. Kate had begun working and was becoming familiar and comfortable with the job's routine. Although she yearned to be back home in 1992, she was getting accustomed to living in 1955. She figured she could make the best of her situation if she held onto the hope that she may return to the time she came from.

CHAPTER TEN

Even though autumn was not officially to begin for a few weeks, the air was dry and cool. The trees were half barren and the sun hid most of the days behind clouds. The crisp breeze blew from the north, causing people in its path to put on sweaters or jackets. Kate welcomed this change in weather. She always enjoyed the diversity the four seasons inevitably would bring: whether it be a sports activity or as simple as new clothes appropriate for the temperatures. She had noticed that people change with seasons also, seeming to be more family-oriented in the winter and more friend-oriented in the summer. Their moods were more positive and exhilarated in the spring, seeming to come alive just like the plant and flowers. People, like animals, want to grow and produce in the spring. Autumn seemed like a time for reflection, a time for people to look within themselves and make an evaluation and any adjustments, if necessary.

Kate's eyes followed the electrical cord up the wall to the clock. Soon she was to have her first date since entering into this place in time. Stephan had apparently taken some serious interest in the questions she had presented him with earlier in the week. He also seemed genuinely interested in Kate as a person. To Kate's dismay, she did not see his interest in her lasting, believing that once she told him the real reason she had come to him, he would believe her to be a lunatic. Even though she intended on trying her best to convince him of her predicament, she realized it was a long shot. Besides, even if he did believe her, a single man in this time may be frightened away by a pregnant single woman. Although she did not yet appear pregnant, she knew it would not be that way for long. Soon her hormones would have their way with her body, preparing for the growing life within her. Actually, the thought started to appeal to her.

As Kate applied a thick, pasty, red lipstick to her lips, she paused to look at herself in the mirror, smiling at the intensity the color gave to her face. How often she remembered her Mother saying, "Honey, you look pale. Why don't you put some rouge on?

At least put some lipstick on." Kate recalled how weird she thought that sounded. Wearing just lipstick made her think that she would look like a vampire or Dorothy Lamour. Now, here before her in a mirror, she was applying lipstick to her lips as though it were going out of style, applying enough of it to last days. A second thought came to mind. Wasn't there some carcinogens found in the red color dye they used in this stuff? Maybe I'm wrong. Maybe I'm not. I think they did ban this dye. In the midst of second and third thoughts on the subject, Kate proceeded to wipe it off. "Why press fate," she said to herself as she laughed at the irony of that statement.

"I can't believe I'm doing this to my hair," she spoke aloud to herself. "This is so terrible to do to a person's hair." Kate grimaced as she continued to rat her hair higher and harder. While applying hair spray at regular intervals, she tried not to think of the damage it was doing to her hair. "To think I've spent years and money using careful hair care products and treatment, and now I do this to it."

As Kate left the bathroom, she thought about the beautifying process and the look it achieved; a look common to the 50's and distressing to her.

I suppose this is one part of this era I will never like or get used to. Maybe after tonight, I will groom myself more how I like to see me. Who knows, my non-conformist attitude may catch on as a new trend. The dawn of a new era will come to pass, and I will be the cause of it.

Kate giggled at the dramatic and pompous surmise that thought related. She was having fun in her own effort at humor, something she hadn't done in a long time.

Kate borrowed a dress from Leala to wear just for tonight. She did not, however, try to attempt putting on the new silk stockings she bought. The garter and stockings presented her with difficulty when she tried them on earlier in the day. I'm sure I'll get the hang of it she thought. I do not, however, want to risk them falling down my legs tonight in public. That would prove to be extremely embarrassing. I guess I'll just have to be daring and go barelegged. "Where are those manufacturers with their giant plastic eggs with pantyhose inside when you need them?" she openly exclaimed.

Before long, Kate heard a car horn beep outside her apartment in the street. That must be Stephan she thought to herself. Picking up her handbag, she took a look around to make sure she had turned off the light in the back of the house. She double-checked the lock on the back door and pulled the window shades down. She double locked the front door upon leaving. As she turned around she realized that this ritual of securing the premises probably wasn't necessary here. Nonetheless, doing so was familiar and made her feel more comfortable.

Stephan waited for her on the sidewalk in front of her home. Handsomely dressed, he wore a three-piece brown suit. His hair was combed back slickly with the help of Vitalis. In his hands he carried one single carnation. He stood patiently waiting for Kate to reach him. Slowly and gracefully, Kate made her way down the path to him. She actually felt a bit girlish, yet sexy by the admiring stare she received from Stephan.

Stephan romantically extended his arm for Kate to take hold of, and he guided her to his vehicle. He opened the car door for her and handed her the flower he had brought as a gift for her. After closing the car door, he went around to the other side and got into the car.

Putting her independent nature behind her and the lessons of the women's movement of the 1970's, Kate began a night to always remember.

The ride to the restaurant passed quickly and they arrived in little time. Kate's thoughts, however, were long and didn't seem to end.

I can't believe this man is happening to me Kate thought. He's so, so . . . . I don't know what it is that he is or that I'm feeling.

90

I've never felt so instantly attracted to any man before. I feel like I've known him for years, yet we've barely met.

"I hope you like Italian food. I've enjoyed the food here for years."

"Yes, I love Italian food." Looking up, Kate saw a large sign, it read: Vincent's Village.

Stephan and Kate were seated and had given their orders to a waitress serving their table.

"This wine you ordered is wonderful," Kate said, sipping from a long stemmed wine glass. She casually glanced around the room.

It was a small and cozy place fashioned in a very Italian decor. Vines grew from the walls and dim lights hovered above every table. Pictures of familiar land sites in Italy hung on some of the walls. The tables, covered in wine red tablecloths, were situated far enough apart from one another to ensure a little privacy.

"So, you come here often?" she asked curiously, wondering who else he had been there with.

As if he had read her mind, he looked at her with a sly grin and replied, "Not really. I stop here for lunch sometimes." Changing the subject, Stephan asked, "How did you get to be so beautiful?" Cupping his hands under his chin, he stared at Kate, making her feel uncomfortable with his uncharacteristic boldness as he starred lustfully at her.

Kate blushed and passed on any response. Instead she began an entirely new conversation. "Why do you do the work you do?"

"It's a simple answer. I don't look at it as work and I enjoy teaching. I enjoy science. I see so many young people come and go, and I know that I've somehow made a difference in their lives, in their thinking. I have the opportunity to open new windows and doors in the minds of these kids, show them new avenues they may have never seen before." Stephan's genuine enthusiasm showed in his face.

"I guess I never thought of it in that way before. I always thought that most teachers hated their jobs, having to deal with the same hassles day after day."

"I suppose some teachers or profesors do feel that way. I think that is because they start teaching as a second calling to what they really want to be doing." Stephan stopped suddenly and paused. "Hey, wait a minute. How come you get to keep asking me all the questions? It seems to me since we've met, I've been doing all the talking and answering of questions. What do you do for a living? I've been wondering what newspaper you work for ever since that day in the cafeteria."

"What makes you think I work for a newspaper?"

"You said you were doing some research and that's why you were interested in time travel."

Kate had forgotten that she had said that. She began, a bit flustered, "Well, I suppose I did say that, but that's not what I meant. To be honest, I was more interested in what you had to say about time travel on a more personal level. I thought if I told you that I was just curious for myself, you wouldn't have made time to meet with me and answer my questions. I'm sure you already have many of your own students taking up a lot of your time with their after-hour questions. I'm sorry if I misled you. It was an innocent deceit."

"What makes you so interested in time travel? Are you thinking of taking a trip?" He laughed.

Kate briefly thought of telling Stephan the truth, she just wanted to tell someone. To have someone truly understand her and what she was going through, but realized the truth would make less sense to him than a lie.

"I just always thought it would be fascinating if we could visit and experience other times than our own. For instance, wouldn't it be marvelous to have been part of our country during the year 1776? I personally would have loved to have been part of the suffragette and in a march with the other women fighting for the right to vote. I can only imagine the personal struggles some of those women were fighting at home while trying to be free as a group. I'm sure it had to be similar to the 60s civil rights struggles the black people had when—," Kate stopped in mid-sentence.

I can't believe I just said that she thought. How stupid can you be, Kate?

Stephan didn't verbally question Kate on what she said, and although listening, he was slightly distracted by the curves of her body and he didn't seem to notice her break into sudden silence. Still, Kate couldn't help but sense he was curious and was being polite in his silence.

Kate began again, "Even more than our past, our history, the future intrigues me. Who knows what wonderful events or inventions will exist in, say, the year 1992."

"That all does sound very exciting, but dangerous."

"Dangerous! Don't be silly. What could be dangerous about experiencing more of life than our own time allows?" Kate interjected amused.

"Sure I'd love to see the pyramids being built. To be able to actually meet and converse with our sixteenth President, but that can be dangerous to our history as we know it to be now."

The smile on Kate's face disappeared and replacing it was a sincere look of interest. "How and why could a person's travel through time be dangerous?"

"Just imagine I get the opportunity to meet President Lincoln. It just so happened to be there on the day of his assassination. I have a very pleasant conversation with him. I like him. I know he is to die that very same day. Does my conscious allow that to happen or do I try and stop it. It could be a moral dilemma."

"Well, obviously you would have to let history take its course."

"True, but it could be very emotionally upsetting for a majority of people. More important than events we know we shouldn't tamper with are the ones we don't know we are tampering with." The look in his eyes became fiery with conviction.

Kate clasped her hands together and started to squeeze her fingers together tightly. She knew she was going to hear something she didn't want to; some important aspect of her situation she hadn't thought of before.

Stephan continued, "An unmarried man is walking down the street and I stop and talk with him for a few minutes. Sounds harmless . . . . The truth being, that on that day at that time, that man was killed. He stepped off the curb and was hit by a truck, but now that hasn't happened because I detained him from what he was supposed to be doing. In those few minutes of conversation with a stranger, I could have had a major effect on the future, even my own timeline history."

"I understand that by being there when you shouldn't have been that you altered things, but I don't see it as necessarily being bad. You did save his life by detaining him. He would have died if you weren't there."

"Kate, think! Yes, I did save his life, but next time the opposite could happen. I might detain someone and cause them to be somewhere they shouldn't be. They step off a street curb, but instead of saving them from a tragedy, I cause one. BAM! They get hit by a car! Just my presence and innocent interaction with that person could prevent someone like our great President Roosevelt from being conceived, because it was his Father who was killed." Stephan drove one of his hands into the other, making a loud clapping noise.

"How horrible! I guess I didn't realize the consequences of one's own actions." Kate sat back in her chair, completely losing her appetite.

"I'm sorry, sometimes I'm a little too dramatic with my explanations. I just see so many angles to some situations that I can't control my thoughts or exuberance. The opposite of that could happen too. Let's say the man I saved by distraction of my conversation doesn't die as he originally had will probablylive onto marry and have children? Then his children will have children, and so on. Who knows, one of his descendants that didn't exist before could grow to be a mass murderer or a Hitler-type."

Kate began to worry. Had she already changed the course of someone's history?

How can I go on and try to lead a normal existence now she thought. I'm afraid to even exist here in this time. What if I cause some terrible tragedy by associating with people here? I'm becoming afraid to even talk to anyone. What would Stephan be doing right now if he hadn't met me and taken me on this date? Have I already negatively affected the course of my parents lives? I never realized how much influence and effect one person could make on the lives of others.

Kate seemed to be lost in her thoughts as Stephan tried to change the subject. She didn't even notice that he was talking to her.

"Kate . . . . Kate . . . . Hello . . . . Are you in there?" He looked in her eyes for a response.

"Oh! Yes, yes, I'm sorry," she said, startled, "you were saying . . . ."

"I was saying a lot of things. All of which you didn't seem to hear. Are you feeling ill?"

"No, really, I'm fine. My mind must have just drifted into thought. I didn't intend to be rude. It's just that . . . . Well . . . .

What you were saying about time and people changing other people's destiny was simply fascinating."

"I'm glad to hear you were deep in thought because you found what I had to say fascinating, not because you thought it was boring. I was worried there for a minute. I thought I was putting you to sleep." He laughed.

The rest of the evening they discussed various topics. However, Kate couldn't seem to be able to separate her thoughts from the subject they had discussed earlier. She secretly kept reviewing all the events that had occurred since her arrival in 1955. She couldn't help but worry she had altered someone else's God-given destiny.

The date was coming to an end as they left the restaurant and entered the night's cool air.

"I had planned for us to go to the movie house, but we seemed to have spent most of the evening talking in there." He pointed to the restaurant. "I regret to say we have missed the movie. It started over an hour ago." He glanced at his watch as if to confirm what he was saying.

"That's alright. We can see the movie another time. I had a very nice time just talking with you and having a delicious dinner."

"I had a very nice time too." He was relieved and happy to hear Kate mention the possibility of a next time.

"Would you be interested in going with me next week to see the movie?" He lowered his eyes while waiting for her response.

"I'd love to."

"Wonderful." He took hold of Kate's arm to escort her to the car.

The cool night air felt refreshing as it swirled past their faces. The half barren trees swayed effortlessly. The glow of the moon shown down brightly, helping to light their path.

"I love the night!" Kate exclaimed. "Most people are afraid of the night with its darkness, but I find it peaceful." Kate tilted her head back and looked up at the sky, allowing the breeze to rush across her face. "Just look at all those beautiful stars nestled in the darkness. See how they shine! I don't recall ever seeing so many stars before." Kate realized at that moment just how all the city night lights and pollution of 1992, had obscured the beauty of the night's sky from her for so long.

Stephan watched Kate's face relax and look content. He found pleasure in just admiring her beauty and listening to her heartfelt thoughts. "Yes, it is nice," he answered.

"Just nice?" she jested as she looked at him through the corner of her eyes with a kidding look of disapproval.

"Alright, it's beautiful." He smiled as he tucked her arm snugly under his, drawing her closer to him.

They found themselves standing before the car, but dawdled a moment longer to admire the sky and hold on to each other's arm.

The drive to Kate's home seemed to take less time than it did going the opposite direction. The poorly lit streets didn't allow for Kate to view much out of her car window. Yet, she didn't mind. She had more interest in viewing Stephan.

"We're home, My Lady," Stephan announced in a playful English accent. "Your court awaits you."

Stephan walked Kate to the front door of her home.

"I've had a wonderful evening," she said.

"I have too. You're very easy to talk to. I enjoyed your company. If it is fine with you, I'll call you in a few days so we can make arrangements for another date?" Stephan leaned in close to Kate.

"That's a very good idea." Kate suddenly felt like a schoolgirl on her first date. Her heart began to beat faster and the palm of her hand felt sweaty and clammy. The anticipation of a good night kiss both scared and thrilled her. Kate leaned in to hug him goodbye while hoping for a kiss.

"Would it be alright if I kissed you goodnight?" Stephan politely asked. He could feel the warmth of Kate's breath against his neck.

Kate's eyes looked up into his and she nodded yes. Instantly, Stephan tilted his head down and pressed his lips softly against hers. His body fought against his intended thought of a short kiss. Instead his hands reached around Kate and drew her body closely up against his own. Kate did not resist, but instead a warm feeling of passion enveloped her. It was a moment that seemed lost in time as they allowed themselves to fulfill their desires of closeness.

Suddenly, Stephan let go of Kate and stepped back.

"I shouldn't have done that. I'm sorry for being so—"

Kate interrupted his words by putting her finger over his lips, "Don't! It's alright; I allowed you to. I could have resisted, but I didn't. It was something we both wanted." Kate thought it was wonderful that Stephan acted so gentleman-like, resisting his urges to protect the honor of the lady he was with.

Things are definitely different here in 1955 she thought. A man in 1992 would not have even had a second thought about a kiss like that at the end of a date. Not only that, he probably would have expected it hoping to finalize the evening with an invite into her apartment and sex.

Kate was actually beginning to feel embarrassed by her honesty, a feeling she hadn't felt with a man in a long time.

"Goodnight, Kate. I'll call you in a few days." Stephan walked to his car and drove away.

Kate stood outside of her apartment a few seconds longer, not wanting the night to end.

Once inside, she glided gleefully across the living room floor to her bedroom and started to get undressed.

This has probably been the best time I've ever had on a date. I can't pinpoint why, but it has been.

Without warning, her thoughts of happiness turned around quickly and became filled with doubt and gloom. I can't see him anymore. What if what he said about one life interfering with another is true? I don't want to change his destiny and possibly harm him. I don't want to alter anyone's destiny.

Kate began to cry profusely. Her tears had only become another reminder that she didn't belong. Her emotions were torn between her desires and reality. What am I to do? She asked herself. It wasn't within my control to come here in the first place. Soon I'm going to have a baby to contend with, besides all this madness. It's impossible for me not to be involved with other people, but.....

Kate threw herself on her bed and continued to weep until her body was exhausted. Without warning she fell and her exhausted body gave way into a night's sleep.

When the next morning arrived, Kate found herself curled up on top of her bed covers. The remaining clothes she wore were disheveled from a night of tossing and turning. Her lips felt dry and chapped and her hair was smashed stiffly to one side of her head. Still drowsy, she got up from the bed and went to the washroom.

"Oh my God!" she said, looking into the mirror above the washbasin. "I'm a mess. My eyes are black with mascara and my hair . . . . ewww." She felt the tacky stiffness of her hair and tried to push it back into place.

Kate tried to put the thoughts of the night before into the back of her mind, at least until she could think more clearly. After she disrobed and showered, she began to feel more clearheaded.

After dressing, Kate made herself a cup of coffee. She sat down on a chair in the living room to think matters through. I don't want to cause anyone any harm by screwing around with their lives, but I didn't ask to come here in the first place. I don't see how it is possible for me to live in this time and not interfere with the natural course of events. I can't live in a cage for the rest of my life or the rest of the time I'm living in this place in history. For all I know, the rest of my life may only be another day or week or hour.

Kate pondered the thought of her life being short-lived and surprisingly found it to be frightening. She got up out of the chair and moved over to the window. She caught sight of her Father doing lawn work in front of the house.

Look at how strong and handsome you are, she thought to herself. I remember always wanting to have to have the chance to meet you when you were younger. Now, I've gotten the chance and found that you are the same person as when I knew you as my Father . . . kind, gentle, and humorous. The real you never really did change with age and time. Only your body and your health didn't see fit to agree with you.

Kate started crying, finding the thought of her Father's forthcoming death to be unbearable. She pulled herself away from the window and tried to catch her breath.

It's just not fair. You were taken away from us by your death. Finally, when I get the chance to be with you again, I can't tell you who I am. I can't tell you how much I love you or how much I miss you.

Although Kate wanted to spend more time speaking with her Father, she didn't. She found it painful to be that close to him and not share her feelings with him.

Kate sat down again and in her mind pretended to have a conversation with her Father. The Father she liked to remember best.

Dad, I just don't know what to do. I'm so confused about my place in this world and this time in it. For the first time in a long time, I'm really beginning to feel happy about my relationships with other people. I am looking forward to the birth of my baby, and I have a new man in my life. Then, why is God making things so difficult for me?

Without warning, an image of her Father sitting in an easy chair from when she was a child popped into her mind and spoke. "Katie, if you always do what you feel is right in your heart, everything else will work out for the best. You must be patient with yourself and others, and time will heal all wounds and allow you the chance to start anew."

Kate sat up, startled by her own recollection of her Father. I suppose you may have been right, Dad. I have been given a new chance in life, and I don't intend on screwing it up again. I can't worry any more, or be concerned about what I'm doing at this very minute. I need to make sure I make the most of every minute, every hour, and every day that I'm through right now.

Kate got up and went to look in the mirror in the washroom. She looked at herself and some other accessories in the mirrors reflection. She saw a stack of makeup left on the sink from the night before. She saw hair spray and curlers and her face.

If I'm going to give myself a chance in this new life, it has got to be done my way. No more bouffant hair-sprayed hair-dos, no more gobs of makeup, no more pretend. I'm not a woman of the fifties. I am a woman of the 90's, and it's about time I start looking like one, looking like me.

She stepped back from the mirror and gathered many of the makeup items in her hands, only leaving a few she thought necessary. She walked to the garbage can and disposed of them.

Goodbye poisoned, red-dyed lipstick.   Goodbye blue eye shadow. Goodbye false eyelashes.

CHAPTER ELEVEN

After fixing her appearance a little, she decided to go over and visit with Leala. As she knocked on the door, she could hear crying coming from the other side. Within a minute or two, the door opened. Kean looked serious as he passed Kate in the doorway. Without even a hello, he continued on his way, leaving Kate and Leala behind.

"What's wrong Leala? What happened? Did you have an argument with Kean?"

"No, not really. I mean we did have words, but . . . . " Leala burst into more tears.

"Take your time. Now, what happened?" Kate patiently tried to probe Leala for some details.

Kean's sister-in-law, Jeanette came over to visit with her baby. She noticed that the painting she painted for us was no longer on the wall. She immediately became defensive and asked where her gift of love, as she put it, was."

"Do you mean that ugly one you had hanging on the wall in your dining room? The painting Kean hates?"

"Yes, that's the one. I was taken by surprise and didn't know exactly what to say. Quickly, I told her I had spilled some water from a filled vase accidentally on it."

"Is that what really happened?"

"No, I threw it in the garbage just yesterday. Can you believe that? Do I have lousy timing or what? I thought about what Kean said, 'Jeanette never comes over,'" she mocked Kean, imitating his voice and actions, as if blaming him.

"Did she believe you?"

"Yes, as a matter of fact, she offered to paint another one for us."

"Well, then, what did you and Kean argue over? It sounds like everything turned out fine," she stated confused.

"Kean insisted that he take her out back and show her what he's been doing in the garden. Well, to shorten the whole story, she saw it."

"Saw what?" Kate was beginning to become annoyed.

"The painting. There it was, sitting on top of the garbage can in plain sight. She saw that it wasn't damaged and became infuriated. She stormed back into the house and demanded an explanation. I was dumbfounded. I didn't know what to say to her."

"Where was Kean?"

"He stayed out back. What a coward! It's all his fault anyway. If he hadn't suggested we remove it from the wall in the first place, if he hadn't insisted in taking her out back, this whole thing would have never happened." Her voice became filled with anger.

"You can't really be serious?" Kate asked in defense of her Father.

"Why not? Then, to top it all off, he leaves me to deal with his sister."

"Maybe he has some good reasons for not coming in the house right away. Maybe—"

Leala cut Kate off in mid-sentence. "Maybe he has just never grown up enough to actually speak to his older sister in an adult manner. Doesn't matter anyway, anymore."

"Oh no, what happened?" Kate shook her head, horrified at the possibilities.

"She was understandably upset, but she immediately became very nasty. She cursed at me, insulted me and wished horrible things upon me. I naturally became enraged. I called her a fat slob who couldn't paint the side of a barn properly if she tried and told her to get out of my house and never come back." Leala's eyebrows furrowed with worry. Although she felt justified, she also felt regretful.

"Did you really say that?" Kate's face lit up in disbelief. Suddenly, she burst out in laughter. "I can't believe you said that to her." Kate wrapped her arms around her stomach that ached because she was laughing so hard.

"Kate! The situation is not funny. How can you stand there and laugh. Don't you realize what my words have caused? I've created a huge family dispute, all because I didn't hold my tongue." A smile began to creep to the corners of Leala's mouth.

"Don't take it so hard. I'm sure over time things will heal themselves. Besides, she deserves an insult like being called a fat slob." Kate covered her mouth and more laughter. She knew her statement to be true, time would heal some of the damage done.

After all these years, I finally find out what happened between Mom and Aunt Jeanette she thought. So this is what caused them to not speak to each other for so many years. I wish I could make Leala feel better and tell her what I know, that the situation will improve in years to come, that it doesn't really matter, that not associating with aunt Jeanette was no real loss to her or Daddy, that Jeanette's kids will turn out just as obnoxious as Jeanette, and no one in the family will ever like any of them.

Kate stayed and visited for only a few minutes longer, until she was satisfied that Leala was feeling better. As she was leaving Leala's home, she saw Kean up the walkway approaching with a bunch of flowers in his hand.

Apparently Mom and Daddy are about to make amends with each other Kate thought.

The rest of Kate's day became consumed with such tasks as cleaning and doing laundry.

I can't believe how difficult it is trying to wash clothes this way Kate thought. Thank goodness Leala has been doing my laundry for me.

Kate struggled with the ringer washer she had access to in the basement of the building. She felt fortunate to have washing facilities in her building when so many people didn't, but was at a loss to function properly with such foreign machinery. She kept getting the clothes stuck in the ringer and twice she almost lost her hand in the ringer press.

The water never really gets hot. The clothes don't seem to get as clean as they do with an automatic washer and I'm tired of fighting with this stupid machine.

Kate pulled one of her blouses through the ringer so hard that she tore it.

"That's it, I quit!" she shouted in frustration. My poor Mother. How could she stand to do this for so many years?

Gathering what laundry she had left, she climbed the basement stairs and returned to her apartment. She spent the rest of the day doing household cleaning chores and grocery shopping. During the evening while she was resting on the couch, the telephone rang. Stephan had phoned her.

"Hi Kate. It's Stephan. How are you doing today?" he politely asked.

"Fine, I suppose." She was glad he called.

"I'm going to have to keep the conversation short, but would you want to go out again with me this coming Saturday night?" His voice sounded hopeful.

"That sounds great, I'd love to. What time should I be ready?"

"Does six o'clock sound like a good time to you?"

"Perfect."

"I'll see you then. I've got to hang up now. Bye."

I suppose this phone call means he really does like me. I hope he will continue to like me even after I tell him I'm pregnant.

Kate knew she would have to tell Stephan soon, but decided to wait a little longer. She thought, if their relationship didn't continue past the point of being casual, it would be pointless to tell Stephan she was pregnant.

The rest of the weekend passed uneventfully, and a few days had passed. Kate's emotional state was deteriorating. She tried to attribute some of her distress to hormonal changes, but knew that was not the reason.

I can't live like this anymore. Something's got to give, and I'm afraid it's going to be me. I can't go on with this charade. I feel like I've been acting in a play or movie. The scenes keep changing, and I just go with the mood, or whatever seems to be needed at the time. I can't pretend this is normal anymore. I just can't . . . .

Kate began sobbing uncontrollably. Her hands trembled against her face as she cupped them over her eyes.

I want to go home. I mean, what I think is home. Everyone thinks I'm a strong person emotionally and mentally, but I'm not. Every day is a struggle just to continue on. I need help. I need . . . .

Kate really wasn't sure what she needed. She tried to put her needs and thoughts into perspective but found it an impossible task. Her eyes quickly became red and achy from her severe crying. Her throat started to feel as though she swallowed an orange whole. Her full lips became chapped and salty tasting.

I wonder if my baby is a girl or a boy. What should I name it? Kate's thoughts took a drastic change of course. Her thoughts became erratic. I like Daniel and it would be appropriate. I secretly wish to have a girl, a petite and precious little thing that I could love and protect. Either way, I just want a happy healthy baby that I can love, and who will love me unconditionally.

"It's just you and me kid against the world," she said aloud to herself, secretly hoping the baby could hear her.

Get a hold of yourself she thought. This is life and it's the only one you've got, so make the best of it. Besides, you have not only yourself to think about anymore, you've got a baby. Getting off the couch she went to look in a mirror.

"So quit crying and feeling sorry for yourself," she said to herself in the mirror, "and get on with living. Don't worry, you'll survive whatever is thrown at you." Her voice hardened, as if almost scolding herself.

CHAPTER TWELVE

Over the next few weeks, Kate had several dates with Stephan. They had enjoyed movies, plays, and museums together. Kate was finding herself falling deeper and deeper in love with him, and the same was true of Stephan's feelings for her.

I wonder if it has been fate all along that Stephan and I be together. Maybe he is the reason I came to this time in the first place. Well, tomorrow will be a test of that fate. I have to tell him I'm pregnant. I'm beginning to show, and I've already waited too long in telling him. I've been very unfair to him by not letting him know much sooner what he was getting himself into. I should have given him a choice in the matter, whether or not to get involved with a pregnant woman, right from the beginning.

Stephan had chosen a quaint Irish pub for their dining and entertainment for that evening. The Gaelic atmosphere was both festive and charming.

"What do you think of the place? I've never been here myself before. I hope you like it," Stephan's voice grew louder so Kate would be able to hear him clearly over the many voices and noises in the crowded room.

"It's very nice, but I was hoping for a little more quiet. There is something important I need to talk to you about."

"Oh, we could leave if you want to," he replied indifferently.

"Maybe they have a back room here. Let's ask the waitress."

Kate asked the waitress when she passed by their table. The restaurant did indeed have a back room which was more intended for dining purposes, so they moved from the pub area and got seating in the back.

"This is much nicer, don't you think?"

"Yes, this is fine."

After they had both ordered their food, Kate directed their conversation to the topic she felt needed to be discussed.

"Stephan, I have something to tell you. It's something I should have told you a long time ago; but to be honest, I was afraid to. I wasn't sure how you would take it."

Stephan reached over the table and took Kate's hand. "What is it Kate? Please don't be afraid to tell me anything. I have hoped that by now you would know how much you mean to me and that you can trust me." His eyes smiled as he looked at her endearingly.

"I'm pregnant. I'm going to have a baby. Before I met you, I was involved with another man. I loved him, but not the way a woman should love someone she wants to marry, and he felt the same way. Needless to say, we broke off any ties with each other and I haven't seen him since." Kate sat back in her chair waiting for his response.

"Does this man know you are pregnant?" he asked, trying to be nonchalant.

"No, he doesn't know. I don't know where he is, and I'm unable to contact him and let him know. Besides, I'm sure it wouldn't make a difference anyway. He never seemed very interested in children, and I don't expect for him to show any interest now. Don't get me wrong, he's a nice guy. He just doesn't want to have children, and I knew that when we became involved. However, accidents do happen."

"Wow! This definitely is something you should have told me sooner. I really care for you, but the idea of raising another man's child . . . . I don't know." Stephan pulled away from Kate.

"Wait a minute. I didn't tell you this because I expect you to raise my child. I told you because I thought—" Kate's words trailed off. Suddenly, she realized what he had said.

He must care enough about me that he had already considered marriage. I suppose the news of this baby has thrown his plans out of whack. I suppose I should be honest with myself, too. The reason I told him is because I love him and want to marry him.

"Believe it or not, I have a hard time telling people my feelings. I guess I'm afraid of being hurt, but I do want to tell you I love you. I'm not saying this now because I am pregnant and want a husband and Father for my child. I'll completely understand if you never want to see me again and want to end what we have together now. I'd be hurt by it, but I'd understand it. I also realize you may need time to think about how you feel about me and what I just told you."

"Look, our food is here." Stephan withdrew his emotions and refused to discuss it any further. He was feeling very confused and chose to shut off the subject of the baby and Kate until he felt he would be able to deal with the situation more effectively.

"Stephan, let me know what you are thinking." She was puzzled by his behavior.

"I think the food looks delicious, don't you?" He looked at Kate directly, his eyes warning her to back off and let it go for the time being.

Kate took heed to his warning and didn't intend on mentioning the subject again until he seemed ready to discuss it with her. Through the rest of their meal they touched upon various subjects, yet said very little to each other; their exchange of words were few and far between. When the meal was finished, Stephan paid the check and they left without staying and enjoying any of the entertainment provided by the establishment.

"Where are we going?" Kate asked, trying to catch up with Stephan who was walking hastily.

"I'm taking you home." He opened the car door for her.

"What? That's it! I've tried to be patient, but you're acting like an asshole. You can't ignore me and push me away like I'm a piece of shit."

Stephan continued to stand and hold the car door for her, pretending he didn't notice her outburst.

"This isn't fair. How can you do this to me? I thought you said you cared about me," she yelled imposingly.

In a sudden burst of rage, Stephan slammed the car door shut and began yelling at Kate. "Damn it! I do care! I wouldn't still be here if I didn't love you. You want me to talk, I'll talk. I'm hurt! I'm angry! How could you keep something like this from me for so long? This is important information….monumental information! Didn't you trust me? What kind of jerk do you think I am?" he yelled, slapping his hands against his chest. "No, I'm not thrilled you are carrying another man's baby, but I'll deal with it. I just can't process all this in a moment…I need time to think…to sort through what it is that I am thinking or feeling. The child is also part of you, and I want to be with you. It's just that I'm getting a lot more responsibility than I bargained for. I've never been very good at committing to a relationship with a woman. My work always came first. You know, that is why I never got married. Then you came along and completely turned around my way of living." His eyes started to fill with tears, but he held them back. Suddenly reflective he lowered his voice and mellowed. "Kate, I've never felt like this before with a woman. I think I've completely fallen in love with you . . . . I'm just going to need some time to think, to get adjusted." He stopped speaking, lowered his eyes, and listlessly reopen the car door for her.

Tears streamed down Kate's face and she slowly and silently got in the car. She was tremendously touched by his honesty. She wanted to reach out to him and hug him tightly in her arms but didn't dare. She understood his feelings and didn't want to make him withdraw from her again. She decided to give him the moment and do with it what he wanted.

He loves me she thought. He really doesn't care that I'm pregnant with another man's child. He's more concerned that he won't be able to deal with being a husband and a Father.

Stephan drove Kate directly home. He saw her enter her apartment safely, watching from the car.

The very next morning, Kate received a telephone call from Stephan. His voice was tired, sounding deep and crackling.

He began, "Hi, it's me. I've been up all night thinking about what happened between us and about what you told me. I'm sorry if I acted like an inconsiderate idiot. I was, or am, just very—"

Kate interrupted him, "No, I'm the one who should apologize. I should have been more considerate of you and your feelings. You were absolutely right. I should have told you sooner. I have just been so confused and scared." Her voice cracked and a tear rolled down her cheek.

"I realize that now. Let's try and put the madness of last night behind us. I love you and one thing I do know for sure is, I want to be with you."

"I love you more than you know. I feel lucky to have found someone as kind and understanding as you."

"I'll call you tonight sweetheart and we will make plans to get together for a very quiet and romantic night. I know we need o talk more about this and so many other pivotal things"

"Alright, I love you, bye." Kate hung up the phone receiver.

The days and weeks seemed to pass effortlessly. Kate had become comfortable with the routines of her days. Her relationship with Stephan grew closer and the bond between them grew stronger. She had become quite content with her life and the people involved in it. She no longer wished to leave her new found home and feared that at any time it may be snatched from her. Consequently, she cherished every waking moment she had, making the most of the moment. Although she questioned the permanence of her existence in 1955, she made plans for her and the baby's future. Plans that included Stephan. She began to believe she had at last found her destiny and the happiness she had had such a difficult time finding.

Kate started to gently rub her stomach and talk to her unborn child, "What do you think of having Stephan for a Daddy? I know, I know, I'm rushing matters. But, I love him so much and he loves me; and I know he cares about you, too. Oh little one, you have given me so much to look forward to. You've helped me to appreciate some of the smaller things in life. I know at first I thought that I didn't really want a baby, but I was wrong. Getting pregnant with you was the best thing that could have happened to me. It forced me to grow up and stop being so self-centered, to look beyond myself and tomorrow and see the many possibilities life has to offer. I love you already sweetheart . . . ."

Kate felt sure her unborn child could hear her. She knew the baby probably didn't understand what she was saying, but knew that it could understand the love that she felt. Feeling serene as though Kate, herself, had made a new revelation about herself through her conversation with the baby, she slipped into a peaceful nap.

Rinnnggg! Rinngg.

The phone startled her out of a sleep. She jumped up off the couch to answer it. She hadn't quite gotten her bearings as she picked up the telephone receiver.

"Hello?" she started drowsily.

"Kate, this is Leala." Her voice sounded weak and frightened. "Please come over. Something's wrong. It hurts—" Her voice trailed off as she dropped the phone to clutch her stomach.

"Oh my God!" Kate dropped the phone and immediately ran next door to Leala's home.

The empathy between Kate and Leala was so intense, that Kate immediately knew what was wrong by the sound of Leala's voice.

How can this be happening Kate thought as she struggled to open Leala's front door.

"I can't get in! Leala, try to get to the door," Kate yelled in desperation.

Leala did not respond to Kate's plea. She lay unconscious on the living room floor. The pain had become so great that she had fainted. Frantically pounding on the door, Kate hoped to get a response from Leala.

What am I going to do? Think! Think! she said to herself. I better phone for an ambulance or the police or somebody.

Kate ran back to her apartment and called the police department and asked to get an ambulance there immediately. She quickly explained the situation, "My neighbor is pregnant and I think she is having a miscarriage. I can't get into the apartment, and she isn't responding to my call. I think she is unconscious."

"Alright, ma'am, just try and calm yourself. We'll send a police car and a first aid responder right away. What's the address?" The police officer's benign voice and attitude did little to calm Kate.

Kate told the police officer the information he needed and begged him that they hurry.

Kate went back over to Leala's and again pounded on the door and called her name. Again there was no response from Leala.

I've got to figure out a way to get in there. I wonder if the back door or window is open.

Kate rushed to the back of the building, hoping there would be some way for her to get into the apartment. When she reached the back, she noticed a window slightly open. It was situated in a

115

place awkward for Kate to reach or even get to. Kate risked her own safety and went and retrieved a garbage can to stand on.

If I can just reach a little further up, I might be able to— Kate strained, trying to get at the window to open it. She felt her fingertips barely reach the bottom of the window. "This is no use," she said to herself.

Kate was stepping down off the garbage can when she felt a terrible cramp on her left side.

"Ooh!"

Kate quickly sat down on the sidewalk on which she was standing. The cramp ceased almost as suddenly as it had started, but she took just a few seconds longer to rest before she got up.

I must have just strained a little too much, she thought. Dear God, please let Leala be okay. I don't understand how this can be happening. I know she is pregnant with me, and she gave birth to me, so why is this happening to her. Unless—

Suddenly, Kate heard a loud commotion in the front of the house toward the noise. She got up and hurried to the front of the house.

The police were already working on opening the front door of Leala's apartment. They had a master key and were trying to unlock it.

"Just kick it in!" Kate blurted out in anger.

"Ma'am, just stand back, please. We don't want to do any damage unless we have to. This here is a master key, fitting most locks and . . . . see, there, it's open." The officer almost gloated in his judgment.

This is a nightmare, Kate thought. I didn't know that emergency services, like ambulances and trained paramedics didn't even exist yet as they do in 1992!

116

Kate allowed the first aid responder to enter the apartment first, but stepped in front of the officer entering through the doorway. She could barely believe her eyes when she saw Leala lying unconscious on the floor. She leaned back against the wall and let the paramedics do what they needed to do in order to help Leala. Within a couple of minutes, the paramedics had secured Leala to a stretcher and were taking her to the hospital in the ambulance.

"Would you like to come with? Or do you want to follow in your own car?" one of the policeman asked, doubting that she would have a car or driver's license.

Kate decided to ride with Leala and they rushed to the hospital.

Kate thought the ride to the hospital seemed long and never ending, even though it was no more than a ten-minute ride.

What in the world is happening? She can't be actually losing the baby. That's impossible because she's pregnant with me and I'm here. I wonder if Stephan was right when he said that a person must be very careful about their interactions with people of another time. I wonder if somewhere along the way I've interfered or changed something that lead to this. I knew that I would have made some sort of effect of the future by being here now. I knew that if I ever got back into 1992 that there might be some little differences, but . . . . Now I'm not even sure if I'm going to ever exist in 1992. Will I be stuck here or will I just vanish off the face of the Earth? Kate's thoughts reeled in panic.

"Excuse me, ma'am, please . . . . we have to get through here." The ambulance driver spoke in a loud tone. Kate had been temporarily lost in her thoughts and did not hear the attendant the first time he asked her to move.

Once inside the hospital, Doctors and nurses rushed Leala into an emergency room and immediately started to examine her.

Leala was still unconscious and her face was pale and wet with perspiration.

Kate stood outside the room in the hall pacing the floor. She was feeling panicky and concerned, not only for Leala but for herself.

Think, girl, think. Calm down and use your brain. It's probably not possible to just vanish from existence. However, I didn't think it was possible to vanish from one point in time to another. If it is possible for me to have indirectly or directly caused this, what was it that I did? Maybe it wasn't one thing, but a series of events that I was involved with. I can't stand this waiting anymore. God, I don't want to die! I want to live!

Kate's thoughts seemed overwhelming. She recalled how she had had a desperate wish to end her life before she was thrown into another time.

Yes, I was unhappy and wanted my life, as it was, to end, but now things are different. I didn't realize the real values and meaning that life has. I was too self-centered to see beyond the moment. I didn't appreciate what I had. Alright! Alright, I admit it. Please, God, you have shown me my strengths and all the many possibilities life has in store for me. Please don't take what I now have away from me. Give me another chance.

"Excuse me. Are you with Mrs. Tierney?" The Doctor's face was sullen. "You look quite pale. Are you feeling alright?"

"Yes! What is going on? Is she okay? Is she going to lose the baby?" Kate's questions flew at the Doctor as if she were cross-examining him.

"Please, I know this is difficult for you, but you must calm yourself. Mrs. Tierney has torn the round ligament, a major supporting muscle of the uterus. It has caused her severe pain, which we are trying to control with medication. At the present time, her condition is stable; however, we have to keep her under close watch. It is entirely possible and probable that this could cause her to go into an early delivery of the baby. The baby at this stage of her pregnancy would have no chance for survival. She is simply not far enough along for the baby to be large enough to have developed the necessary life-sustaining body functions."

"What are the chances of the baby dying?" Her eyes filled with tears.

"At this time it is very difficult to predict anything. I must add, however; that there is no immediate sign of danger. Mrs. Tierney's vital signs look fine and so do the baby's. Both their conditions seem to be stable. It is our hope that if we keep her immobile and sedated that we may be able to pacify the situation and give the ligaments time to heal somewhat. I know you don't want to hear this, but only time will tell. We have to wait and be patient."

Kate wanted to scream. She felt frustrated and afraid. No one, including the Doctor, realized how much was at stake. Thirty-six years of living may become non-existent if that baby dies.

Kate suddenly felt a numbing of her fingers. Her head began to spin and her heart raced. The room around her seemed to be enclosing her, and her vision grew dim.

This can't be really happening she thought. Calm down, you're just panicking. Take a deep breath she told herself repeatedly.

Kate's real fear was not that she might be fainting, but that she was about to leap from this point in time, back into her own. Her fear seemed only to grow as the walls around her began visually to cave in.

The Doctor caught Kate in his arms before she had completely fainted. Just as the Doctor was ushering Kate to the nearest seat, Kean entered the emergency room in a panic.

"I left work as soon as I got the call from the nurse. I got here as fast as I could. How is Leala and the baby?" Kean just noticed Kate lying ill on the couch while the Doctor tried to revive her. "What the hell is going on here? What's the matter with Kate?" His tone became harsh as he stood there confused and worried.

"Your friend here is just having an anxiety attack. In her condition, all the excitement and news must have upset her terribly. While I was speaking with her, she became pale and started to faint. She's already beginning to look better. I'm sure she'll be just fine." The Doctor approached Kean to shake his hand, greet him and calm him.

"How's Leala and the baby?" Kean urgently asked again.

Trying to make the explanation as simple and quick as possible, the Doctor responded, "Your wife has a muscle that supports the uterus, it's been strained, torn. The trauma of this upon the uterus and baby could cause her to deliver the baby prematurely. I want you to know that we are trying to stop her from doing that. I don't mean to scare you, but the baby could not survive outside of the womb at this stage of its growth. Your wife seems to be a little more stable, now that we've given her something for the pain."

"Pain? She's in pain?" Kean rubbed his hand back across the top of his head in an anxious and worried way.

"Mr. Tierney, you must stay calm. Your wife needs your support now. You must stay strong for her." The Doctor looked firmly at Kean.

Kean put his hands in his pockets and stood rigidly, but assured the Doctor he was calm and would be supportive to his wife no matter what happened.

"I must get back now and check on Leala's condition." The Doctor disappeared behind two doors that led into another part of the emergency section of the hospital, leaving the doors to swing on their hinges behind him.

Kean saw that Kate still appeared ill and distressed. He leaned over her and asked if there was something he could do to help her.

"Just take my hand and don't let go," she whimpered.

Kate felt comforted that Kean was there. It reminded her of when she was a little girl and he would try to comfort her when she was sick. Kate was afraid to close her eyes. She feared if she did, she would never be able to open them again. She held tightly onto Kean's hand, assuring herself that he would not let her slip away into oblivion. As she lay there, she recalled a fond memory from her childhood.

"Katie, how in the world did you get up in that tree?" Kean, as a young Father, asked.

"Daddy! Daddy, I can't get down! I'm scared!" Katie looked down at her Father frightened and helpless.

"Katie, if you climbed up into the tree, you can climb down." He almost looked amused at his daughter's situation.

"No, I can't! I know I'll fall," she yelled. Her Father's smile made her angry.

"Alright, alright, I'm coming up to get you." He made his way up the tree to get her.

He grabbed her and tried to help her descend down the tree.

"No, Daddy, I'll fall."

"Katie, I won't let you fall. Just hold onto my hand tightly, and if you start to slip, I'll stop you from going anywhere. I promise I won't let go, and you'll be safe." Kean started to slowly move down the tree until they both reached safety on the ground. "See, I told you that you would be just fine."

"Thank you, Daddy, you saved me just like a prince would do for a princess. You're the best . . . ."

The memories of her past faded as the voice of Leala's Doctor got her attention.

".... rest. I'll allow her to go home, but she must remain on bed rest. Her condition is stable, but, and I stress again, she must have at least a week more complete bed rest. It will give the ligament a better chance to heal. As for this young lady . . . ." He paused and looked at Kate. "She needs to get some rest too. You still look a little peaked."

"Thank you, Doctor, for all your help." Kean sighed in relief.

"You take this lovely Mother-to-be home, and you go home and relax. I'll call you if anything in her condition changes, which I assure you it won't. Leala will be much better suited for visitors in the morning. She's sleeping soundly now." The Doctor shook hands with Kean and helped escort him and Kate to the door.

Kate was more relieved than anyone else knew. Not only was Leala going to be fine, but Kate knew she would be fine, too. She now knew she had just been feeling faint and sick due to the excitement and worry. She was relieved she no longer had to worry about the threat of annihilation.

Once they arrived home, Kean thanked Kate for her help with Leala.

"I'm sorry you had to go through this whole ordeal today, but I'm glad you were there for Leala. Thank you doesn't seem to say enough for what you did today." He motioned as though he wanted to give Kate a hug, but refrained from doing so. Instead, he bid her a good night and wished her well.

As soon as Kate got inside her front door, she walked straight to the telephone. She called Stephan to inform him of everything that happened. He managed to console her during the phone conversation and lift her spirits. By the time Kate hung up the telephone, she was feeling much better and looking forward to a good night's rest.

The next day, Kate went to check on Leala.

"How are you feeling today?" Kate asked Leala.

"Much better. Thanks for asking. I think part of my problem was the fear I had of losing this baby."

"Do you still think that will happen?"

"No, I know God wouldn't let that happen to me again. He knows how much I want this baby. He wouldn't be that cruel." Leala looked over at the vigil candle she had burning in His honor. "I'm glad to see that you're spirits are up and that you are feeling better. Since Kean is home today to be here for you, I thought I would catch up on some cleaning around my apartment. Besides, Stephan is coming over tonight for dinner, and I want to make him a fabulous, tasty meal." She smiled and raised her eyebrows.

"I just want to let you know you don't have to worry about me. Kean is going to take a few days off work to take care of me. Anyway, I'm sure the Doctor will allow me to get back on my feet by the end of the week."

"Can Kean afford to miss so much work? I know neither of you are wealthy people."

"We'll manage. We've both decided that having this baby is the most important thing right now."

"Since you seem well taken care of, I'm going to get going. Call me if you need anything, *anything*." She kissed Leala on the cheek and went home.

CHAPTER THIRTEEN

All day long, Kate cleaned the house and prepared for Stephan's visit that evening. She found herself constantly thinking of Stephan throughout the day. She wanted to share every detail of her life with him and hope that he was feeling the same. She wanted to share herself, but was feeling very awkward in her pregnant condition. Still, she left the possibility of intimacy an open option for the evening.

Stephan seemed to be preparing for his evening with Kate in his own way. After work he went to the barber and got his hair trimmed neatly. He bought a dozen white roses, Kate's favorite flower, to bring with him that night. On the way to her apartment, he stopped and picked up a couple of baby toys for her unborn child. Once back in the car on the way to her home, Stephan couldn't stop himself from thinking about Kate and the baby.

I wonder if she would consider marrying me? I'm sure I love her, but does she love me enough to want to marry me? Besides, the baby will need a Father. I don't know if I'm ready to be a Father though. Still, I can't imagine my life without Kate in it now. Is this true love? Is it enough that I should make a lifelong commitment to her and a baby? I know I'll never meet anyone else as special and unique as Kate. She's so different from any other woman I've dated. I don't know what it is exactly that makes her so different and special to me, but she I miss her when I'm not with her. We have such an incredible connection and…. Maybe I should slow down my thinking and take things as they come. All I know for sure is, I've never wanted anyone as badly as I do her.

When Stephan arrived, for some unexplainable reason, conversation at first seemed awkward.

"Thanks so much for the beautiful flowers. Why don't you sit down and get comfortable while I put these in some water." Kate knew she was acting strangely. She thought maybe she had put too much emphasis on their date this evening that she wasn't acting like herself. She was acting too cautious and impersonal.

Stephan seemed to feel uncomfortable at first, too. He had been feeling confused about his feelings for Kate and was using this particular date as a basis for a judgment on their relationship.

This is ridiculous, he thought. We've had months of dating . . . why now should things become controlled and calculated? This isn't a courtroom, and I shouldn't be here to judge.

Resigning to that fact, Stephan eased up and began to enjoy the evening. Kate seemed to pick up on his change of mood, and let down her guard, and no longer seemed to be on the defense.

During dinner, they had long talks about their aspirations for the future. They always included each other in their plans.

"You look beautiful tonight." Stephan admired her.

"Thanks. I just wish I could fit back into my old clothes. I feel so fat and—"

"Stop that! You're pregnant! That's the way you should look when you're pregnant. Most women would wish that they look as attractive as you, pregnant or not. Besides, you should be proud of being able to carry and nourish another life. It must be a wonderful feeling." He reached across the table and took Kate's hand in his own and held it.

Kate looked at Stephan fondly. "You're so sweet to say that."

"I mean it. You are the most incredible woman I've ever met." He stood up and helped Kate out of her seat. He pulled her in close to him and spoke more softly. "I love you, Kate Taylor." He leaned forward and kissed her.

Arm in arm, they both walked over to the couch and sat down. Stephan grabbed Kate snugly in his arms and kissed her long and passionately. His need to have her grew greater and he couldn't seem to stop himself from making further advances. Kate did not reject him and was feeling flattered and womanly. Becoming consumed with the desire to be part of her, his hands left her full breast and began to unbutton her blouse. Then suddenly, while he was kissing his way down her neck, he stopped.

"I can't," he pulled away from Kate a little, but his breathing continued to be heavy and accelerated.

"It's because I'm pregnant and look the way I do, isn't it?" Tears swelled in her eyes.

"No! God, no! That has nothing to do with it. Don't even think that way. At this moment, I've never wanted anyone as much as I want you." He started to reach for her again, but stopped. "I just don't think it is right for me to put you in this situation without a commitment from me."

"What do you mean?" Her eyes lit up and she waited in anticipation for him to finish what he was saying.

"Will you marry me?" He slid off the couch and got down on one knee.

Kate was too overwhelmed with sentiment to answer immediately. She would never have imagined such a wonderful proposal of marriage when she lived back in 1992. The whole gesture of him not wanting to consummate their relationship without marriage being involved pleasantly surprised her.

Stephan looked worried waiting for her answer.

"Are you sure that is what you want?" She could have slapped herself for questioning him. "I mean . . . yes, I will marry you, but I want to be sure —"

Stephan interrupted her, "Yes, I really want to marry you. I'm not just saying I want to marry you because I want to . . . . you know . . . . make love to you. And to prove it," he got up off the floor and sat down, "I won't make any more advances to you . . . . tonight," he added, unsure of how long he would be able to keep his word.

Kate was a little amused by his gesture. She thought that kind of male honor had been gone since the dinosaur. Yet, she was extremely touched by his chivalry.

"Just so you know, I wasn't doubting your intentions with me. I just wanted to make sure you were making a conscious choice, not one you felt you had to." She leaned back and rubbed her stomach that had a few cramps in it.

"For your information, I'm not as ruled by my male hormones as you may think!" He jokingly displayed an insulted look on his face.

"I'm glad to hear that," she replied with a sly and enticing smile.

Both sat silent for a moment trying to decide what they should do or say next.

"Do you want something to drink?" Kate asked, standing up to go get herself something to drink.

"Yes, a tall, cold ..very cold, glass of water would be nice." He smiled and took a deep breath.

"Do you want that in a glass or would you prefer to just get it from the shower?" she retorted while smiling smugly. She was having fun with the sexual tension between them. She left the room flashing a false look of innocence in her eyes at Stephan.

By the time Kate had gotten back from the kitchen with their drinks, the intensity of their previous mood had diminished. Stephan once again joined Kate, who was sitting on the couch.

"So, you want to marry me, huh?" He wanted to make sure she hadn't changed her mind.

"More than I can tell you," she responded with loving sincerity.

Stephan didn't say a word, but sat back and gently wrapped Kate in his arms.

"Do you remember what we were talking about at the table?"

"Which subject?"

"You started to tell me about something you wanted to do when you were a kid."

"I did?" He looked puzzled.

"Yes, you did. Don't you remember?"

"Sure, I remember." He looked vague. "Maybe you could refresh my memory, though," he teased.

"You don't remember at all do you? Boy, for a genius you have a lousy memory." She playfully slapped his arm. "It had something to do with what you wanted to be when you grew up."

"Do you really want to hear what I wanted to be when I grew up?"

"If I didn't want to know, I wouldn't have brought up the subject. I think it's kind of fun to find out things about people when they were a child. So in getting back to our dinner conversation, what did you want to be when you grew up?" Kate asked as she stayed contently cuddled in Stephan's arms.

"Everything." He laughed.

"Be serious. Did you always want to teach?"

"I'm not sure. I know I always loved to learn new things. I was probably the only child on the block who wanted a transistor radio, not so I could enjoy the music and stories, but so I could take it apart to see how it worked." Stephan stared into the room with a vague look. "Believe it or not, at one point in my childhood I wanted to be a garbage man. I thought . . . . what a great job. You get to look through other people's belongings, drink beer and swear, and you even get paid for it."

"Has anyone ever told you that you're strange? I think you chose the right profession. I just can't imagine you being a garbage collector." She giggled.

"What about you? Did you ever want to have some sort of a career? I know some women actually would rather be doing something else other than being a wife and Mother these days."

"When I was four, I wanted to be a dancer. When I was eight, I wanted to be an actress, like ….Marilyn Monroe. By the time I was a teenager, I just wanted to grow up and be on my own."

"Did you have trouble at home?" His arms snuggled Kate tighter.

"No more than the average teenager has. I just always had this feeling that something better was waiting for me. That I had to keep moving to find what was waiting for me. I guess I was just never content or happy with what I had, so I kept searching."

"Are you still searching?" His voice was gentle and hopeful.

Kate turned herself around and faced Stephan. Her eyes warmly glowed as she looked at him and spoke, "Not anymore." She laid her hand on her pregnant stomach and looked deeply into the eyes of the man she loved, " I think I've found what I've been looking for all these years." Her lips pressed softly against his as she felt years of fear and loneliness melt away. Time seemed to stand still as they became swept away with passion.

"I love you Kate." He ran his fingers through her hair.

"I love you, too." Her eyes filled with tears.

"I want you to know how important you are to me. I can no longer imagine my life without you." He allowed his hands to slip down from her hair and he caressed her body in his arms. Kate felt safe buried in his muscular arms, as she laid her head upon his broad chest and shoulders. Seconds grew into minutes as they found themselves content in just holding each other in silence.

"Oh, Stephan, there is so much I want to tell you," Kate thought, "if only I could be sure you would understand."

Kate's lips began to move, but no words came out. She knew in her heart that the time wasn't right just yet for her to divulge her shocking story of time travel.

Stephan's thoughts wandered, too. He was becoming very confident about his feelings for Kate, yet something bothered him. Something seemed out of place and not right, but he couldn't figure out what.

"There seem to be so many mysteries about you Kate," Stephan thought. "Where is your family? Where did you really grow up? You say things or name places I've never heard of. Sometimes you are so odd. You're kind of an enigma."

Stephan broke the silence with a quick and urgent incidental question he had that came to his mind.

"Kate, did you say when you were eight, you wanted to be a movie star like Marilyn Monroe?" His face appeared puzzled.

"I suppose I did, why?" Kate pulled away from his shoulder to look him in the face.

"Marilyn Monroe is younger than you." His facial expression became grim and he released his arms from around her.

"Stephan, what are you so serious for? I obviously made a mistake. I meant to say—" Kate's face turned pale as she struggled to think of another actress quickly.

"Damn!" She thought, "Who was popular when I should have been eight years old?"

She became flustered and her eyes filled with tears. She was unable to think clearly under the pressure of the situation.

"I'm not feeling very well. I think you should leave." She got up off the couch and started to pace the floor.

"What's wrong with you? I just asked you a simple question and all of a sudden you're upset and not feeling well. Did I say something that offended you?" he asked, his voice rising in pitch.

"No! You didn't say anything. I'm just feeling ill, and I would like you to leave." She began to cry.

"I can't leave you when you're so upset like this. Just tell me what to do for you."

Stephan tried to think calmly, "This has to be related to being pregnant. I've heard of women acting irrationally and emotionally when they're with child. Maybe I should just leave."

Kate softened her tone of voice and responded to Stephan. She knew she had to get a grip on her behavior.

"I'm sorry if I sounded hysterical, but all of a sudden I've got this terrible headache and stomach ache." She said with straining puppy eyes.

"Do you want me to call a Doctor?" Stephan went over to put his arms around Kate.

"No! Please, I think I just need to lay down quietly for a while." She pushed his arms away.

"If you think that is best, I will abide by your decision . . . . Even if I think it's wrong," he mumbled to himself.

Stephan gave her some strong looks of concern and bewilderment. Without saying another word to Kate; he grabbed his overcoat and left the apartment.

Alone now, Kate began to think about what just happened. How stupid can you be? How could I make such an obvious mistake like that? If he didn't already, for sure he will now suspect something unusual is going on. Maybe it was a subconsciously and intentional slip of the tongue. I'm going to have to eventually tell him the truth about myself.

Later that evening, Kate called Stephan on the telephone and apologized for her behavior earlier in the evening. She didn't offer an explanation for her behavior, other than she was feeling very sick at the time she had her outburst. Stephan graciously accepted her apology and made plans for them to get together again soon.

The next morning, before Kate went to work, she stopped by and visited Leala.

"You look much better today. Are you feeling well?" Kate asked.

"Yes, I'm doing alright. What's going on with you? You look very chipper and cheery this morning. You almost look *too* happy . . . . Did something happen with Stephan during your date last night?" Leala grinned and waited for Kate to answer.

"Yes, something happened with Stephan last night," Kate answered, trying to temporarily deceived Leala.

"You mean . . . . You went to bed with him?" Leala's mouth fell open in a shocked manner while her eyes smiled.

"No, no, that didn't happen. Why you nasty minded little girl. Shame on you for thinking I would do something like that," Kate teased Leala.

"Well, you can't tell me you don't want to . . . . you know. He's gorgeous and despite all the old-fashioned women there are, times are changing. Even though I waited till marriage, I know some women do have . . . . you know, before marriage now."

"Leala, sometimes you are so naïve. I'm sure there are lots of women having sex before marriage. They just don't go around and tell everyone they did it. Because if they went around telling others, soon they would have a bad reputation." Kate shook her head in disbelief at Leala's innocence.

"If you didn't . . . . you know, then what did happen with Stephan last night?" She sat up straighter in bed.

"He asked me to marry him!" Kate could barely contain herself from a girlish scream.

Leala, however, did scream. "Oh my God, I don't believe it! You must be so happy. You are a very lucky girl to get a catch like that."

At that moment, Kean came rushing into the room all out of breath. "Are you alright? What's wrong?" He heard Leala scream and thought something wrong was happening to her.

"Oh, I'm sorry, Honey; I'm fine. I was just so excited about the news Kate told me. Go ahead, tell him."

"Stephan asked me to marry him last night." Kate felt odd about telling Kean. Yet there was a part of her thrilled to be telling her Father that she was about to get married.

Kean didn't appear as thrilled as Leala did about the news, but politely congratulated Kate.

"I'm very happy for you. You tell that guy he better treat you good or he'll have to answer to me."

Kate thought how unusual it was that Kean said that. She always imagined her Father saying something like that to her at a time like this.

Kean left the room mumbling over his shoulder, "Women? I come running because she's screaming . . . . She's getting married . . . . Poor guy, I wonder if he realizes what women are really like . . . . Can't live with them, you can't live without them." He continued to slowly walk away while shaking his head in bewilderment.

Both girls quietly laughed at Kean's reaction as he left the room.

"No, I haven't given it any thought. I'm just happy that he loves me and we'll be together. I'm in no rush to make it legal. That will all happen in good time. Besides, I want to have a real wedding and I don't think they make maternity dresses for brides yet."

"Don't you think it would be nice if your baby has a name before it's born? Not only that, but you can't be serious about having a big wedding. It just wouldn't look right, especially if you intend on wearing a white wedding gown." Leala looked quite serious.

Kate was stunned by Leala's comments. For the first time, she began to see Leala as her Mother. She hadn't seen that side of Leala before, a side she considered to be narrow-minded and old-fashioned.

"How can you say that?! You're supposed to be my best friend and here you are insulting me." Her voice quivered with anger. She was feeling betrayed.

"Kate, dear, you know you're my best friend, that's why I feel I have to be honest with you. Do you realize what people will say? Do you realize what they say now?" Leala accidentally let it slip that Kate had already been talked about by others.

"What do you mean, 'they say now?'" For the first time during her pregnancy, she felt embarrassment about her condition.

"Kate, please! I love you, but people just aren't as liberal as you might like to think. I've never joined in it. I've even corrected

134

it, but there has been gossip. All I'm trying to say is maybe you should reconsider your plans, at least for the sake of the baby." Leala lowered her eyes and cautiously waited for Kate's response.

"To hell with all those people! What do they know about me? Let people, you included, think what they want. I know the truth. I know who I am and what kind of a person I am." Kate was feeling embittered. She abruptly began to leave Leala's bedroom.

"Kate, wait! Please don't leave like this." Leala started to cry.

Kate stopped instantly when she heard Leala begin to cry. She didn't want to upset Leala anymore than she had and possibly worsen her condition. Kate turned around and went back to Leala's bedside. Still angry, Kate listened to what Leala had to say, not only for Leala's sake, but for her own.

"I'm sorry, Kate. I should have been more sensitive. The only reason I said anything was I thought you should know. Right or wrong, most people, including myself, just aren't as accepting as you may have thought. I have to admit, I didn't see how prejudiced and thoughtless I was myself until this moment. Your friendship means more to me than . . . . well, please forgive me." Leala unfolded her arms and opened them to reach out to Kate for a hug.

Kate accepted Leala's apology, but insisted she needed to leave for work or she would be late. Although Kate didn't want to admit it, she still felt disconcerted by the whole incident.

Kate comforted herself on the way to work with thoughts of revenge.

"Just wait! All those people who think the way they do will learn their lesson when their children grow up and become a product of the 60's: free love, sex and drugs."

That evening, Stephan joined Kate for dinner again at her apartment. Stephan brought up the subject of their marriage and arrangements that should be made.

"Not to sound pushy, but when would you like to set the date for our nuptials?" Stephan inquired.

"I've been thinking about that quite a lot today. I've decided that I would like for us to get married right after the baby is born."

"After?" He was a little shocked and disappointed.

"Yes, after! Don't tell me that you're going to lecture me, too. If you are, I'll save you the trouble. I know it would look better in today's society if we got married immediately. That way the baby would have a last name and wouldn't be a—" She stopped herself in mid-sentence. She knew she was being sarcastic, but didn't want to say anything she might regret later.

"First of all, I don't know who's been lecturing you, but I certainly had no intentions of doing that. Second of all, you've made it very clear what you want to do in concerns with your marriage and your baby. Have you ever stopped to consider my feelings in this whole matter? Did you ever think that I may want to start OUR family as soon as possible for no other reason than I love you? You keep talking about your baby, maybe it would be nice if you started to consider it ours. This morning when the jeweler thought I was the Father, well . . . . I felt very proud. It was a good feeling and now you seem to want to take that away from me. It's as if you're trying to exclude me from everything important in your life, our life." Stephan looked down to the floor. He was feeling sad and resentful toward Kate.

Kate realized that she had over reacted. "I'm sorry. I didn't realize how selfish and insensitive I have been. I guess I've been alone for so long and hurt so many times by others that I tend to be selfish as a defense. Can we start all over again with this conversation? I promise to listen instead of just talk. I love you more than anything. I'm sorry I hurt you." She approached Stephan for a hug.

"At times like this, I think we both need to stop our own thoughts and really listen to the other person. Sometimes, I think we're on the same wave length and then I find out that we think like we're worlds apart from each other." He pretended to reach into Kate's head as if to pull out her thoughts.

That statement is more true than you know, Kate thought to herself.

Kate knew that the time for her to reveal the truth about herself was approaching fast. It was becoming apparent to her that it was imperative that Stephan know the truth about her before they got married. Still unwilling to expose her true identity, she wanted to put off their marriage for a while longer. She feared if she told him the truth, he might leave her.

I know he loves me, but will he believe me when I tell him I'm from another place in time? A time with a little more change and distance than that of California or France.

"The reason I want to wait is, I wanted to have a real nice wedding, with a gown and all. As you can plainly see, I can't do that in my present condition. I want our wedding to be a day I'll never forget. I know that according to the rules of some others, it would be proper if we got married right away; but I don't see the harm in waiting. I love you and nothing can change that and it shouldn't matter what other people say. What matters to me is what you say and feel. So, I'm asking you with true concern and regard in my heart, what do you want?"

"I want for us to be together for infinity and whether or not we get married tomorrow or a year from now truly doesn't matter. As long as I'm able to be with you and share in your life, I'll be happy." He still looked a little disappointed.

Kate could see there was more on his mind than he was saying.

"You don't sound very convincing. Something is still bothering you. You're not being completely honest with me. Please tell me what still is on your mind," she urged.

With slight hesitation, he answered, "What about the baby? When you have the baby will I . . . ." He felt like a child asking, "I mean to say, will the birth certificate state me as the Father or will the baby have your last name on the document? Not that a piece of paper should make that much difference, it has more to do with the meaning behind it."

"Are you trying to say are you going to be named as the baby's Father? If you are, of course. I'm honored that you want to be. Let's get one thing settled right now. In my mind and for all purposes, you are the baby's Father. I feel badly that you had to even ask a question like that. I think we both need to work on this area of our relationship a little, but from now on, we will think of ourselves as not only a couple, but a family." Kate put her arms around Stephan's neck and hugged him tightly.

The evening ended soon after and Kate went to bed still worrying about how she would tell Stephan about her time travel. When she had finally managed to fall asleep, it seemed to her, that it was already morning and she had to get up and out of bed.

Kate had stayed away from visiting Leala for a couple of days until she felt she no longer harbored any ill feelings toward Leala. Conversation was awkward at first, but within minutes the two women were chatting like the good friends they were.

"Are you getting ready for Christmas? You know it's only two weeks away," Leala asked.

I've been so busy, I haven't prepared at all. The holidays seemed to have snuck up on me this year, Kate thought. I haven't experienced any of the constant advertising over the last two months I'm used to. In 1992, all the stores start putting out Christmas decorations by the end of October. By November, a person becomes swamped with television commercials advertising everything from children's toys to electric toothbrushes to give as a present. I have to admit, although I always hated Christmas being so commercialized, I was always prepared when Christmas did arrive. Still, the simplicities of Christmas in 1955 has some pleasant virtues that people are going to miss in the future.

"Maybe this weekend, if the Doctor says it's fine for me to get out of bed, we can go shopping together. I have a few gifts I need to purchase yet. I'm really glad I got an early start this year and did most of my shopping last week."

"That sounds like a good idea. If you don't mind though, I think I better start my shopping today after work. Let me know what the tomorrow when you see him what the Doctor says. I've got to go to work now. Talk to you later."

The cold weather continued, but the first snowfall of the season had yet to be seen. Kate walked to work a little slower than usual and admired the giant wreaths and other Christmas decorations that lined the streets and sidewalks. She noticed that there were many more people dressed up in Santa suits collecting for charity than she was used to seeing in her own time. She saw stores displaying nativity scenes in their store front windows and a lot fewer strings of lights than she remembered ever seeing.

I guess things do really change with time, no matter which direction you travel in it.

CHAPTER FOURTEEN

During the next two weeks, Kate finished her Christmas shopping. Her finances made her purchase of gifts less than what she wanted, but she felt that she had gotten everybody she bought for something they would like. She purchased a special gift for Stephan that cost more than the other presents did. It was a gold plated pocket watch, which she had inscribed. It read: You are the light before my eyes which shall never flicker out. With all my love, Kate.

Kate spent the holiday with Stephan. Leala and Kean went over to her ailing Mother's house and Leala made dinner for the three of them. Kate wanted to stop by and visit her Grandmother she never met. However, she wasn't invited and thought it would be awkward to ask. She knew Leala would wonder why she would want to meet and spend the holidays with a stranger.

If only I could have explained it to Leala Kate thought to herself the day after Christmas.

When New Year's Eve arrived, Kate was in good spirits. She had awaited the bringing in of a new year with anticipation. She and Stephan went out together that evening and celebrated at a local restaurant near Kate's home.

The restaurant wasn't very crowded, but the mood of the people there was gay. The flamboyant party decorations dazzled Kate's eyes as she and everyone else there prepared for a countdown to midnight.

"Are you ready to bring in the New Year and say goodbye to the old?" Stephan spoke loudly over the noise of the crowd.

"As long as you'll be part of it." Kate and Stephan toasted each other with a glass of champagne.

Soon the roar of the crowd's voices grew louder. "Ten, nine, eight, seven, six, five, four, three, two, one, Happy New Year!"

Many of the couples there kissed each other, including Kate and Stephan. Within seconds everyone started to sing. During the song, Stephan and Kate left the restaurant and went outside.

"Just look at that clear sky tonight, isn't it beautiful?" Kate had always loved the beauty and immensity of the sky.

"Yes, but not as beautiful as you." He leaned over to share the warmth of his body with Kate who was beginning to shiver from the cold.

"If you keep spoiling me with all these compliments, I might just get too accustomed to them." She giggled.

"Let's go back inside and get our coats and head home." He motioned by moving toward the door.

"I'll wait here while you go get our coats, if you don't mind."

"Are you sure? You're starting to look as if you are getting awfully cold."

"I'll be fine."

Stephan went inside and got their coats and within a couple of minutes, returned to meet Kate outside. During the drive home, Kate stayed more silent than usual.

"Are you feeling alright?" Stephan placed his right hand on her left and patted it affectionately.

"I'm fine. I've just been sitting here thinking what a wonderful time I had tonight. I guess I don't want it to end." She looked out the car window up at the sky again.

"It doesn't have to end." He squeezed Kate's thigh and looked at her sheepishly.

"Do you see that?" Kate started to look frightened.

"What?" Stephan could feel her become tense and rigid.

"The sky! There looks like there's a terrible storm brewing. It's so clear over there." She pointed to the south. "And over there it's all clouded and dark. The weird part is, that although the sky is clouded and dark, there seems to be an unusual glow about it." In her mind she instantly compared it to the storm she experienced before her leap through time.

"I never knew you were frightened by storms. Don't worry; I'm sure it's nothing. You have to remember this is winter and the sky usually isn't that clear to begin with. It's probably just a cold front moving in from the north." He could see he was having little effect in reassuring her.

"That could be it, but why does it seem to be moving in on us so fast?"

"Kate, don't take it so personally. I don't think the storm is moving in on just us. It's not out to get you," he stated as a joke to try and soothe Kate.

"This isn't funny!" she snapped.

"I'm sorry, I didn't realize you are so sincerely frightened. Please try and relax. We'll be home in a few minutes and then you'll be safely inside your home."

"I'll never be safe," Kate thought.

Kate watched the storm intently. Her eyes never veered from the sky during the rest of the drive home. She watched the storm move overhead and felt herself become more frantic.

Two blocks from home Kate couldn't take it anymore; she yelled for Stephan to stop the car.

"What?" He responded in surprise.

"You heard me! Stop the car!" She noticed the cloud seeming to move downward in the sky.

"Kate, this is ridiculous! I'm not going to stop the car. We're two blocks from home."

"If you love me, you'll stop the car and let me out!" Her eyes pleaded with Stephan.

"Alright, alright." He pulled the car over to the side of the road and turned off the engine.

"I can't believe this," he thought. "I've never seen her act so irrationally. This is the most bizarre behavior I've ever seen her display.

As soon as Kate got out of the car she started to cry. She ran over to Stephan and grabbed him for the tightest hug her strength would allow for.

"I love you, Stephan! I've never loved anyone as much as I love you. No matter what happens, I want you to always remember that." Tears streamed down her cheeks.

"Kate, I love you, too. I just wish I could do something to make you calmer, something to take your fear away." He looked bewildered.

"Now, I only wish I would have told you the truth about me a long time ago," Kate thought.

She buried her head in his shoulder and continued to sob. Stephan didn't know what else to say, so he kept silent. He just held her tightly until his grip started to slip.

"Kate, look!" He pointed up to the sky. "I've never seen anything so beautiful before." He was amazed by the sight.

Kate looked up hesitantly and for a moment was shocked.

"It's beautiful!" She released her hold on Stephan.

The sky suddenly burst with the full mass of snow. It fell so thickly, neither of them could see a foot in front of them. The first snowfall of the season had come with more than it had promised every child.

"I have never seen a snowfall so heavy and vast. It seems as if the heavens suddenly opened up and poured all its purity and glory upon us," Kate marveled.

Stephan looked at Kate to make sure she was alright. He noticed she still had a few tears in her eyes.

"Are you alright?" He again approached her.

"I'm wonderful! I'm marvelous!" Her eyes filled with more tears and she began to laugh.

"You're a nut cake, you know that, don't you?" He was even more confused than before by her actions.

Kate backed up slowly away from Stephan. Suddenly, without warning, she reached down and grabbed a pile of snow and threw it at Stephan. Hitting him right in the face, she knew he would be looking to even the score. She turned and ran.

"Why you little brat!" he teasingly yelled. "I'll get you!"

During the next ten minutes they both had fun in, and with, the snow. They acted like children teasing and enticing each other with play. Stephan finally, but gently, caught Kate and pushed her into the snow that had quickly accumulated on the ground.

"Now, I've got you!" He held Kate helplessly down.

"And you can keep me!" She kissed Stephan.

"Is that a promise?"

"You have my word."

"In that case, I'll let you up." He helped her get back on her feet.

"You look awfully cold and tired, I'm taking you home now."

They both got back in the car and went home. Stephan saw Kate safely inside the door and left for his own residence.

Kate took off her coat and went to look in the mirror. She talked to her image, "You really freaked yourself out tonight, didn't you? Stephan probably thinks you really are a nut." She walked away from the mirror and went into the bedroom to get undressed from her street clothes and ready for bed.

After she tucked the covers snugly around her body, she lay and thought for a while.

I have to stop freaking out every time something seems a little unusual. I can't let myself go through the rest of my life being afraid. I have to realize and adjust to moments that seem out of the ordinary. Otherwise, I will go nuts. No one can live their lives in constant fear.

Beginning to feel emancipated, she fell peacefully asleep.

CHAPTER FIFTEEN

January did prove to be a very cold and snowy month. Kate was beginning to feel more awkward because of her physical limitation. She and Stephan spent most of their time staying indoors, especially at Kate's home. Leala and Kean came over occasionally to visit with Stephan and Kate, as did Stephan and Kate frequent the Tierney home. By month's end, the main topic of conversation was the birth of their babies. Although Stephan and Kean were very proud Fathers-to-be, they usually went into another room and played cards and left the girls to finish talking about baby care and such.

Before they knew it, February was upon them and they were celebrating Valentine's Day. The weather had taken a drastic change, causing it to be unusually warm that day. Kate and Stephan had made special plans to celebrate the day and evening. At the last moment, because of the beautiful, warm weather, they added going to the beach on their agenda. The plans they had made earlier lasted longer than they had expected and they didn't make it to the beach until a few minutes after dusk.

"Aren't you tired?" Stephan asked, wanting to make sure the day's pace had not been too tiring for Kate.

"No, I feel fine, except my feet are killing me." They walked from the car to the beach and started strolling.

Kate had been planning for several weeks to confront Stephan with the truth about herself. She had tried to tell him a few times before, but something always seemed to distract them. A few days prior to Valentine's Day, she knew that she would have to make the time and definitely tell him. Now, as they strolled, it seemed like the perfect opportunity to tell him. Still, she feared his reaction and thought matters out in her head before she dared say anything.

If I'm going to spend my life with him, I have to be completely honest with him about who I am and my past. On the other hand though, if I didn't tell him it would make matters a lot easier to deal with. Yet, could I really live my life constantly telling lies? I'm sure that soon I would get to the point when I wouldn't know where the lies ended and the truth began. I have to tell him; it's the only fair thing to do, for both our sakes.

After a few minutes of walking, Kate stopped and sat down on the sand. Stephan joined her assuming that she needed to rest.

The ebony sky sparkled with a full array of glowing stars. A cold breeze occasionally rushed over the frozen water in the lake subsiding the effect of the night's warm air.

"What unusual weather we're having. It's so weird to be sitting here at this time of the year. Don't get me wrong. I'm not complaining. I love it!" Kate kicked off her shoes and lay back on the sand.

"If you could have one wish, what would it be?" Stephan asked gazing out past the rolling waves.

"To stay here on a night like this forever." Kate smiled.

"Am I included in this night?" Stephan raised an eyebrow as he looked longingly at Kate for an answer.

"I wouldn't have it any other way." She leaned in closer to Stephan.

"Kate, I have something to ask you." Stephan stopped and paused so long, that Kate teasingly urged him on.

"Wake up, Stephan. Are you in there?" She made a fist and knocked gently on his forehead.

Stephan grabbed her hand and held it tightly in his own hand. "Kate, this is serious. Please don't interrupt."

Kate's face became serious. She had an uneasy feeling about what Stephan was about to say to her. She anticipated that he would tell her something she didn't want to hear. She suddenly felt very insecure again about his intentions and was sure he was going to end their harmonious relationship.

"I promise, I won't interrupt you. I love you," she added, hoping she wasn't about to be crushed emotionally.

"We've been dating for a while now. We've had some wonderful times together, but it got me to thinking . . . there has to be more."

Kate's heart fell. This is it. He's dumping me. When there's a, 'but . . . .'

"I mean, with you being with child and . . . ."

Kate interrupted. "You don't even have to say it. Just go. Leave. You told me it didn't matter if I was pregnant with another man's child. You said you loved me and I believed you. How could you...?" Kate burst into tears as she abruptly stood up and began walking away.

Stephan stood up dumbfounded for a few seconds. He put his face into his hands and shook his head from side to side in disbelief.

She said she wouldn't interrupt. Women! Who can figure them out? He thought.

Stephan began walking quickly, trying to catch up with Kate.

"Kate! Kate! Wait! Will you stop?" Stephan broke into a run and caught up with Kate. "What are you talking about?"

"What am I talking about?" she snapped.

He grabbed Kate's arms and swiftly turned her around.

"Will you just shut up for a minute?" Kate began to speak again, but Stephan silenced her immediately. Placing his hand over her mouth, he continued with what he was saying.

Kate allowed him to silence her. She stood, shocked in silence by his actions.

"Finally, you're quiet. You are the most unusual and impossible woman I've ever met. Just when I think I know you . . . . I don't. I just can't figure you out. However, there is one thing I am sure of. I love you and I want to spend the rest of my life with you. I want you to marry me before the baby is born. I know we agreed to wait, but I want us to get married sooner." He let his hand drop away from her mouth.

Kate's mouth fell open and now she stood dumbfounded. She was sure he was going to end their relationship; and, instead, he wanted them to get married sooner than they had planned.

"If that is what you really want, of course, I'll marry you sooner. I love you. You mean the world to—" Stephan once again silenced her with his hand.

"Do you ever stop talking woman?" He released his hand and drew her in closely and kissed her.

Kate wrapped her arms tightly around his neck, gently caressing him. Stephan didn't seem to notice her bulging stomach pushing against him. He only felt arousal by the general touch of her body against his own. His hands seemed to freely caress every inch of her body, as they both glided down onto the sand. After a few moments of tender and passionate kissing and touching, Kate pulled back a little and spoke.

"I'm sorry for the way I reacted. I love you so much, and I thought—"

"I know what you thought. I don't know how you could think that I would leave you. Don't you know how much you mean to me? I've never felt this way about anyone before. I have such a deep, unspoken connection with you. It has gotten so I can't imagine my life without you. I love you so much that sometimes it scares me." He looked like a young boy discovering the meaning of life for the first time.

Kate pulled away and sat up, looking at the sand beneath her feet.

"I have something to tell you. It's something I've wanted to tell you for a very long time, but didn't know how. I've been afraid that you would think I was crazy. Before I even begin, I want you to know, and really believe, that I am not crazy. I want you to be prepared for a hard-to-believe story that isn't a tale, but part of my life, a part of my being what I am and where I am right now. I also want you to realize that this is the most difficult thing I've ever tried to tell and explain in my lifetime." Kate paused trying to collect her thoughts.

Stephan sat forward with his hands resting in his lap. He listened intently as Kate began to speak again, unaware he was about to be confronted with the most unbelievable story he ever heard.

"I guess there is not an easy way to say this without being direct and pertinent. My name is Kate Taylor. I was born in Chicago in February of 1956. My parents' names are Leala and Kean Tierney. My Father died on—"

"What? Kate, this is ridiculous. This isn't funny. What do you mean you were born in 1956? This is 1956." His face contorted with confusion.

"Please, let me continue. I used to work for Chicago Title & Trust until—I was married a few years back to a lawyer, for two years, before I caught him repeatedly cheating on me and got a divorce. Since then, I've only had one relationship with a man . . . until you. He is the baby's Father."

Stephan had a difficult time following along with what Kate was telling him. His emotions swelled up only to get caught in his web of confusion. He babbled out a question without even realizing why he asked that particular one.

"Who is the Father, and where does he live?"

"His name is Daniel Wolski, and I don't know where he will live."

"What do you mean, 'will live'? This is nonsense."

"He's a year younger than me and hasn't been born yet. I know this doesn't make any sense. Let me try and clear things up for you. I was born in 1956, and I'm 36 years old. Somehow, some way, I was transferred through time and space and landed here in 1955, about a year before I was actually born. I don't really belong here in this time, in this year. I had a whole other life I was leading in a completely different era than this one. My Mother is old and my Father is dead. I lived in my own apartment on the north side, a part of the city that has yet to become very populated."

"Stop! Just stop. Why are you doing this? Do you actually expect me to believe this farce?" His voice raised and grew louder, releasing some of his built up frustration.

"No, I don't expect you to believe me. I'm just hoping that you know me well enough now, and love me enough to try and believe me. I wouldn't make up something like this. Haven't you noticed me saying unusual expressions? Haven't you noticed my way of dress or hairstyle to be different than the other women you know? Maybe just slightly off? Haven't you ever noticed I never speak of my past? Don't you find it unusual that I have no family anywhere? I have no IDs, no birth certificate, no social security card. I have no past here. My past hasn't come to pass yet, and it won't even begin for another couple of months. I'm an orphan of time." Kate fought to hold back her tears.

"I don't know what to say. I want to believe you, but this all sounds so impossible, so . . . ." He thought about the many times Kate had said unusual things in the past. He recalled several instances when she seemed to predict what would happen. Even small instances like in the Mayoral elections, or knowing all the words to a just released song now came to the forefront of his mind. Things said that made no sense about people like Gloria Steinem had been mentioned as important historical figures. I've never heard of her or others mentioned in the past.

"Crazy. Go ahead, just say it. I don't blame you. I would think I was crazy, too, if I didn't have it happen to me." Tears rolled down her cheeks.

"I have to know more. When? Where? Why? How? How is this possible? I know you aren't crazy, but . . . . Kate..... I believe that you believe. That's the best I can do for now." He reached out in for her hands.

"That's the best that I can expect." She grabbed his hands and held onto them tightly. "I'm not sure how exactly I traveled through time or what caused it. That's why I originally came to talk with you. Do you remember our very first conversation in the cafeteria at the University? I was hoping then that you would be able to give me some insight on time travel. I was hoping to understand it and figure out how I got here and how I might be able to get back home."

"Yes, I remember that conversation. I thought you were doing some research for a newspaper or magazine article, but later you told me you were just interested on a more personal basis."

"Exactly, it all started when I was taking a vacation at a friend's cabin near Wooster Lake. I was out walking when suddenly, and out of nowhere in particular, a storm started. It looked like tornado weather. I've never actually seen a tornado before, so I lingered a little longer than I should have; and stayed to watch. It came in around me so fast and furiously it frightened me. I thought it would be wise to go back to the cabin for safety. I started walking quickly back when something large—I think a tree branch—came down from above and hit me on the head, knocking me unconscious. When I woke up, it was 1955."

"Isn't it just possible that you suffered amnesia from the bump to your head. Maybe you just think you lived differently, or in a different time, and actually you've been remembering a book or combination of books you once read."

"You may think I'm crazy, but I'm not an idiot. I know the difference between reality and fantasy. Let me try and prove it to you." Kate paused trying to think of some events that haven't happened yet, but will in the near future.

God, I wish I listened better in history class, she thought. I can't think of one world or political happening in 1956.

"Movies! I don't remember much from history class, but I do have a memory for movies and actors. This is 1956, right? When the Academy Awards are given, Yul Brynner will win for best actor and best picture will be *Around the World in Eighty Days*."

"Anyone can take a guess at that."

"If I had a TV, I could prove it to you. Some of the most popular shows are airing for the first time now I've seen a dozen times in reruns."

Stephen interjected, "What's a rerun?"

"I could tell every story plot and some of the actors' lines before they happen. *I Love Lucy* will become one of the most popular and well-loved shows in the world, airing in many different countries. *Gunsmoke* will air on television for another twenty-something years."

"Kate, this is really getting us nowhere. If this were all true, why would you have leaped through time? There have been scientists trying to accomplish such knowledge for years, searching for the ultimate answer to their questions, such as a hole in space. A vast hole is what many of us believe, but we've never been able to find it."

"Maybe because it continually keeps moving like a storm," Kate added smugly, trying to prove her point.

"I know you are trying, but this isn't getting any easier to understand or believe," he stated, becoming discouraged.

"I just wish you would believe me. There are so many exciting and wonderful things I want to tell you about. Things and events that haven't happened yet, but will." Her voice was mixed with enthusiasm and frustration.

"Like what?" He tried to be encouraging.

"Like, the U.S. will send a spaceship into outer space in 1958. By 1969, 3 astronauts one of them named Neil Armstrong, will land on the moon, and Armstrong will be the first man walk on the moon. In 1962, the first sugar free, but still tastes sweet using artificial sweeteners, diet soft drink will be available at the market. In 1989, an item called the microwave oven will be a common household item. People will use it daily to cook food more easily and quicker, in much less time than it would take now. You could cook a hamburger in 4 minutes and a baked potato in less than 2 minutes. There will be cordless telephones, 2-inch and 90-inch television screens with all programs aired in viewable in color. Personal sized computers will be on every work desk in the office place. Something called the World Wide Web has begun to change the way in which the world connects and communicates. I'm used to having things in my household you couldn't even comprehend: VCRs, personal answering machines, compact disc players, dishwashers, cable TV—" Kate sat back catching her breath.

Stephan sat quietly amazed by all the things Kate talked about so naturally. Although not convinced, he knew with certainty

Kate was not lying or insane. Kate wanted to continue with what she was saying, but felt it was futile.

"Stephan, please say something. Let me know what you are thinking."

"I don't know what to say. Some of the things you have talked about seem so strange, yet believable. Still, you have to understand how difficult this is for me to to put this whole situation into perspective. I came here tonight to ask the woman I love to marry me and share the rest of her life with me. Instead of a simple yes and a night of bliss, I'm given to contend with a future wife from another world that can't guarantee she will even be here tomorrow. I don't know what to say, because I don't know what I think, feel, or believe." Stephan pulled away from Kate and stood up.

"There you go again, pulling away from me. Last time we had some difficulties you pulled away and hid from me and yourself."

"What do you expect? This is the most outrageous tale anyone has ever told me."

"I thought if anyone would believe me and understand, it would be you. You've worked most of your life searching for the answer to the possibilities of time travel. You've spent years teaching your own theories, and others' theories on the subject matter. How can you not believe, unless you've been a hypocritical dreamer your whole adult life?"

"You're right, I am a dreamer. I do believe time travel is possible, but I'm also a man of logic, first and foremost."

"So that's what you want . . . . facts, proof? I'm not sure I can give you the proof you want. However, it is fact that I know about many inventions, events and history that has yet been made. Do you know what the Star Wars in government versus the movie is all about? If you were to actually think about some of the things I've told you, you might realize they are more than just possibilities. Why would I make up this whole story in the first place and how could I come up with such far-fetched inventions so easily?"

154

"I'm not saying I don't believe. I believe that you believe. I know it makes no logical sense for you to make up such tales, but it is just so difficult to undeniably say that I don't have my doubts."

"I could tell you some more things that will be in the future. There is going to be another war—this time in Vietnam—nuclear power plants, and one of them, called Three Mile Island, has a major accident. Presidents Ronald Reagan and George Bush make some real strides with our relationship with the Soviet Union and their leader named Gorbachav. We're actually friends with them." Kate's mind reeled with so many thoughts, she couldn't organize them.

"Ronald Reagan the—"

Kate interrupted him. "Don't even say it, yes.

The sixties are going to be unbelievable. So much happens. There are going to be so many conflicting political and cultural differences it would blow your mind." Kate held out her hand to use her finger as markers to count off statements. "The civil rights movement gains strength. Its leader, Reverend Martin Luther King Jr., is assassinated. A president named Kennedy is assassinated. Make love, not war. Flower power. The Vietnam War. Twiggy, and the Beatles. Mini skirts and bell bottom jeans. Disco and yuppies, hair bands, Black Panthers, Desert Storm"

Letting her enthusiasm get the best of him, he began to ask some questions.

"Have we rid hunger or found a cure for cancer?" His eyes began to light up like a little boy's.

"Unfortunately, there will still be plenty of hunger and homeless people still living this way. We have found a cure for a couple of cancers; all in all, the treatments are much better and much more successful, but not much in the way of cures. We can do heart transplants and create human babies outside the Mother's womb."

"It all sounds encouraging, though."

"Not all. We are still looking for a cure for a disease that doesn't exist yet in 1956 or for many year yet to come, but is a killer. It's called AIDS, a horrible disease that ends in death. There will be a severe problem in our country with an illegal drug called cocaine and a cheaper, more addictive version, called crack. We have to worry about acid rain, fluorocarbons eating a hole in our atmosphere, and the possibility of nuclear war."

Stephan stood, stunned by all that Kate was saying. He suddenly realized that the woman who stood before him was indeed from the future.

No one can make up all the things she has so effortlessly just told me, and why would she want to? He thought.

Stephan stared up into the night's sky becoming completely absorbed in its vast beauty and depth.

"I've waited my whole life for something like this to happen. The strange thing is, I always imagined I'd be the star of the adventure. My mind is reeling with so many questions, yet I don't seem to be able to single out one of them to ask." His eyes turned from the sky and gazed at Kate almost as if in awe of her.

"I've wanted to tell you for a long time, but I didn't want you to think I was crazy. I've been so scared and lonely at times with this secret that I wanted to burst. I feel relieved to have finally shared it with you. Do you still love me?" she asked, feeling insecure.

"Of course, I still love you, nothing will ever change that. My heart and soul have been committed to you for a long time and they always will be."

"Stephan, there is something else I have to tell you . . . . The baby's Father lives in 1992 and he and I were never married."

"Do you love him, and did he know that you were pregnant before you came here?" He lowered his eyes waiting for her response.

"I thought I loved him, but I didn't really know what love was until I met you. As for your other question, no, he didn't know I was pregnant. I didn't know I was pregnant until I was already here." Putting her soft hand against his face, she pulled him to her and kissed him gently.

"How exactly did you travel through time? What caused you to leap from one year to another, and why?"

Kate explained everything the best that she could, including the fact that she didn't know exactly how and why. "I'm sorry to be so vague about some of it, it's just that I don't know myself what the answers are."

"Do you realize the importance of something like this happening? I know so many people in the government and in the private sector that would kill to get hold of you and the information you have."

"Please, stop. I'm not an experiment waiting to be prodded and poked. I don't want to be a freak. I'd be called everything from an alien to a crazy liar if anyone else found out."

"You're right. I'm sorry. You have to forgive the scientist in me." He changed the subject abruptly, getting himself out of trouble, "I do have one meaningful and urgent question to ask. What is a compact disc player?" Stephan smiled childishly and Kate laughed.

The stars continued to shine as the night air became cool. The rush of air blowing increased and the waves rose high above the water level in the lake. An hour or more had passed before either of them had thought about time passing. Although their conversation was discursive at times, they were very intent in listening to one another's speech.

"It's getting rather chilly, isn't it?" Kate rubbed her hands up and down her arms trying to warm them.

"I suppose it is; let's head back to the car." He looked at his wrist watch to see how far into the night it was.

While they slowly walked, Kate had some more pressing questions to ask. She didn't feel she really understood the process of how time works.

"What's wrong?" Stephan asked, noticing how worried Kate still looked.

"If we're not sure how I got here, what's to stop me from going back to when I started? I'm sure it's like you explained to me a few months ago. It was an accident. I'm sure I'm not supposed to be here. Otherwise, why would I have been born when I was? Somehow, I must have fallen through one of those spaces, holes in time. What would stop me from going through another hole? It may not even be back to my own time. It could be one hundred years ago, or ten years ahead of where I am right now." Kate's back became rigid with fear, as her forehead wrinkled with worry.

"I know it all sounds frightening, but you have to realize that the chances of your going through time again are very miniscule. What happened to you was a phenomenon, something rare. So rare know one even thinks it is possible. Besides, the timeline can't work so illogically or the world would be in constant chaos. There's a balance to what occurs and when. A series of events that must unfold accordingly. A continuum of time."

"I'm here now, aren't I, screwing up some series of events? Therefore, just by my being here, I have changed the future by disturbing the master plan."

"That may be true, but who's to say that you shouldn't be here. It just may be possible that it was meant for you to come here and meet me just as you did," Stephan responded with his heart.

Kate reached out to hold Stephan, seeking to assure herself of reality.

"Sometimes, I wake up and I think this has all been a dream, that you are just in my imagination, and all this is just scenery I once saw in an old movie." She looked around.

"It's not a dream for you, only a dream come true for me." He smiled and kissed her lovingly.

During the drive home, Stephan elaborated on the subject of time. "Some scientists, one in particular, Dr. Francis Boulivia, have published several papers explaining how time works in dimensions. To simplify it, would be today that all time occurs in diminutive dimensions. Basically, all events, or years in time, happen side by side along the timeline. So, while 1956 is happening here," he demonstrated with his hand, "1992 is happening here, next to it. The

158

same would be true for every other year past and future. They are just occurring in different dimensions."

"It all sounds all so confusing. I think that's why it frightens me so at times."

"Please try not to be frightened. I'll always be here for you."

"And little Sonya or Stephan will always be here for me, too," she said, surprising Stephan with the choice of his name for the baby.

"Stephan, huh? I'm flattered. Well, if it is a boy, he'll be darn lucky to have such great parents as us." Stephan placed his hand on Kate's stomach and laughed.

"You know, if somebody would have told me a year ago that I would be sitting in a car with the man I love and be talking about our baby, I would have said they were crazy. Yet now I can't, or should I say don't, ever want to imagine it any other way. My long search for happiness and the feeling of wanting to find my place in this world have come to an end. Thank God that I didn't get what I wanted when I first came into 1955."

"What was that?"

"To go back to the year 1992. If I had, I would have never found myself or you. I would have still been searching for home."

"Well, you know what they say, 'home is where you hang your hat.'"

"Whoever 'they' are, they must be very intelligent people." She chuckled.

That night Kate went to bed with the feeling of elation. She had a difficult time falling asleep. Finally, around three in the morning, she nodded off into a peaceful sleep.

Stephan had a difficult time falling asleep too. His mind kept going over and over all that was said that evening.

He contemplated: I wonder what that locket looks like. I wonder if finding the locket has any significance to Kate's travel through time. Maybe it belonged to someone here in 1956. Maybe they lost it and it was so precious to them that they . . . . Oh boy, I'm starting to think like a mystery writer or a kook. I think I better try to get some sleep. I'm exhausted. I just wish my brain would stop thinking and go to sleep. Too much to think about and so little time. Time . . .

CHAPTER SIXTEEN

The next day, Stephan and Kate took the locket Kate found to a jeweler to be repaired. They both viewed the locket as a good luck charm and wanted it to be repaired to look like new.

"Is this silly?" Kate asked, worried that a gift like the locket was foolish for a baby.

"No, I look at it as a symbol of love. If it's a girl, she'll be thrilled to have it when she gets a little older. If it's a boy, well, he can give it to his wife when he gets married. Either way, they'll both feel greatly loved and know that their Mother went through the trouble of doing this even before they were born."

Kate took the locket from her pocket and gave it to the jeweler to look at.

"Do you think you can match the missing piece of the locket with the old?" she asked hopefully.

The owner looked over the locket carefully. "What a beautiful locket. With a little cleaning and a new back side, sure it can be fixed as good as new."

"Are you sure you'll be able to match the two sides?" she asked.

"Mr. Lombardi doesn't take on a job he can't handle," he stated proudly in his Italian accent.

"Wonderful. How long do you think it will take to complete the job? I don't mean to sound pushy; I'm just inquisitive." Kate was concerned that it would not be finished by the time she had her baby.

"Do you need it for a particular occasion? I can worka fast ifa I have to."

"Not really. I know this will sound silly, but I wanted to have it ready by the time I'm due to have this baby." She looked down at her stomach.

The jeweler also looked at Kate's stomach. "I thinka I better worka fast. You look likea you gonna have that baby soona." He laughed.

"Not fast enough for me," Kate confessed, feeling extreme discomfort at the moment.

"I thinka I cana get the job done in a weeka, maybe ita take ten days. You leave it a here witha me, and have the papa here takea you home." He pointed casually to Stephan.

For the first time, Stephan felt proud of being known as the unborn baby's Father. He got a great big smile on his face as he thanked the jeweler, and he and Kate left the store.

Stephan took Kate home and headed off to the University. He had a few classes to teach that day and didn't want to be late. Later that evening, he and Kate had made plans to see each other again. When Stephan arrived that evening, he had some good and bad news to tell Kate. He waited to tell her until after dinner when they were relaxing comfortably in the front room.

"So, how was your day?" Kate asked politely as she walked across the room to turn on the television set.

"It went very well." He hesitated mentioning his news yet.

"I have to tell you, this is one thing I'll never get used to, or like." She pointed to the television set with her eyes. "I miss my T.V. I miss color and my remote control. Call me spoiled if you want, but there are some things I can't wait until they're improved." Stephan looked at her, baffled.

"A remote control, huh? What are you going to mention next? Seventy channels to choose your viewing selection from?" he joked.

"Try one hundred twenty-two." She looked at him smugly.

He didn't respond verbally. He only looked back at her, feeling embarrassed by his ignorance.

"Do you want to watch *The Honeymooners*?" she asked. Personally, she didn't like the show and would rather not watch it.

"If you don't mind, I wouldn't mind if we didn't watch it right away. I have something I have to tell you."

Kate sat down next to him on the couch and waited for him to continue.

"I have some bad news. I have to go to Washington D.C. for a conference in two weeks. The good news is, a renowned professor who is an expert in the field of time exploration will be there." He lowered his head and tilted his eyes up to look at Kate.

"In two weeks! I'm due to have the baby in about four. What if I deliver early and you're not here? How long will you be gone?" The pitch of her voice rose with anxiety.

"I'll only be gone for four days. If I didn't feel that it was absolutely necessary for me to go and attend, I wouldn't go. To be honest, this conference was in the making long before I met you, and I was one of the people who initiated the original planning for it. I can't not go now. Besides, I'll be able to meet with this professor, and may be able to obtain some very useful information from him."

"You're not going to tell him about me, are you? Remember you promised that you wouldn't turn me, or our lives, into a freak sideshow for a bunch of scientists."

"I did want to bring your story up for discussion, but only as a fictional in theory. I wouldn't violate you or your trust, unless you said it was okay for me to tell him?" he asked, wanting to make sure she hadn't changed her mind. Secretly, he did have a desire to explore her time travel at the conference.

"No! I haven't changed my mind. I suppose though, it wouldn't hurt anything if you talked about me as if I weren't real. Still, this still doesn't solve the issue of me having the baby. I want you to be here when the baby is born." She looked sadly at him.

"I don't mean to sound unconcerned, but I'm sure you won't have the baby while I'm gone. If you do, we'll have to deal with it when, and if, the time comes."

"You don't care if you don't see the baby being born?" Kate was disappointed and shocked. She hadn't realized she was thinking like a woman of the nineties.

"See the baby born? What are you talking about? They're not going to let me see the baby being born; and even if they did, I'm not sure I would want to." He looked puzzled at Kate.

Suddenly, Kate realized what she was thinking and saying. "How foolish could I be? Of course he's not going to see the baby born. This might as well be the stone age when it comes to childbirth. I bet he is actually frightened, maybe even disgusted, by the thought of seeing a baby being born. Wouldn't he be surprised to learn that men in my time actually help with the birth of their babies?"

Trying to be understanding, rather than offended, she explained herself to Stephan.

"You're joking, right? I guess time does change a lot of things." He was still trying to understand why birthing had changed so much over time.

"To get back to the original subject, I suppose you have to go. If, by chance, I have the baby, you can always fly back home on the next plane. Unless, of course, you are in the middle of something; and, then, I'll expect you back as fast as possible." She tried to be reasonable and understanding.

"That's more than fair. How did I luck out and get such an understanding wife-to-be? Speaking of which, when are we going to get married?"

"When we originally planned, after the baby is born. I know you wanted to get married sooner, but you have messed up your own plans now. There simply isn't going to be any time for us to get married before you leave. By the time you get back home, it will be too close to the time I'm supposed to deliver. I guess we will just have to wait." She wasn't disappointed, but she felt she couldn't let him feel completely guilt free.

"I guess you told me," he stated, feeling a little guilty.

Their conversation ended, and Kate turned on the television as a distraction for them both. They were both feeling hassled by their feelings and emotions. They were temporarily overwhelmed by the events that lie ahead of them.

Looking at the clock, Stephan noticed that they had missed most of *The Honeymooners* show. "Oh well, I suppose we can just watch the last few minutes of it, even if we've missed most of the story."

Kate watched the show for a minute, and recognized seeing it before in reruns. "If you want, I can tell you what happened over the last twenty minutes you've missed. I've seen this show before, at least twice." She told Stephan the main parts of the story that he had missed.

"Sometimes you amaze me. I all too often forget just how special you are." He listened to Kate intently, not even bothering to watch the rest of the show.

CHAPTER SEVENTEEN

During the next couple of weeks, Kate and Stephan saw less of each other socially. Stephan was very busy preparing for the conference, and time didn't allow him much leisure. He felt extremely guilty spending so much time away from Kate, but due to his work he had no other choice.

Kate stopped working at the gift shop. Her feet and ankles were constantly swollen, causing her much pain and discomfort. Most of her time was spent resting and doing what she could to help Stephan prepare for his trip.

The day of Stephan's departure arrived. The weather was moderate and the sky was cloudy and drab.

"I wish I didn't have to go. I know I'll only be away from you a few days, but it already feels like it will be an eternity." He held Kate tightly in his arms, hugging her.

"I know, me too. I'll miss you very much. Do you realize that this is the first time we will have been separated since we've met? It'll probably do us good to be apart. You know what they say, 'absence makes the heart grow fonder.'" She held back tears.

"That may be so, but I can't imagine my heart growing any fonder of you than it already is. I love you Kate." He kissed her briefly and grabbed hold of his suitcase. "I better get going. I don't think the taxi driver appreciates being kept waiting." He started to walk out the front door of her home.

"I'll make sure I water your plants and . . . I love you. Please have a safe trip." Tears had finally managed to escape her eyes. She could no longer hold them back.

Stephan dropped his suitcase on the sidewalk and rushed back to Kate's side. He grabbed her into his arms and kissed her lovingly.

"Don't cry; I'll be back before you know it."

He felt his heart feel her sadness.

"I know, I know. You better get going, you don't want to miss your plane." Stephan quickly kissed Kate again and departed for the airport.

The remainder of that day, Kate moped around the apartment. She had no desire to do anything. Mostly, she watched television and read some magazines Leala had given her. She went to bed that night feeling drained and exhausted.

I wonder what will happen when I'm born in 2 days? It will be so strange to see myself as a baby. The neat part of this whole thing is that I can help myself and correct any mistakes before they happen. I mean, the possibilities seem endless. I will actually have the chance to live my life over again, sort of. I can be my own mentor, guardian angel, teacher. Who else but me could better understand what I will need as I'm growing up?

Early the next morning, Kate woke up feeling much better. She felt well rested and immediately started to get some chores done around the apartment. Leala stopped by to visit Kate.

"How are you feeling today? I didn't mean to be nosey, but I looked out of my front room window yesterday, and I saw how bushed you looked. I could tell you were feeling tired and sad. I didn't come over because I thought maybe you needed some time to yourself." Leala sat down in a brown tweed chair.

"I was feeling awfully tired yesterday. I was also feeling sad because Stephan was leaving, but I'm feeling much better this morning. I still miss Stephan, but I don't feel exhausted like usual, except my back aches. I must have slept oddly or something and cramped up some of my back muscles." Kate continued to clean while she talked with Leala.

"I can see you are doing better today. You're just a busy little bee today. I was wondering . . . ." She saw that Kate was standing on a chair, reaching to dust some cobwebs that had built up in the corner of the room. "Kate, get down from there! You are going to hurt yourself. You should know better than to—" Her reprimand was interrupted by Kate's yelling.

"Ooooh!" Kate doubled over, bending in half at the waist. She stayed like that for a moment.

Leala immediately rushed to Kate to help her get down from the chair. "What's wrong?" Leala assisted Kate down from the chair. "Are you going to be okay? What can I do for you?" She was very concerned that Kate had pulled a muscle from straining to reach.

"I'm feeling better already. I'm not sure, but . . . ." She cringed with pain again. "I think I'm in labor." She squeezed the words through clenched teeth.

"Really? This is so great I think I'm going to blow a gasket. You know I can't drive, but I can get hold of Kean at work, and he can take us—I mean you—to the hospital." She was gleefully delighted with the news.

"No, don't bother Kean. I can call for a taxi. It will take a taxi as much time to get here as it will Kean. Besides, I'm not going to deliver the baby right away. Unfortunately, I'll probably be in labor for several hours." Kate called the Doctor, then called for a taxi to pick her up.

"Do you want me to try and call Stephan for you?" She had momentarily forgotten he was out of town. "Oh, I'm sorry! With all the excitement, I forgot he's not here. Don't worry, I'll stay with you for as long as they will allow me to at the hospital."

"I knew I could always count on you," Kate began to feel anger at Stephan for leaving.

Within the hour, Kate and Leala arrived at the hospital. Kate's labor dragged on painfully for nine hours before she started to get ready to actually deliver the baby. Kate was becoming used to the cycles the pain came in and was able to carry on a conversation between contractions. During the last moments before she was whisked away to the delivery room, she and Leala talked nervously.

"Are you scared?" Leala asked.

"Wouldn't you be? At this stage, more than anything, I just want to get this baby out . . . ."

"Hang in there; it won't be much longer now." Kate squeezed Leala's hand tightly during the contraction she was having. For the first time during her labor, Kate started using some breathing techniques she had seen other people use on TV during labor.

"Are you alright? Do you want me to get the nurse?" Leala stopped talking to Kate and started speaking aloud to herself, "She's hyperventilating, I better get a Doctor before she passes out. The Doctors never warned me that your breathing can become so erratic like this." Leala turned and tried to pull her hand away from Kate who was still clutching onto it. "Kate let go! I have to get you help!"

When the contraction was almost over, Kate suddenly burst out with laughter. "I'm fine, don't get a Doctor. I was just using a breathing technique that helps relax you during a contraction. I always thought it wouldn't help, but it did a little. I must have looked like an idiot, huh?" Once again, she was able to take long, deep breaths.

"You scared the hell out of me. Where in the world did you learn that breathing like that would help? It looked to me like you were hyperventilating. A person could make themselves faint doing that. Whoever told you to do that must be an idiot. Promise me you won't do that anymore, at least until I'm not here with you." Leala sighed.

"But it seemed to help!" Kate's eyes smiled. She knew how helpful it really was and knew that Leala would be shocked if she were to tell her about Lamaze.

"You just think it helped. Probably because you weren't getting enough oxygen, you were beginning to not feel anything. Kate, dear, that is called being unconscious."

Within a couple of minutes, a nurse came in the room and asked Leala to leave. The Doctor needed to check Kate to see how far dilated she was. Following the exam, the nurse prepared Kate to go into the delivery room.

By the time Kate got to the delivery room, the pain of her contractions seemed unbearable.

"It hurts! It hurts!" She was now convinced that the breathing was a stupid idea and didn't have any real value when she most needed help.

The nurses and Doctor got Kate on the delivery table and put her legs into stirrups that at the ends of the table.

"It won't be much longer now, dear," the Doctor spoke to her gently, trying to soothe her.

"I have to push," her face turned red as she felt her stomach swell hard and tight. "I have to push now!" She couldn't withstand the pain and the urge to push.

"Okay dear, we're ready now. You can push." His response, made as a statement of permission, angered Kate.

Kate pushed as hard as she could. Her face felt as though it were going to burst, and her legs shook from the strain.

"You have to try harder. Push with everything you got, I can almost see that baby's head."

"Oh shit! You can't even see the baby's head yet? I can't, I can't do this." Her fingers wrapped tightly around the delivery bed's guardrails.

"I hate to break this to you, but you're going to have to, whether you want to or not. This baby is going to come out one way or another, and it's not going to be another." He intentionally tried to get Kate angry so she would push harder.

Kate pushed long and hard, several more times. Finally, the Doctor was able to grab the baby's head and guide it out of the birth canal. With one final push, Kate let out a loud, piercing scream and fainted.

"It's a girl. Kate you had—Nurse, she's fainted. Try and revive her."

The pudgy face baby girl came into the world screaming loudly. A nurse took the baby to the side to remove any mucous that may have been left in the lungs and to clean her.

The nurse was able to revive Kate within a couple of minutes. "You had a girl and she's beautiful. Do you hear her crying? She's perfectly healthy."

"Can I see her?" Kate still felt dizzy, but wanted to hold her daughter.

"In a minute. The other nurse is cleaning her and checking her over right now. Are you feeling alright now?"

"I still feel light headed, but I'm okay."

The other nurse walked over and placed Kate's baby in Kate's arms. "Here she is. What's her name?" she smiled.

"Sonya, her name is Sonya." Kate stared at her baby in glory.

"She's so beautiful," Kate thought. "She couldn't be more perfect. I just hope I can be a good Mother and give you all the things you'll want out of life. Most of all, I hope you grow up healthy and happy."

The nurses let Kate hold Sonya for a couple of minutes before taking Sonya away to the nursery so a Doctor could examine her.

Kate was brought back to her room and helped into bed. The Doctor suggested that she remain in bed for at least the rest of the day. He explained that she may need to stay in the hospital for a week before being able to go home. Kate had no intentions of following the Doctor's advice. She knew that if she were feeling well, it was not necessary for a woman to remain in bed, or the hospital, for the length of time he prescribed.

On that thought, a delivery boy carrying a dozen white roses came into her room. With the flowers was a card from Stephan that read: "Leala called. Thank you for giving me a wonderful daughter. Sorry, I'm not there. I love you and will call later today." Signed Stephan. How swee,t she thought.

Within seconds, the delivery boy was back in her room with three more dozen of assorted flowers, all in beautiful vases.

I can't believe this, she thought. I am so lucky to have found someone like Stephan.

Kate thanked the delivery boy and tipped him. She sat, looking around the room at all the beautiful flowers for several minutes. When Kate noticed how much time had passed, she became concerned, because the nurses hadn't brought Sonya into her room yet. She pressed the nurse's call button attached to the wall and waited a couple of minutes for them to respond. When they didn't, she left her room and went to the nurses' station down the hall.

"Is there a problem? Why hasn't my baby been brought to my room?" Kate waited, in an irritated manner, for an explanation.

"Taylor, right? I'm new here; we met this morning in the delivery room." The blue-eyed nurse grinned widely but didn't answer Kate's question.

"You didn't answer my question," Kate responded curtly. She wasn't in the mood to be charmed by the giddy nurse.

"I'm sorry!" Her grin turned to a scowl. She was offended by Kate's attitude. "The nurses from pediatrics haven't brought you your baby because the Doctor is examining her right now. I'm sure when he is done, they will bring her in to see you. If there isn't anything else, I must return to my duties." She turned away abruptly.

Kate returned to her room and waited patiently again for Sonya to arrive. She now understood the delay and she was again feeling at ease.

A few minutes had passed when Kate heard a scuffling noise outside the door of her room. She got up to see what the source of it was. To her surprise, the same delivery boy from before was at the door. He had dropped several bouquets of flowers.

"Here, let me help you." She bent over to pick up two of the fallen bouquets.

"Thanks ma'am. I'm sorry I've made such a mess of your flowers. You must be one special lady to keep getting all these flowers from the same man." He put the bouquets he had in his hand in her room. Kate followed.

"These are all my flowers?" She felt flattered and spoiled since Stephan had sent her more flowers only hours after the first floral delivery. The card she received with this delivery read: "Hope you're both fine. I'm going to try and wrap things up here early. I might be able to get home by tomorrow. I love you. Yours for infinity, Stephan."

Kate felt very moved by Stephan's card and flowers. She couldn't help herself from overreacting, and she began to cry. Kate stopped crying after a few seconds when she heard the squeaking of the nurses' white wedge, rubber soled shoes rub against the floor as she entered.

Kate looked up and suddenly broke into a bright and cheery smile. "There's my little girl!" She rose from the bed to take Sonya from the nurse's arms.

"I'll be back to get her when visiting hours start." The nurse immediately left the room.

"How's my little girl today?" She spoke to Sonya in a quiet and high-pitched voice. Sonya began to cry.

Kate played with Sonya for several minutes before she was interrupted by the ringing of the telephone in her room.

"I bet that is your Daddy calling to say he is coming home," she said to Sonya in a babyish manner.

Kate picked up the telephone receiver. "Hello?"

"Hi, Kate?" Leala wanted to make sure the operator had connected her to the correct room.

"Hi, Leala, how are you?"

"Never mind how I'm doing. I called to see how you are feeling and how your precious baby is doing."

"We're both fine. Are you coming by to visit us later?"

"Don't hate me, but, no. I haven't been feeling very well today. I don't know what it is, but I'm simply exhausted and a little nauseous."

I know why you're not feeling well, but I can't tell you, Kate thought.

If I could only tell you, Kate thought. Tomorrow is the day you're going to have your baby. Tomorrow is the day my life began and you became my Mother.

Secretly, Kate became excited about Leala's condition. She knew all was going according to plan.

"Don't worry about it. Your health and the baby's are the most important thing right now. You get plenty of rest, and I'm sure I'll see you tomorrow." She thought, one way or another you will see me, too.

"Thanks for being so understanding. I know you have no one to be with you right now and . . . ."

"Don't be silly. I have Sonya, and we'll be just fine. I want you to take care of yourself. I'll talk to you later."

"Sounds great. Before I let you go I have to tell you what Stephan did." Kate proceeded to tell Leala about the cards and flowers she had received from Stephan. When she was finished with her story, she thanked Leala for calling and bid her goodbye.

As Kate hung up the telephone, she felt as though the room began to spin around her. After a few seconds of feeling distressed, the dizziness ceased.

My, what a horrible feeling that was! Although it lasted only seconds, it was worse than any hangover I've ever had. Must be my hormones going wild or something. I better put Sonya in her crib and lie down for a minute.

CHAPTER EIGHTEEN

Kate placed Sonya, who was still crying, in her crib and started to go to her own bed to lie down. On the way to her bed, she began feeling light-headed.

I wonder if this is normal she thought. Maybe I should call a nurse.

With those words, Kate's vision blurred, and she became dizzy. The room began to spin around her and the objects in them began to fade from her view. Chimerical objects and people moved before her eyes, and she became frightened. She felt as though she could touch them; but when she tried, her hands passed through them as if they were apparitions.

This is preposterous! How can these images seem so real and yet move by me like they're not real? This is just my imagination. This is all some sort of weird dream and I'm going to wake up. I'll just close my eyes and when I open them all this nonsense will have stopped.

Kate closed her eyes and tried to breathe deeply. She still felt dizzy and began to lose her balance. Quickly, she re-opened her eyes.

"Aahhh!" Kate yelled, her own voice echoing eerily.

As Kate opened her eyes, she saw one of the phantoms pass through her own body. It was apparent that the phantasms didn't notice her. More scared than before, Kate looked over to where Sonya lay. She saw that Sonya had stopped crying and was asleep.

At least she seems to be safe from this madness. I can't take this much longer. Stop! Please stop!

Kate fell to her knees and cupped her face in her hands. She began to cry hysterically. Overwhelmed with the situation, Kate kept her face buried in her hands. She was afraid to look up again.

Just as suddenly as it had started, her dizziness ended. She looked up from her hands and saw the room had returned to normal. She heard the sound of Sonya crying coming from behind her. Kate returned to her feet and tried to regain her composure.

What was that all about? I've never experienced anything like that in my life.

Kate wanted to go and soothe Sonya, but she felt drained and exhausted. She went to her bed and sat on the edge trying to get her strength back. She tilted her head back and closed her eyes for a minute. When she opened them again, she was shocked.

Her head had stopped swooning, but her eyes continued to play tricks. She stared with incertitude at her surroundings. The walls in the room seemed to disappear at times. People seemed to be able to pass through the walls, leaving no distinction where the hall and the adjoining rooms began or ended. Some of the nurse's faces were muted, appearing as chimera.

Kate closed her eyes and she felt her stomach turn, creating a nauseous feeling.

What is happening to me? What is happening to the room? This is the most bizarre illusion I've ever experienced, Kate thought.

Kate reopened her eyes as she listened to the cries of Sonya fade in and out. Trying to evaluate the situation, she paid closer attention to what she was seeing and hearing. Her goal was made more difficult by a phantasmagoric view of her surroundings.

Why do I hear several different conversations at one time, when I only see two nurses?

In an instant, things changed. She saw several nurses and a few visitors all at once. They passed through each other as if they were apparitions. Finally, Kate was able to identify some things and distinguish the people's faces more clearly as her eyes began to adjust.

Am I ill? Am I having a hallucination?

Suddenly, a different reality exposed itself by what Kate saw and heard. Oh my God! I'm seeing everyone and everything in different time. That is why I'm hearing so many voices and seeing things so absurdly.

Kate had noticed the many different styled clothes. She saw some wearing padded shoulders and others wearing bell-bottom jeans. The hairstyles were diverse too. Some men wearing long hair and sideburns while others sported crew cuts. The women's hair was styled many ways, from a bouffant to being shaved on one side of their head.

I bet the walls keep moving, because there has been construction over the years which has changed the physical appearance and boundaries of the rooms and their divisions.

I must be traveling through time or . . . . Sonya, I have to get to Sonya!

Kate reeled around and went to get Sonya out of the bassinet. Her head began to swoon again, due to the preposterous situation she was being forced to deal with. She almost fell over from dizziness before reaching Sonya. Kate managed to get to Sonya's bedside but was unable to lift her from the bassinet. She watched helplessly as her hands tried to grab Sonya who faded in and out just like all the others she saw. Kate cried and screamed, not knowing what to do next to help herself. Her only consolation was that Sonya had stopped crying and seemed to be peacefully sleeping. She felt comfort in knowing Sonya was not having to witness the senseless madness she was enduring. Thinking she had no options left, she fell to her knees and prayed.

"Dear God, please! I don't understand why You are doing this to me. What can the purpose be in so cruelly separating an innocent baby from its Mother? Please don't let Sonya grow up without a Mother. Please don't let her grow up without knowing me."

Kate buried her head in her hands and sobbed. As she tried to get up off the floor, she lost her balance and fell onto the bassinet.

The bassinet! I can feel the bassinet!

Kate quickly stood up. She could see the bassinet and Sonya clearly. She swiftly reached down to retrieve Sonya. She felt Sonya's body radiate warmth beyond the blanket she was wrapped in. Placing her hands firmly around Sonya, Kate grabbed Sonya up and held her tightly in her arms. Sonya seemed startled and began crying as fervidly as she had been before she had fallen into a peaceful sleep.

Feeling exhausted, Kate sat down on the hospital bed. She still clutched Sonya in her arms as she reached for the telephone.

I have to try and contact Stephan in Washington, D.C. I have to tell him what just happened. I wish he were here right now. I'm so scared and I have no one here to confide in. I wonder if I was actually experiencing some altercation in time, or if I was just hallucinating? It all seemed too real to just be my imagination.

Kate had the operator dial the appropriate phone number and tried to wait patiently for an answer to her call.

"Hello, this is Holiday Manor. May I help you?" a pleasant voice answered Kate's call.

"Yes, I'm trying to reach a Professor Stephan Adler. Would you please connect me to his room?" She gulped for air, still feeling out of breath.

"Right away." The line seemed to click dead before it rang through to his room.

Stephan was on his way out of the room, but stopped to answer the phone.

"Hello?" he asked curiously.

"Stephan! Something is wrong!"

Stephan interrupted her, "Are you alright? Is the baby alright? Damn it! I knew I shouldn't have left you when I did."

"Please, listen to me. We're both fine, except that . . . . Well . . . . I don't know how to explain this, but I think I experienced some altercation with time. I mean, I saw things and people as if they, or I, were in different dimensions. I don't know what it means, and I'm frightened. What if it happens again and things don't return to normal? Will I be trapped in limbo, being neither there nor here? I don't know what to think or do." Her voice pleaded for help.

"Are you sure it wasn't your imagination? I don't mean to doubt you, I just want to make sure that you don't doubt what happened yourself."

"If I'm to be honest with myself, it all really happened. What should I do?"

"Tomorrow morning, I'm meeting with a man who is very knowledgeable about time travel. He has written a book about the time-space continuum and understanding different dimensions. It's fair to say he's probably the world's foremost leading authority on the subject. If I could, I would ask him to fly back to Chicago and meet with you, but I know he can't. He's leaving right after my meeting with him tomorrow to go to Europe. He has a very busy schedule, and I just know he wouldn't agree to change his plans for me. I hate to ask this, but do you feel well enough to come here to Washington to meet with him?"

"I don't know about this . . . do you really feel there is no other alternative? I can't take Sonya with me, and I don't want to leave her. She's not even a day old. How can I just leave her behind?"

"If I didn't think it was necessary, I wouldn't have asked. I don't know what to tell you about what you experienced. Maybe if you explain what happened to him he might be able to give us an explanation. I understand that you don't want to leave Sonya. How

180

do you think I feel? I haven't even seen her yet. I don't want to lose you Kate; and I hate to admit this, but I'm afraid, too."

"I suppose I could ask Leala to pick up Sonya tomorrow from the hospital when she is released. I'm sure she would watch over Sonya and take good care of her while I'm gone. If we plan it, I could take the next plane back to Chicago right after I meet with this professor. If I can be assured that I will only be gone for half a day, I suppose it would be okay to leave Sonya." Kate looked down at her baby and coddled her, trying to stop her from crying. "Oh my God, I almost forgot! Tomorrow is the day Leala actually give birth to me. The 29th is the real day I was born. I knew I never explained any of this to you before, so let me do so now. Leala will give birth to me tomorrow, February 29th—remember this is a leap year and the 29th. Anyway, Leala had to choose either the day before or the day after as my legal birth date. She chose the 28th."

"It's your birthday and you didn't tell me?"

"I thought you were already feeling guilty enough. I didn't want to add to it by reminding you it was my birthday."

"I feel terrible. I'm sorry . . . ."

"That's alright, you can make it up to me tomorrow. Technically, it's still my birthday. Besides, I've already gotten the best present I could have received, a baby daughter. Now, she and I can celebrate our birthdays and rejoice together every year."

"Kate, this may not all be a coincidence. Maybe this whole incident that happened to you today is a result of Leala giving birth to you tomorrow. Maybe you shouldn't be there when you are supposed to be born tomorrow."

"I never thought of that."

"I'm sure Leala will arrange something for the care of Sonya while you're gone. It sounds cruel leaving Sonya under these conditions, but I don't know of another way. I think you need to get away from Chicago, and you need to get some answers to this whole situation." "As soon as I'm off the phone with you, I'll make the arrangements for your flight out of there."

"You realize, Leala and the Doctor, and whoever else, are going to think I'm crazy for suddenly flying to Washington. How am I going to explain why I'm leaving Sonya and going out of town?"

"Don't! Just tell them something very important that you can't explain has come up and you must leave. If you have to tell them something, tell them your Mother or Father has passed away and you need to go and make arrangements or something."

"That sounds like a good lie. I'll tell them my Father died. At least they won't question my intentions then. They'll have to understand why I must leave."

"I want you to know I love you. I'll call you back in a little while with information on your travel plans."

"Don't say it like that. When you say 'travel,' it makes me think . . . ."

"Please try not to worry. I'm sure there is a reasonable explanation for what happened to you earlier. We'll get some answers and everything will be just like it was."

"Stephan, I don't think there is a reasonable explanation for anything that has happened to me. I just hope that someday, I will be able to put this all behind me. I love you, and I'll talk to you later."

Within the hour, a telegram came to the hospital for Kate from Stephan. It read: "I have you scheduled to leave on a chartered plane from Sky Harbor Airport. Stop. Be there at 9:30 am. Stop. A ticket will be waiting for you there. I'm sorry things have to be this way, and I love you. Give Sonya a kiss for me. Stop. I'll kiss you myself when I see you later. Forever yours. Love, Stephan."

Kate started to become nervous about her plans to leave Sonya but knew it would benefit them both if she could finally have some answers. She knew she had to do something to protect Sonya and herself from ever being permanently separated, and this trip seemed to be the only possible solution.

A nurse came to get Sonya, who still seemed distressed.

"She's been very cranky. I think she may be colicky. Would you ask the Doctor to check up on her?" Kate handed Sonya to the nurse.

"Very possible. He'll probably just change her formula, because when he checked her this morning, she was the picture of health. I'm sure it's nothing more than indigestions." Kate stopped the nurse who started to leave the room.

"I have to leave out of town early tomorrow morning. My Father has died and I have to go to Washington and make some arrangements. I know that Sonya is too young for traveling yet, so I'm going to ask a very dear friend of mine to take care of her in my absence. I'll have to sign any release forms or whatever papers that are necessary tonight." Kate looked away from the nurse nervously.

"Are you sure you're strong enough, Dear? You did just have a baby. I realize that something like this isn't planned, but I want to make sure you will be okay. I'm so terribly sorry that your Father has passed away." The nurse patted Kate's shoulder.

"I'll be fine, and thank you for your sympathy. Could you just make sure that any arrangements that will be needed for Sonya's and my release will be in order by morning? I'll make sure that I tell the Doctor what is going on when I see the Doctor later today. I'll probably have to have special permission to get Sonya released so early, but at least then I'll be able to give Sonya directly to my friend Leala."

A little later on, Kate called Leala on the telephone. She asked Leala if she could come to the hospital right away. Within the hour, Leala and Kean showed up at the hospital. First they both went to the nursery to see Sonya, and then they went to Kate's hospital room.

"Thanks so much for coming on such short notice," Kate welcomed them.

"We were going to come and visit anyway today. Your little one is so cute," Leala replied smiling.

"So what do you think, Kean?" Kate asked feeling delighted that her Father had gotten the chance to see Sonya.

"She's beautiful! I only pray that we're blessed with our own child. I hope she's as healthy and happy as your little girl." He kissed Kate on the forehead.

Kate felt her body become warm and tears filled her eyes.

I always dreamed that my Father would be able to see his first grandchild be born, and my wish has come true, Kate thought.

"Are you alright, Kate?" Leala asked, noticing Kate becoming teary eyed.

"I'm fine. I'm just so happy that we are all here together like this." Kate thought that now was the perfect time for her to bring up the subject of her departure. "There is one thing though; I need for you to care for Sonya while I'm gone. I would be honored and extremely grateful if you would take care of her for a day, maybe two. I hate to burden you especially in your condition, but I have no one else."

"What? Where are you going? Are you crazy?" Leala asked, feeling both puzzled and annoyed.

"My Father has passed away. I have to go to Washington and put his affairs in order." She pretended to look sad as she lowered her eyes downward.

"Oh Kate, I'm sorry, I didn't know. I'm a little confused though, you told me that you didn't have any family to speak of," Leala asked.

"We weren't close and was a tumultuous relationship so I have preferred over the years to not even acknowledge his existence, but now I must take care of matters." Kate tried to think quickly. "To be honest, I never mentioned him because . . . . well . . . . we weren't speaking." She thought to herself about what a lame explanation she had just given.

"What happened between you two that caused you not to speak to each other?" Leala inquired.

Kean interceded with a statement of his own, "Leala, don't be so impertinent. It's none of our business. If Kate wants to tell us, she'll do so when she's ready to talk about it." However, he secretly wanted to know what happened too.

Kate was thankful for Kean's remarks. She shyly avoided answering Leala's question by pretending to cry.

"I know it's a big imposition to ask you to take care of Sonya, but I don't know what else to do." She began to feel dizzy again, reminding her how necessary her trip was.

"It's no imposition you're like family." Kean insisted.

"As far as I'm concerned, you are family. It will be no trouble at all for us to tend to Sonya in your absence. We'll be glad that we will be helping you in some way, especially with a crisis like this at hand. Just tell me the details of when I should come and get Sonya and when you will be leaving." Leala hugged Kate.

"First thing tomorrow morning."

Kate was interrupted by Leala, "So soon? Must you leave right away?"

"I have no choice, it's urgent that I leave immediately. Besides, tomorrow morning is the only time I can get a flight to Washington. Stephan made the arrangements for me, and I'm sure if he would have been able to get a different flight time he would have," she partially lied.

"The Doctor has agreed to this?" Leala was shocked that he would release Kate and the baby so soon.

"Not exactly, but he'll have to. I will give him no choice. I'm a little weak, but fine. Sonya is perfectly healthy, except the nurses think she is a little colicky. She's been crying an awful lot. As soon as her formula is changed, she should be fine. The Doctor will just have to understand this is something I don't want to do, it's something I have to do."

"So, I should be here first thing in the morning, right? Should I get some of the baby clothes you have at home and bring—"

Kean interrupted Leala again, "Ladies, I'll leave you two to talk about this stuff. I'm going downstairs to have a smoke. I'll meet you downstairs when you are through talking up here. Congratulations, Kate, on your new arrival, and you have my sympathy about your Father." Kean kissed Kate on the forehead again and left the room, leaving Kate with the biggest of smile for that display of affection from her Father.

The two ladies finished their conversation and made all the final plans. Leala would meet Kate down in the lobby of the hospital at 6:30 in the morning. At which point in time, Kate would have a taxi waiting for her outside.

Later that day, towards evening, Kate talked with the Doctor. He reluctantly agreed to discharge Kate and Sonya from the hospital. He signed all release forms needed for the hospital's records. He asked Kate to sign a form releasing him from any further responsibility in regards to her health and well-being. He explained it was against his better judgment to discharge her; but due to the circumstances, knew it was necessary. However, he needed her to sign the release form to protect himself legally.

Kate requested that Sonya be left in her room for that evening and night. She felt the need to spend as much bonding time with Sonya as she could before leaving tomorrow.

Kate held Sonya in her arms as she looked out the window at the world beyond it.

She thought aloud so Sonya could hear her, "This isn't such a bad place to grow up, huh? I think you're going to like it. As a secret between you and me, I liked it the first time I was here, when I was growing up. You'll be lucky to have such a great Dad like Stephan. Besides, you and I are both lucky to have family like Leala and Kean near us too. You'll get a good start in life here, much better than if you were in 1992. I promise you right now that I'll do my very best to provide you with love, understanding, and a good home. Remember, kid, home is where you hang your hat."

Kate stayed awake past her usual bedtime. She sang songs to Sonya and told her tales she remembered hearing as a child. She tried to soothe both Sonya and herself with pleasant distraction. Reluctantly, Kate finally put Sonya to bed for the night so that she could get some sleep, too. Although Kate was nervous about the day ahead, she fell fast asleep.

In her sleep, Kate had nightmares about the eerie experience she had had the day before. In her dreams, she was unable to stay in the year 1956 and was forced to leave. She saw herself passing through the hospital wall, unable to stop herself. Once on the other side, she was again living in the year 1992, and the wall behind her was solid. She desperately tried to get back through the wall to get to Stephan, who was holding Sonya in his arms. She was unsuccessful and failed to reach them.

When the nurse woke Kate in the morning, Kate was still feeling as tired as she had the night before.

"Are you sure you want to make this trip today? You look very tired. Did you have a bad night's sleep?" the nurse asked with concern.

"I had a horrible night's sleep. I kept having the same nightmare all night long. I kept dreaming . . . . well . . . . I have to go to Washington today." Kate's fear had grown, and she wanted for her situation with time to somehow come to an end more than ever before. She wanted to finally find peace.

The nurse bowed her head as if she understood and left the room.

Kate got out of bed and got dressed while Sonya was still sleeping. She thought it was odd that Sonya had never woke up for a middle of the night feeding, and she went to her bassinet to see if she was alright. Just as she got there, Sonya started to cry. Sonya's wails got the attention of a passing nurse, and she went to get a bottle for Kate to feed to Sonya. When Sonya was done being fed and burped, Kate dressed her in an outfit that she had brought to the hospital when she came. Soon, a nurse came in the room with a wheelchair, wanting to escort Kate and Sonya downstairs into the lobby.

"Sonya is still crying a lot, isn't she?" Kate asked, concerned, "She never seems at peace."

"The bottle you gave her this morning was the soybean based formula. It should help ease her stomach discomfort, but it'll take about 48 hours before you should be able to tell the difference, maybe less. She just needs time to adjust, that's all," the nurse reassured the worrying Kate.

Once the nurse got to the lobby with Kate and Sonya, she left them with Leala and Kean, who were waiting patiently, and returned to her duties.

Kate looked at her watch and saw that the time was fleeing. She quickly went over some last minute details about Sonya's care with Leala.

She desperately wished she could warn Leala that she would go into labor within hours. She wanted to somehow make sure Sonya would be cared for in her absence.

"Just in case you go into labor, do you know someone you can trust to care for Sonya?" she tried to be casual with her question.

"I doubt that will happen. Don't worry so much."

"But, it could. Do you know someone who could care for a newborn?" her heart felt heavy.

"I suppose my sister, Vera, could care for Sonya if such an emergency arises. I haven't seen her much in the past two years, but she's very good with children. She has a two-year-old boy of her own. If I need to, I'll ask her for help, but I know I won't need to. This is so silly for you to worry about. I'm not due to deliver yet."

"I'd rather be safe than sorry." Kate resisted the need to discuss the subject more thoroughly.

"I don't know how I can thank you enough. I don't know what I would do without you." Tears formed in Kate's eyes as she put Sonya in Leala's arms. "Do you have a car seat?" She realized immediately that she posed a stupid question.

Of course they don't have a car seat Kate thought. I looked for one myself in the stores not realizing it hadn't been invented and used yet, and obviously I couldn't find one. They don't even make them yet. I wish they did make them. If people only knew now what I know, they would certainly start making car seats. When I get back from Washington, I think I'll start educating people on the dangers of a baby or child traveling in a car unprotected. Maybe I can get someone to listen and take heed. Maybe they'll start making car seats. It's the least I can do as a responsible Mother.

"A car seat? What's that?" Leala looked baffled.

"Never mind, it would take too long to explain. I see that my taxi is here. I best be going. I don't want to miss my plane." Kate kissed Sonya and Leala on the cheek. She hugged Kean goodbye.

Kate wiped the tears from her eyes and started to walk to the waiting taxi.

"Wait!" Leala called out after Kate.

Kate stopped and turned around to find out what Leala wanted.

"The jeweler called from the place where you brought the locket to be repaired. Do you want me to pick it up for you?"

"The locket is ready! No, I'll pick it up on my way to the airport. Thanks anyway." Kate was happy the locket was ready.

She turned around one last time before getting into the taxi and waved goodbye.

Although Kate was sad and disheartened about leaving, she knew she was doing the right thing for all involved. She knew she couldn't truly feel safe and provide a good home for Sonya and Stephan without having some satisfying answers to her problem. Possibly, she would get some help in Washington.

CHAPTER NINETEEN

Picking up her blue pin-flowered overnight bag that lay on the ground by her feet, she got into the taxi.

"Where to, ma'am?" the twenty-three-year-old taxi driver asked as the taxi drove away from the curb.

"I need to go to Sky Harbor Airport on Milwaukee Avenue, but first take me to Broadway and Foster."

The taxi sped off while Kate looked back with sadness and waved to Leala and Kean. She continued to wave as they disappeared from her sight.

The guilt Kate was feeling was beginning to overwhelm her. Leaving her one-day old baby girl behind was more difficult than she anticipated, even though she knew Sonya was too young to travel and this trip was necessary to their future well-being. Trying to be more cognitive than emotional, she sat back on the cold leather cab seat and tried to relax.

The buildings were blurred from the moving taxi as she leaned her head on the cold glass window and closed her eyes. The moistness of her breath caused patches of fog to build on the window, creating images of abstract objects.

Kate was tired, but at the same time she was feeling a new strength, a mental and emotional strength one discovers when they bring new life into the world.

Despite her current problem, in general, whole new aspects of life and herself were brought into light during her pregnancy and Sonya's birth: An appreciation for the simple which spawns the extraordinary; a new faith in mankind and a drive to make life good and fulfilling; a new worth and sense of belonging; a love of, and for, life.

Pulling up to a curb at the corner, the taxi driver announced, "We're here. You want me to wait for you, right?"

Stepping out of the cab, she nodded and replied, "Yes, I'll be back in a few minutes. I just have to check on something at that jewelry store." She pointed to a small glass enclosed storefront thirty feet from where she stood.

Upon entering the store, Kate felt a chill travel through her entire body. She attributed it to the drastic changes her body and hormones were going through. Changes more commonly known in her era as postpartum, a term still not used or familiar to people of this era. Regardless of its name, she knew her physical and mental state were in havoc due to having just given birth.

"Ah, Miss Taylor, how well you a look, and how nice it is to a see you again," the elderly store owner flattered in his slight Italian accent.

"Thank you. Is it ready?"

"Most certainly is. I told a you we are a small but efficient jewelers," he answered in a jestful way.

"Wonderful, may I see it?"

"Let me a go in back and get it for a you."

In his absence, Kate thought about her daughter and the locket that would be her daughter's someday.

"Oh, it's beautiful!" Kate exclaimed after he returned and placed it in her hands.

The gold locket now shined fully. It had been perfectly repaired, with the new back panel appearing perfectly matched with the original front panel. Mr. Lombardi had even matched the script writing technique. She couldn't believe her eyes. It looked brand-spanking new, sparkling in the bright lights that illuminated from fixtures mounted on the ceiling above.

"Look at a the inscription, Miss Taylor. Make a certain every word is accurate. I do a aim to please here."

Taking a more intense look at the locket, she began to read the inscription. Aloud, she read, "'Tis wise to learn. 'Tis God-like to create."

Turning it over, she saw the initial of her name engraved on the backside of the locket.

"I don't know how to thank you enough. You've completed it beautifully."

"No, no, I just a fix it, and did what a you asked. You're the one who a completed it. What an inspiring message to a place near one's heart."

"Thank you; but, unfortunately, I can't take it with me today. I don't have the money to pay for it yet, so I'll have to return next week to pick it up and pay for it."

"Nonsense. You a nice a girl. I trust you. Please, take it with you a now and give it to a your daughter. You a pay when you get the money and please a take your time. I'm a not a go anywhere. You bring the money when you a can."

"I don't know what to say."

"Say, 'thank you, Mr. Lombardi,'" he replied as he took her hand and pressed it closed around the locket in her palm. Then he led her to the door.

"Thank you very, very much. I promise I will be back as soon as I can."

"I know you will, Dear. Now go. You're a young woman with a baby thata needs her," he said as he opened the door and ushered her out of the store.

When she reached the taxi, she suddenly felt dizzy and nauseated. Noticing something was wrong, the driver immediately got out of his cab and offered his assistance.

"Ma'am, are you alright? Here," gesturing with his arms, "let me help you," he offered as he helped her back into the taxi so she could sit down.

"Thank you. I'll be okay. I just got a little dizzy there for a moment. I'll be fine; I just need to sit for a little while."

"Are you sure?"

"Yeah, it's probably because I didn't eat breakfast this morning, that's all."

Feeling absolutely ill, she started to have second thoughts about this trip. She knew it was important to talk to Professor Szabo, but she wasn't so sure she was physically able to continue on such a venture.

"I'll be back in two shakes of a lamb's tail," the cabby told her as he dashed away.

"Where is he going to?" she questioned in her mind. Kate laid her head back to rest, trying to regain her composure. In what seemed like seconds, the cabby returned holding a white paper cup filled with water.

"Here, drink this. It will make you feel better."

Taking the cup in her hand, she slowly drank the water. Beginning to feel better, Kate, again, thanked the driver, while he was getting back in the taxi.

People behaved so differently in this era than they did in her own, she thought. By comparison, the people of this time were more trusting, compassionate, and helpful. The children, in general, were more polite and well mannered. I guess Vietnam, terrorist attacks, racial violence and Watergate all have a way of changing people and their views, besides all the more personal culture change caused by women's lib, divorce, recession, drugs, and crime.

Feeling happy to be a part of this place in time, Kate spoke aloud trying to use language of the time she had heard others use. "Gee, you've been real swell to me. You know who you remind me of? Shirley MacLaine's brother when he was younger."

"Excuse me, who?"

"You know that actress who . . . ." Stopping herself in mid-sentence, Kate suddenly realized she had just compared him to an actor who was probably about eight- years-old at the present time, a man who wouldn't become an actor of any fame for years to come. Feeling a bit embarrassed at her inadequate attempt to seem keen, she continued on no further.

The cab driver's face was contorted in confusion as he shrugged his shoulders, and started the engine.

"Never mind. I think I'm still a bit disorientated from that dizzy spell I had. I think it's best that we leave for the airport now," she said, her face blushing.

Settling back in her seat, she reached in her purse for a brush. Kate brushed her hair gently as they drove towards the airport.

Looking out of the taxi window, she once again began to admire the simplicities of life, watching a small boy gather coal from the railroad tracks and place it in his wagon. Apparently, some had fallen off the coal car that had passed minutes before.

Out further west, the houses were placed far apart with a lot of open land surrounding them. They were so few, the land almost seemed bare of life. A large wooden sign caught her attention. It read, "J. Connolly Construction, New Homes of the Future. Complete with modern conveniences." It amused Kate to think of what those modern conveniences that the sign referred to, possibly such things as gas heat and storm windows.

Driving along Milwaukee Avenue was like a trip through the Prairie State, but not the same Prairie State she remembered. The one she remembered only existed on the pages of textbooks she read as a child in school. Looking around her, Kate commented, "So this is what they mean by 'Prairie State.' The wild flowers are beautiful."

"They sure are, ma'am."

The land surrounding them looked vast and untouched by anything or anyone but nature. It was a sight she knew she would always remember. The colors and fresh smells lingered as she once again closed her eyes to rest.

Half of an hour had passed when they reached the airport. The airport was small and unimpressive, only servicing private, chartered planes. There was no immense tower like the one she remembered pillaring at O'Hare Airport. The airport was modest, a one story, level, brick building with two designated runways for the planes to use. The grounds were unkempt, garbage swirling freely around the building entrance.

"That will be three dollars and twenty cents."

Pulling a five-dollar bill out of her wallet, Kate gave it to the driver. "This is for all the trouble I've caused you."

"Thanks, thanks a bundle; but you were no trouble at all. Have a safe trip, and thanks, again." His face lightened with gratitude.

Kate turned towards the airport office building as the cab driver shifted gears and drove away.

After entering the airport office, she saw three other people huddled in a corner of the room. She wondered if they were traveling together and would be on the same flight as her. Having always been hesitant about plane flights, she secretly hoped she would have company on the plane to preoccupy her.

Uncertain where she should go to obtain flight information, she stood still to survey the surroundings.

The room was cold and damp, causing her to pull her coat tighter around her body and shift the coat collar up around her ears to keep warm. Three chairs were situated against the wall, along with a full-size cooler labeled with a *Coke* logo on it. To the left of her, she saw a counter with an electric perk, silver plated coffee pot on it. A sign above it read, "Please help yourself." Behind the four-foot green tiled counter stood a man directing her with motions to come over by him.

"Hi, my name is Kate Taylor. I'm supposed to have a ticket waiting here for me," she said, walking to the counter.

"Let me check," the fortyish man replied. His features were plain except for a two-inch scar he bore above his left eyebrow. He wore a blue cap, which was a size too small, causing the hat to perch on his head awkwardly. His eyes were dark and he sported a small mustache in a popular style of the time.

The two women who were chatting with the man they stood near looked as if they could be Mother and daughter. Both women wore fur hats with long knit flaps on the sides that they tied under their chins.

"Excuse me, Miss Taylor," he spoke trying to gain her attention. "I have your ticket right here in front of me. You'll be leaving on flight 229. It'll be departing in just a few minutes. Please try and make yourself comfortable 'til then. Pour yourself a cup of coffee, or get a bottle of soda pop, and sit if you like. It won't be too long of a wait. "Here," he said, extending his hands out to her, "Let me take your luggage and check it in."

"That sounds fine, thank you. Will those people standing over there be on the flight with me?"

"They surely will," he replied as he took Kate's bag and walked into a back room.

"I heard they named the song, *Let There Be Peace on Earth*," Kate overheard the older of the two women say.

The elder woman wore a black wool coat with small white specks on it, which was quite a contrast of the bright red, large-buttoned coat that the younger woman was wearing.

The gentleman that conversed with them looked neat and trim. His hair, slightly grayed at the temples, was visible beneath the wide brimmed gray hat he was wearing.

"I can't believe it has become so popular already," the girl in the red coat said.

"Well, I think it's a marvelous song," the elder woman commented. "To think a group of teenagers felt that emotionally moved by the Christmas season that they wanted to convey a message of love and peace through song to others."

"Mark my words, Ladies, someday that song will become a favorite traditional Christmas song. Its meaning is pertinent to all the people of the world unlike those new rock n' roll Christmas tunes that contain little or no meaning. I just can't figure out most teenagers these days. They listen to that loud, obnoxious music and—"

"Now, Dear, calm down. You know what the Doctor said, and you're getting carried away with yourself again. Mary, your Father and I have a surprise for you," the Mother interceded. "Your Father will be starting a new job this coming summer."

"How neat!"

"The best part is that while you will be starting college in Chicago next fall, your Father will be working in his new job . . . . in Chicago, too! Won't it be wonderful that we will be able to still be together as a family? We're going to move and reside here when the job transfer is finalized," she gleefully exclaimed, her face glowing with excitement.

Grabbing her daughter with open arms, she then proceeded to embrace her in a hug.

"Oh, Mother, this is so swell! I can't believe what I'm hearing. It's such a relief. I didn't want to tell you and sound like a sissy, but I was a little frightened about moving away from home and starting college."

Their conversation ended abruptly due to an announcement being made by the flight coordinator. "The plane is fueling up now. Prepare yourselves for departure. You should be leaving in about ten minutes."

Instead of sitting down, Kate paced the dirty green linoleum floor. Although feeling a bit unnerved about the flight ahead of her, she still felt intense excitement about seeing Stephan, causing her to smile. Although it had only been a week since she last saw him, she missed him tremendously. His love and support was of great comfort to her. She knew he would always be there for her no matter what happened, and she cherished him for that.

Settling herself, Kate leaned upon the wall in silence until she heard an announcement to board the plane.

CHAPTER TWENTY

Once aboard the plane, Kate was shocked at the pilot's appearance.

The pilot, a pugnacious sort of character, looked grubby. An unshaven, two-day growth of facial hair made him look as non-conforming of middle class social ideals as did his attitude. His eyebrows, thick and bushy, almost met at the center of his furrowing forehead. His eyes, dark and bloodshot, showed no signs of a being benign. His voice was gruff and his speech blatant.

The pilot closed the plane hatch and turned around and stood, looking sternly at his passengers.

"I got three rules on this plane. One, no smokin or eatin'; two, once we're in the air, don't bother me unless someone is dyin'. I'm not a tour guide, so don't expect sightseein' information. Flying a plane ain't easy; it takes concentration and skill. Three, stay belted in your seats for safety reasons, and don't bother to ask . . . . there's no toilet. Oh, and have a nice trip and welcome to Chicago Charter Planes."

Looking over at the others and feeling like a fellow plane inmate, Kate could see how offensive this pilot was to them. Mary's mouth hung slightly open in vexation. Her Mother, while rolling her eyes to the side, tugged at her husband's arm, pleading with him to contain his outrage. Kate, rubbing her neck with her hand, was not angered, but astounded, amazed that a man like Pete Bonner was allowed to charter C.C.P. company planes.

Kate's next thoughts pertained to Stephan's arrangement of this flight. He obviously wasn't aware of the company's lack of responsible hiring standards. I'm sure he thought I would be traveling in better class.

Mary's Mother looked over to Kate and into her eyes as if she were searching for an answer to the pilot's belligerent attitude. In response, Kate shrugged her shoulders and lowered her eyes as she seated herself on a bench in the back. There were two more bench type seats in the plane, one in front of the other. Each bench was capable of accommodating two people.

The sound of the engine starting up momentarily startled Kate as she watched the others seat themselves. Mary, sitting in a seat by herself, leaned on the window next to her to peer out. Her parents sat together in silence, both staring ahead at nothing in particular.

Kate became increasingly fretful about leaving her baby behind. Even though she knew she would be gone for a day, maybe two, she anticipated it feeling like an eternity. Tears swelled up in her eyes as she thought of holding Sonya in her arms.

Kate had become very happy and content living in 1956. Her new family and friends made her life seem fulfilled. Yet, part of her always felt out of place, not quite belonging, like an orphan in time. Still unsure and inquisitive, she desperately wanted answers to her own transfer in time.

She thought: Did I die in 1992? Was my travel through time a freak accident? Am I and everyone else existing in another dimension? More importantly, could I return to 1992?

The plane was up in flight by the time Kate had noticed. Traveling by plane was commonplace for her and to people of her time, yet she was a bit skeptical of the safety of this particular plane and pilot, causing her to be a little tense.

Kate preoccupied herself by rummaging through her carry-on overnight bag. She stopped after a few minutes, deciding she wanted to wear the locket she had been admiring.

I wonder if Sonya will think this locket is as lovely as I do? Did I just use the word lovely? In my entire life I never used such a corny word. I guess I'm getting more with the times than I thought.

This damn thing, she thought. She leaned her neck even further down to get a better grasp on the chain of the locket. Her fingers continued to fumble as the chain slipped between them. The locket fell to the floor as she grabbed into the air trying to catch it.

"Damn it!" she cursed aloud, drawing looks from the others, who were as nervous as she about the infringing storm.

As she reached for her seat belt to unbuckle it, she thought only of the safety of the locket. I would just die if I lost or ruined it before I gave it to Sonya. With all the jumbling the plane is doing, it would be safer around my neck than in my purse, and now look what's happened.

Initially unnoticed, a storm that had been brewing became increasingly worse, causing the plane to jerk wildly. Kate looked out the window as her heart started to beat faster. Her fingers trembled against the cold glass as she watched the storm over take the sky, surrounding the plane from all sides. Fear swelled in Kate. She had been afraid of storms ever since the one that had brought her back in time.

The clouds mixed with rain and snow swirled relentlessly around. Lightning lashed out striking the left engine of the plane. The internal combustion within the engine could no longer be contained as it burst into flames, instantly burning it out. The passengers were jerked violently about in their seats. Kate, already being unbelted, was tossed to the floor. The plane took a dive forward and down.

"What the hell?" Pete Bonner shouted as he tried to regain control of the aircraft.

Mary's Mother, in confusion, unbuckled herself and instinctively went to check on her daughter's safety.

In a panicked voice, which was barely audible over the thrashing noise of the plane and storm, Pete yelled, "We're going down! God help us! Hang on . . . . Son-of-a-bitching thing!"

The pilot struggled to maintain what little, if any control, he had of the plane. Suddenly, the plane descended at alarming speed, throwing the passengers about the plane.

"We're going to die! Oh, my God, we're going to die!" Mary screamed.

"Paul," her Mother called out to her husband, "where are you?" she cried out, laying helplessly injured and dazed on the floor.

Paul had bumped his head on the sidewall of the plane during the thrusting of the plane. Blood trickled down the side of his face and his chest heaved with every breath he took. He was barely conscious and unable to respond to his wife's plea.

The sky grew dark and mystical. Suddenly, Kate knew what was happening. The horrendous force of the storm was too similar to the one she had experienced before. She again was entering some sort of hole in time. She knew she was going to be rejected from the existence, the life she was now leading.

"I won't let it happen again! I can't, I just can't go through this again!" she shouted, fear overwhelming her.

The next thought coming to her mind was the locket. She recalled how she found it, old and broken, just before the storm that whisked her back in time. Now here, just minutes earlier she had dropped the locket, possibly losing it.

The locket! I've got to find the locket!

That's how—It was a plane crash she thought. I didn't die in 1992. I died in 1956. That was Sonya's locket I found.

"Noooo . . . . I won't let this happen. Not now, not again. I have a life now and people I love and who love me. You can't do this!" she yelled. Her eyes, red and swollen, poured out with tears as she pleaded with God.

"I'm not going to let you. The locket!" she ranted, almost babbling. In a panic she began to desperately search for the locket on the floor. Unmindful of her immediate, impending death, she felt all around the floor for it. I've got to find the locket!" Kate thought it may be her connection to 1956 and that it would save her from a date with destiny.

"I'll stop you! Where is it?" she cried, continuing the search.

Her eyes were so flooded with tears, her vision was blurred. With little fight left in her, she exerted herself to make a far reach. While trying to attain the locket, the plane plummeted.

Reaching as far as she could under one of the seats, her fingertips felt the cold touch of the chain. She strained her body and arm as far forward as she could, then wiggled her fingers trying to grab the locket. Abruptly, the plane made another jerk, tossing her to her side. Savagely, she scampered, trying to get back to where she had felt the locket. Crawling and fighting her way through scattered objects and broken glass, she received several cuts and bruises on her legs and face.

Indifferent to her pain and the surroundings, her only objective was to get the locket. She believed conclusively that retaining it would stop this vicious cycle she seemed destined to be part of.

Feeling distraught with little strength left, she willed herself to find it and within seconds had it in her sight. She reached for it with a quick extension of her arm. She caught the sleeve of her blouse on a protruding metal hinge from beneath the seat. Reaching again, she felt the locket caught on something under the seat. She tugged on it with desperation until she felt a release. Almost sighing with relief, she grabbed it and pressed it firmly into her palm. Holding it tightly in her hand, she released a sob.

Just then, lightening again hit the plane, blowing a large hole into the side of the plane directly across from Kate. Simultaneously, Kate felt a jolt of energy surge through her. Feeling lightheaded and oblivious, she helplessly watched her weightless body being extracted out the aperture.

Destiny had finished what it had begun.

Once outside of the plane, Kate seemed to transduce from her human body into something like an apparition. She felt no negative emotions, only a warming tranquil feeling as she began to transcend the limits of time and space.

Seeming to be in an endless hallucination of billowing clouds, reality meant nothing. She was distal from everything she knew as real or logical. Feeling free and uninhibited, Kate, in a trance, hovered for what seemed hours as time, past, present, and future, unified as one.

As in urgency, without control, Kate began to soar. Vivid visions emerged all around her. Passing them in a whirlwind like waves, she continued to journey. Faces and places, both familiar and not, began to loom as she passed through time.

Without warning, her surroundings went black. Familiar smells of baked apples, wet cool, new grass and pine trees delighted her senses. In a peaceful transition, she again became aware. Noticing her body take form and enjoying the sensations it gave to her, a feeling of structured power had been renewed. Yet, in the darkness, she could see herself as whole, and relished the moment, contently curling her body, assuming a fetal position as if being reborn.

Involuntarily, she suddenly released a scream as the darkness turned into light.

No longer were the clouds in a gentle billow. They moved fiercely, crashing into each other, as she passed through them at an alarming pace. Becoming fearful, she searched with her eyes for something familiar. The sun's intense light stung her eyes and blurred her sight. Smells of exhaust fumes permeated her nose and thoughts of death overwhelmed her. Her body became straight and rigid as she felt herself falling. Within seconds, gravity had taken her hostage and was forcing her to the ground below.

In panic, her thought raced. Terrifying questions came to mind as she retraced her life in her mind.

The rate of her travel was making it difficult to breath. Feeling faint and crazed, she drew her arms about wildly, grasping into the air, reaching for something to stop her. With one last gasp for air, her lungs and hearing stopped functioning leaving her limp body to travel alone on a preset course with destiny.

Awakening from a coma-like state, Kate was momentarily paralyzed; her body and mind vacant of feeling and thought. Unaware, she still clutched the locket in her hand. Although she lay stifled for only a few minutes, it seemed much longer to her.

Becoming more conscious, she stretched and moved her limbs. She tried to bring feeling back into her numb hands and fingers.

Kate scanned her surroundings with her eyes. The wooded area in which she lay was all too familiar. However, she could not place the direction of anything or anybody. Confused, Kate didn't realize she was only a short distance from Sara and Jim's cabin.

The large sun in the sky was hot and intense, instantly warming her face. The sound of birds singing echoed in her ears. Sitting herself up, she watched the air ripple with waves from the sun's heat, giving the trees in her view a distorted look. Sitting a while longer, she began to convince herself this was all a delusion. Kate knew something was wrong but was unable to comprehend her situation.

Perspiration ran down her temples and onto her face. Feeling hot and uncomfortable, she wiped the sweat from her face with her scarf, instantly causing her to question why she was wearing a scarf in such hot weather.

Without thinking about it, she placed the locket she clutched in her hand in her pocket. Her body was covered with bruises and cuts, and her muscles ached. Despite feeling weak and sore, she exerted herself to stand. Dizzy and disorientated, she tried to focus her thoughts. Her legs felt wobbly as the muscles in them strained to help her walk. In a slow and feeble way, she struggled to walk, searching for help. Half dazed, Kate felt void of her senses, power, and reasoning. She was lost, distraught.

Where am I? What has happened to me, the plane, the people . . . and my baby?

Suddenly feeling as though a dam of reality had broke in her mind, Kate screamed and thrashed her arms about wildly. Her slow trod broke into a fleeing, undirected run that caused her to stumble around in a misguided way. Her whole body trembled as she embraced her head with her hands. Her chest heaved hard as she shrieked.

"Noooo . . . ., no! My baby! Where's my baby? Why are you doing this to me? What have I done? If you exist and can hear me, God, I want an answer!" she yelled, crying in rapt, her voice cracking from the volume of her overtones.

Her anxiety seemed only to build as she wandered about further. Feeling like a pawn in a game of chess, some of Kate's bewilderment turned into anger.

"What is the reason, God? What have I done wrong to deserve this? I'm not a toy or a game piece to be moved around as you please. I'm a person with real feelings and emotions. You can't jerk me around like this! I won't let you, you bastard!" Shaking her fists, she fell to her knees. She pummeled her fists on the ground and threw her head back and sobbed.

Her heart filled with rage. She was becoming determined to somehow, someway, seek her rebellion for the injustice that had been wrongfully served to her.

Kate cursed toward the heavens until, with one last outburst, she was drained of her strength. Feeling empty and exhausted both mentally and physically, her head reeled, bringing her to the ground. Exhausted, her body relinquished its effort to sustain her any longer. Still fully clothed in winter garments, she fainted. The bright sun beat upon her face, as she lay sprawled on her back.

CHAPTER TWENTY-ONE

"Hello, Mrs. Tierney?" the caller began, "My name is Sheriff Dowling."

"Yes, this is Mrs. Tierney." Leala waited curiously for him to respond.

"I wish I weren't making this call, but—" his voice became deep and quiet, "I'm sorry to inform you, but your friend Kate Taylor has been in a plane crash."

"Oh my God! Is she alright? Please tell me if—" Suddenly Leala realized Kate was probably dead.

"We obtained your name as the closest of kin from hospital records. We found several scattered pieces of paper and one of them was a hospital bill with Kate Taylor's name on it." Sheriff Dowling kept trying to put off telling Leala the point of his call.

"For God's sake, man, tell me what has happened to Kate!" Her voice became loud with fear.

"I'm sorry to tell you there were no survivors from the crash."

"NO! NO!" Leala dropped the phone receiver and ran to get Sonya from her bassinet. Grabbing Sonya up into her arms, tears swelled in Leala's eyes and poured down her cheeks. Holding Sonya tightly and safely in her arms, she rushed back to the telephone.

"I want to see her. Where are you?" her voice trembled.

"I'm afraid that won't be possible, ma'am."

"What do you mean that won't be possible? I'm the closest person she had to family. I said I want to see her!" Leala repeated with conviction.

"Ma'am, I didn't want to tell you this, but the plane crash was a mess. We've already found pieces of the plane as far as five miles from the sight of the wreck. Please don't make me be more graphic than I already have been. Try and understand there just isn't any way for you to see her."

Horrified and numb, the color drained from Leala's face as she tried to absorb the shock of the news.

"Ma'am, is there anyone else I should notify of her death?"

Barely able to speak, Leala answered. "I'll call anyone that should be notified." Her arms began to feel limp, so she placed Sonya on the couch, cradling her snugly in its cushions.

"We'll be in contact with you. We have a lot of people searching through the wreckage right now. If we come across any of her belongings, we'll make sure they reach you. Any remains we find will be brought to Forseyth's Funeral Parlor. I'm sorry that this happened and my sympathies are with you." Feeling horrible about being tactless and crude at times in the conversation, the Sheriff quickly hung up the phone.

Leala, still in shock, hung up the telephone slowly. Her thoughts seemed to race wildly, yet she could not focus or concentrate on even one of them. After a few moments of confusion and mental numbness, she began to regain some control of her thinking and actions.

"I must call Stephan," she thought. "How do I tell him?"

Reaching for the phone, her arm and hand trembled making it difficult to dial. However, she did make the call and got in contact with Stephan.

"Hello, this is Professor Adler."

"Stephan, this is Leala." Leala found it difficult to continue and her silence seemed long.

"What? What's wrong?" Stephan knew that Leala would not be calling him unless something was wrong.

"Kate's dead. The plane crashed," the words burst out of her mouth before her throat swelled shut from her own denial.

Stephan didn't respond at first and the silence between them was agonizing for them both. Stephan was the first to finally break the silence.

"Where did the plane go down?" The words choked in his throat.

"I don't know."

"Well, where did you get the call from?" he asked impatiently.

"I don't know." Her voice grew frantic.

"What do you mean you don't know?" He became angry at her ignorance.

"I just got a call and . . . . his name was Sheriff Dowling. He didn't say and—" Leala started a howling cry. Tears streamed from her eyes. She became so choked up she was unable to speak.

"I'm sorry! Please calm down. I'm just as upset as you are, and I should have realized what you must have been thinking and feeling when you heard the news. Please just calm down. I'll find out where Kate is." Stephan dropped the phone after he couldn't get any response out of the sobbing Leala.

This can't be happening, he thought. Maybe Kate's still alive.

Stephan rushed out of the room to find out where Kate was and to go be with her. Even though he was concerned about Leala, his own grief over Kate took charge over his actions.

Leala still could not control herself and she became more and more frantic. She called Kean at work and left a message for him of Kate's death and to come home immediately. By the time Kean had reached home, he found Leala in a frenzy, curled up on the floor clutching her stomach. Sonya lay awake but peacefully on the couch.

"Oh my God! Leala, Leala, what is it?" Kean's voice blared.

Almost unconscious, Leala managed to mutter a few words. "Get me to the hospital. Something is wrong, it hurts—" Leala fainted.

Kean grabbed Leala up in his arms, feeling her warm and sweating body become limp. After he put her in the car, he rushed back and asked their neighbor, Mrs. Connolly, to watch Sonya while he rushed Leala to the hospital.

Once they reached the hospital and Leala was in the care of her Doctor, Kean temporarily emotionally fell to pieces.

Kean prayed, "Dear God, this isn't fair. Why did you have to take Kate? Why is this happening to Leala and me? Please make her and the baby be alright."

Kean placed his head into his hands and quietly sobbed for a few minutes. Over an hour passed before the Doctor came to talk with him.

"Mr. Tierney?" The Doctor asked to make sure he was speaking to the right man.

Kean looked up at the Doctor.

"Your wife has gone through a great trauma. She has gone into labor and the baby and her seem to be in some distress. We are going to do a cesarean section."

"What is that? Is she going to be alright?" Kean looked worried.

"It's an operation where we surgically open up your wife's uterus and remove the baby. It's much safer than trying to have her deliver the baby naturally now. Please don't be alarmed by the word surgery. We've performed many of these cesareans. Your wife and the baby will be just fine as long as there are no other complications involved." The Doctor tried to be reassuring.

"How long will it take and can I see her?" Kean asked feeling overwhelmed.

"It would be best if you didn't see her now. We have given her something that has made her quite sleepy. The whole procedure should take about two hours. I'll have a nurse inform you when we are all done. Then, as soon as Leala is in our recovery room, you can see her and the baby." The Doctor shook hands with Kean and gave him a quick pat on the shoulder for reassurance before he departed the room

Stephan took the next plane home. When Stephan reached the site of the crash, he had some difficulty getting past the police officers on the scene. With some persuasion, he managed to convince them to allow him through the rope barriers they had placed up around the area.

Stephan interrupted him, "You don't understand, I have to look for her. Please . . . ."

"I suppose it wouldn't hurt, if you promise to stay in the area. We don't want to have to send a search party out looking for you."

"Thank you." Stephan walked away from the officer without saying another word.

Stephan searched for over an hour before becoming distraught. Feeling discouraged, he dropped to his knees in dismay.

"NOOOO!" he yelled, as loud as his voice would allow. Cupping his face in his hands, he sobbed and thought.

"Why? Damn it! Kate, you can't be dead. Please . . . . Where are you? I need you."

"Mr. Adler, sir, are you okay?" the officer asked.

Stephan looked up at him, but didn't answer.

"I found this while searching; does it belong to Miss Taylor?" He held out his hand to show Stephan.

Stephan looked startled and just nodded a yes to the officer who then placed it in Stephan's hand. Suddenly, a new reality began to form for the grieving Stephan.

"Is there something I can do for you, sir?" the officer asked, trying to be helpful.

"No, no, you've already done more than enough." The officer turned and walked away.

Stephan stared into his hands for a while before his thoughts fell into place.

This is so unfair. I finally find someone I truly love more than life itself, and she's taken away from me. Kate, I love you and I always will!

Shaking his fists towards the sky, he damned the Heavens above. Crying, his whole body shook and he abruptly walked away to his car.

CHAPTER TWENTY-TWO

When Kate awoke in 1992, she found herself lying in a hospital bed. Her friend Sara had been patiently staying at her bedside for a couple of days while Kate had lay unconscious. Sara smiled with relief as Kate opened her eyes and looked around.

"Kate, Kate, can you hear me? Are you alright? I've been worried sick about you." Sara's voice urged Kate for a response.

At first, she could not verbally respond. Instead she continued to lay motionless as tears swelled in her eyes. After a few minutes, her tears broke loose and she began screaming. Sara became frightened by Kate's behavior and pushed a button to summon a nurse.

"It's alright; you're home now. I'm here, and you're okay. Please stop and tell me what's wrong. What happened out there?"

Sara didn't know what to think. What happened out in the woods? Why was she dressed so unusually?

Sara's thoughts were interrupted by the entrance of three nurses. They rushed in, one of them carrying restraints, and the other a syringe filled with a sedative.

"What's going on here?" one of the nurses asked. "We could hear her all the way down the hall at the nurse's station."

"I don't know. She woke up and just started crying and screaming, and I'm not able to calm her down. She just freaked out." Sara stepped back out of the nurses' way.

The nurses tried to reason with Kate for a few minutes to no avail. Finally, as a last resort, they tied her arms and legs to the bed with the restraints. After they got her secured to the bed, one of the nurses attempted to inject her with the needle, pausing only for a moment to try and comfort Kate with words who looked terribly frightened.

"It's okay, dear, this won't hurt you. This is just to help you relax a little. All you'll feel is a slight prick and a little burning sensation for a few seconds." The nurse cleaned a spot on her arm and gave her the shot. "There . . . . isn't that much better?"

Kate's body fell limp instantly and her eyes rolled a little upwards in her head.

"Is she going to be okay?" Sara asked, concerned.

"I'm sure she'll be just fine. This sort of behavior can be normal. Many trauma patients respond this way at first. Do you know exactly what happened that brought her here in this condition? It is always easier to deal with the patients if we know what caused them to become traumatized in the first place. I hate having to guess, which I find myself having to do more often than I would like to admit. Let me tell you, the Doctors have the easy job. They come in a few minutes a day and help mend people's wounds. We nurses are here around the clock trying to mend not only their bodies but their minds, trying to give patients some sort of peace of mind." She stated with contention.

"No, I wish I did. I've never seen her look so weak and frail." Sara walked over to Kate's bedside to take a closer look at Kate's face.

"I'll have one of our resident Doctors look in on her. Her own Doctor will be in to see her later today." The nurse removed the mild restraints she had placed on Kate earlier.

"Good, I wanted to ask him a few more questions. He wasn't very specific when I spoke with him earlier. All he told me was Kate was very dehydrated and seemed to be suffering from heat exhaustion. He also asked me an odd question. He asked me if I was aware that she had been pregnant and that she seems to have had a late, third trimester miscarriage or delivery. I was not aware of any of this at all."

"Oh, before I forget, I wanted to ask if there are some family members we can contact and notify of her condition?"

Sara paused for a few seconds, hesitating to mention that Kate had a Mother nearby.

"She does have a Mother that lives near here, but I think it would be better if I told her the news. She's very excitable, prone to panic attacks, and well . . . ."

"It is hospital policy to contact the patient's closest living relative."

"I know, I understand; but her Mother can be very difficult to deal with at times, especially when she gets upset."

"Well, I suppose I can make an exception. I just won't write it down, for now anyway, that there is any family for us to contact." She looked sheepishly at Sara and winked.

"Thanks, thank you very much," Sara responded sincerely as the nurse left the room.

Suddenly, but slowly, Kate reached out and grabbed Sara's hand and spoke softly.

"Sara, I need your help. Where is the locket?" Kate licked her lips that were dry and parched.

"What locket?" Sara was baffled.

"Sonya's locket. I know . . . . I thought I grabbed it before the crash."

"Kate, you are talking nonsense. What crash? And who is Sonya?" Sara began to reason that it was probably the sedative that Kate had in her system that was confusing her thinking.

The medicine has to be the only explanation. I have no idea what and who she is referring to.

Kate felt that it was futile to try and explain herself in the condition she was in.

"Never mind, just tell me where the locket is," she insisted.

"I don't know. Do you want me to ask at the nurses' station?"

"Yes, please go ask." Kate's eyelids fell shut as she waited for Sara to return from the nurses' station.

Hours had passed before Kate regained consciousness. At first, she didn't realize she had been asleep for so long a time.

"Are you feeling better?" Dr. Howell asked his patient.

"Where's Sara? She said she would get something for me."

"I told her to go home and get some rest. She said she wanted to stay, but when you didn't wake up for hours, she accepted the fact she did indeed need some sleep herself."

"Doctor, when can I go home?" The word home stung in Kate's mind.

"Hold on Kate, slow down. You are in no condition to be released from the hospital. You were severely dehydrated and traumatized when you were brought into this hospital. Besides, I have a few legitimate questions that still need to be answered about your pregnancy." His eyebrows raised.

Kate suddenly became controlled and calculating. She was getting used to finding herself in new or different environments. Everything that had occurred in her life over the last year had trained her to no longer be shocked by what is her present situation or what may be in store for her in the future. She seemed to be completely capable of handling and dealing with herself and the Doctor. She chose to temporarily vacate her mind of her own memory and experiences as if to allow an alternate self to take her place. Her reactions, however, were a direct result of her not being able to deal with all that had happened to her in the past year and as a resistance to accepting her present.

"Do you recall what happened to you before you were hospitalized? Did something or someone frighten you? Why were you dressed in winter clothing? Do you recall fainting? When did you miscarry or was it a stillborn birth? Did you feel ill prior to when you passed out?"

"Now, who should slow down?" Kate retorted. "Well, it went like this . . . ." Kate fabricated a story about all that happened during her vacation and about her pregnancy. She also expressed her wishes that confidentiality be held and none of this was to be discussed with anyone but her.

Kate stayed seven days longer in the Doctor's care at the hospital. Sara visited everyday and tried to bring cheer into Kate's mood. Although Kate recovered physically, her soul and mind suffered every waking hour. She thought about Sonya and Stephan every waking moment, yet was unable to share her sadness with anyone. At times, she felt her grief swell so much within her, she thought she would burst. On the last day of her hospital stay, Sara came to take Kate home.

"I'm glad you're doing better and can go home today," Sara said smiling.

"You never were able to locate the locket, were you? I know I didn't have any success in finding it. I know I had it when . . . . when I had the accident. I just can't figure out what happened to it after that. I wonder if I dropped it? Did the hospital lose it on me?" Although still despondent her eyes reached out and looked sadly into Sara's eyes.

"I have a surprise for you. It's a surprise that has both good and bad news. I'm hoping the good will outweigh the bad for you." She held out her hand and placed part of the broken locket in Kate's hand.

"Where did you get this? What happened to it? It wasn't broken in half. I mean, I thought I—" Kate thought back to when she reached for the locket on the plane.

I must have broken it. When it was caught on something under the seat, I pulled it. I must have broken it then and didn't realize it because of everything that happened next.

Kate thought it was apropos that the piece in her hand was the same piece she had originally found on the ground near the cabin. She wondered what happened to the other half of the locket. The half she had put together which made the locket complete and beautiful.

"Kate, you never really answered me when I've asked you about the importance of this locket. What's the big deal about this locket?" She looked curious, glancing back and forth from Kate to the locket that Kate held in her hand.

"It's very simple. When I found this locket my life seemed to just start to fall into place. I gained a better perspective on who I was as a person. My life became happy for the first time in years. I guess I thought of the locket as a good-luck piece." She began to cry as she realized the irony of the locket now.

"I don't mean to push you, but you have to try and put yourself back together. I know what you said happened out there, and I also know that there is more you aren't telling me. You're leaving something out of your story. I don't know what it is, but I've known you long enough to know when you are concealing and lying. If you feel you can't tell me, fine; but please let me help you get your life, and you, back in shape. I guess what I'm saying is, you can always count on me being here to help you." Sara grabbed Kate's hand and squeezed it tightly and affectionately.

Kate had difficulty responding to Sara's gesture of comfort and friendship. She knew in her heart, no one is forever and always there for you, except yourself.

"Let's get out of here." Kate grabbed a few things Sara had brought for her to use while in the hospital and threw them in a bag. "You still haven't let my Mother know where I am or what happened to me, have you?"

"No, as a matter of fact, I've had trouble getting hold of her. I tried calling about something else and couldn't reach her."

"You don't think she's ill do you?" Kate asked, concerned.

"No, because I called a neighbor just to make sure of that. She said that she had spoke with your Mom the day before I called."

"That's comforting to know." Kate bid her goodbyes to the nurses as Sara and her checked out.

Once she was back in her own apartment, she still felt lost. Everything that was once familiar to her now seemed foreign and strange.

Am I expected to just continue on with life like nothing unusual has happened? Not only have I just lost my baby and Stephan, I've lost me, myself, and my life.

Kate became lost in her own thoughts, unable to cope with her present reality.

Everything looks the same, but it just doesn't feel right. I don't feel right. Am I destined to spend my whole life searching for the half of me that always seems to be left behind?

She sat down on the edge of the couch, keeping her back rigid. She felt overwhelmed with a crushing feeling of emptiness. Yet, in her sadness, she found herself unable to shed any more tears. Instead, a vacant stare took their place.

"I can't stay here any longer," she said to herself as she stood up.

Without really thinking about where she was going, she grabbed her purse and car keys and fled her apartment. She got in her car and drove for hours, until she finally found herself at her Mother's house. "I have to find out what happened to Sonya," she mumbled to herself in the car. She stepped out of the car and was startled to see the sign on the front lawn of her Mother's home: Millennium Realty, Sold.

"What?" she said aloud to herself. "This can't be. When did she do this? Why? I can't believe she did this without consulting me. Damn that woman! She went ahead and sold the place, even after what I told her. Then, to top it off, she doesn't even tell me!" Kate stomped her way across the lawn to the front door, her face flush with anger and resentment. She repeatedly pushed the doorbell harder than was necessary.

"Damn it, Mother, answer!" Kate felt enraged about her ignorance. She felt it was her right to know that her childhood home was being sold. To Kate's dismay, no one answered the bell and opened the door. She instantly began searching through her purse for a set of house keys she had.

After unlocking the door, she entered and tripped over a box in the front hall. The house looked barren of furniture, and dozens of boxes were stacked around the room, and throughout the house.

She paused in her tracks to take a better look around and to try and fully comprehend what she was seeing.

I just don't understand. Why? She thought to herself. Why would Mom do this and not tell me?

Suddenly, nothing seemed real anymore to Kate. She felt as if she were trapped in a movie and someone else was playing her role in it. She kept waiting for the Director to yell, "Cut, stop. You've done a great job. Let's call it a wrap and all go home."

Although Kate was still angry with her Mother, she was just as curious as to what was going on and why. More than anything now, she needed to get some answers, not only about Sonya, but about her selling the house. She decided to wait at the house until her Mother came back for the evening.

Suddenly Kate thought about the ruby family heirloom ring she used to wear all the time. It wasn't on her finger when she was ousted from 1956 due to her fingers being swelled up from her pregnancy. I bet Mom got that ring from my belongings back in 1956 and gave me that ring telling me it was my Grandmother's ring. Why wouldn't she just tell me about her friend who died and that it is special to her because it was her friend's ring?

Helping time to pass more easily while she waited for her Mom to return home, she started to browse through some of the boxes lying on the floor.

The first box she opened contained her Mother's very first set of new china dishes. The set Kate had helped her Father pick out as a present for her Mother. The next box contained odds and ends.

My first-grade report card, she thought to herself. I thought that was long gone. What the heck is this? Kate held an object that was odd looking. She had no idea what its purpose was.

Becoming a little bored from the wait, she went to sit down on the couch to rest her eyes for a while. She pushed a small tightly wrapped box to the other end of the couch so she would have room to sit. Laying her head on the back of the couch, she began to rest. Within minutes, however, her curiosity got the better of her, and she couldn't resist the urge to see what was in the sealed box. Her head perked up, and she reached to pull the box closer.

Well, I've always been a busybody, too nosy for my own good. Why should I stop now?

Tearing the tape, she managed to get the box open and peer inside. The box was filled with letters and documents of different sorts, and a newspaper clipping. Kate grabbed the newspaper clipping and read it first. It contained a brief paragraph about her own apparent death from a plane crash and how her body had never been recovered from the crash site, although she is confirmed as being dead.

Kate held the yellowing pieces of newspaper in her hand and became flooded with memories of that crash.

Here I am holding this old and brittle piece of paper, and for me, it was only a short while ago that I lived through the crash. This is a long forgotten piece of history for most people. It is still a current and painful for me to cope with and not a distant memory that creeps up on one like a reoccurring nightmare.

Kate felt a warming of her heart when she thought that her Mother still cared enough to keep some memory, even if it was a tragic remembrance. Kate began to wonder if there were other pieces of her other life as her Mother's best friend hidden among the boxes.

I find it so odd that in all my years growing up, Mom never mentioned a friend named Kate. Undoubtedly, I was probably named after her. Why would she keep her friendship and the death of her friend such a secret?

Kate began to search deeper into the box. She came across a sealed envelope with no markings on it. Immediately, without the hesitation of guilt, she opened it. Kate's eyes instantly focused on the piece of the paper's titled information, "Certificate of Birth." As her eyes lowered down the page, she saw that it was her daughter's birth certificate. Temporarily passing over the birth certificate, she searched for more papers that might help her find out what happened to Sonya and where she might be today. The next official looking document that Kate opened would cause her great confusion and alarm.

"Certificate of Death?" she asked herself aloud in a high and nasal tone. Quickly, she unfolded the bottom half of the paper that would reveal who's death certificate it was, although she already assumed it was hers.

Kate became extremely distraught and a little confused by what she read.

"Deceased: Susan Tierney." Kate read on quickly, "Born: 2-29-56. Died: 2-29-56."

Mom said I was actually born on February 29th, but because the 29th usually doesn't exist, leap year and all, they had to choose the day before or the day after as my legal birth date. If I was born that date, how could this Susan have been born on the same date in that year? I don't understand. This whole thing doesn't make any sense.

Kate pushed the paper to the side and looked through the box for more information. She came upon an entire package that was tied together that contained a bunch of papers and documents.

Maybe this has some answers in it. Maybe I will at last be able to find out what happened to Sonya and find out who the heck Susan is.

Kate was not ready for the ultimate shock her ventures through time was about to produce. Although she had learned many lessons about herself because of her travels, she was not prepared to be confronted with the truth of her existence. She was not yet able to understand that complete knowledge of her own being would more than suffice the pain she had to endure to be at peace with herself.

Kate read through each piece of paper without interruption. Although she had difficulty confronting the truth and understanding it, she needed to know all there was to know. She read through all the papers as if it were an unquenchable thirst. Finally, when she had finished, she sat back feeling stunned and overwhelmed as she reviewed in her mind what she had learned.

Kate had learned that Susan was her Mother's baby, the one Leala had been pregnant with when Kate was back in time with her. The baby apparently died a few hours after delivery. Kate learned that her Mother had adopted the baby she gave birth to, Sonya, after Sonya's Mother, Kate Taylor, had died in a plane crash. During the adoption, in remembrance of her friend, Kate, Sonya's Mother, she changed Sonya's name to Kate. Sonya—Kate—was born on 2-28-56, the date known to Kate as her birth date. Apparently, Kate's real birth date had always been 2-28-56, not the 29th as she had been told and believed.

Kate thought more about the confusing and twisted reality of facts she was learning. Then that wasn't me that Leala was pregnant with. She was pregnant with another baby she named Susan, and Susan was born and died the day my plane crashed. I don't know exactly how it is possible, but the baby I gave birth to was actually myself. Maybe that's why I was having all those episodes after Sonya—I mean—I, was born. Two equal entities cannot occupy the same space in time. This must have caused some type of space-time continuum quandary. It was meant for me to go back into 1955-56, but not to stay there in the same form in which I came. If I hadn't gone back in time from the exact point in time when I did in 1992, I wouldn't have given life to myself in 1956. Therefore, I would have ceased to exist.

Kate couldn't keep her composure any longer. The momentous information she had learned was too overwhelming to cope with. She suddenly not only was confused, she felt very alone and afraid, more than she had ever before. For the first time in her life she realized she was completely responsible for herself and, in many ways, for her own destiny. She wrapped her arms around herself and sobbed for a few minutes until she saw her Mother approaching the house. She emotionally wasn't able yet to process the loss, the gain, and the absurdity of the situation.

I have to get out of here! She stopped crying and stood up, looking around as if searching for an escape. She ran toward the front door, not knowing where she was going to go once she went through it. All she did know was that she needed to get out of the house and get away, away from her Mother, the past, and her present. When she reached the front door that was still open from when she had entered her Mother's house, Kate ran into her Mother who was entering. Kate stared into her Mother's face for several seconds and then slipped past her, brushing Leala to the side.

"Kate! Kate! Where are you going? What's wrong?" Leala called out after Kate.

In despair, Leala entered the house and immediately saw the box of papers she had tried to keep a secret for so many years exposed and scattered across the couch. Startled, she didn't know how she was going to explain to Kate why she had kept her adoption a secret for so many years.

"Oh shit," she thought, "why did Kate have to snoop and find those papers? I know I shouldn't have kept everything about her and my friendship with her Mother a secret, but it just became more difficult to tell her as each year passed. Now, she probably hates me. God knows what she is thinking about me and the truth I've hidden from her for so long."

As it was, Kate didn't know what to think of the situation. She continued to run for several city blocks until her lungs and weakened body could no longer keep up with her racing mind, and frantic pace. She finally had to stop and catch her breath. Dripping with sweat, she stopped and bent over, placing her hands on her knees, trying to physically recuperate from her run.

Without warning, even to herself, she burst out in a mad laughter.

This is unbelievable she thought. I'm a freak! My whole life has been spent living out someone else's insidious idea of a joke. I'm completely alone and the last laugh is on me! I'm an orphan of time and space, with no beginning and no end.

Just as suddenly as her laughter had begun, it ended, and she began to cry uncontrollably. Kate began to walk again, slowly and aimlessly down the sidewalk, following its path wherever it might lead.

After several hours of walking Kate eventually found her way back to her apartment. Once inside, she sat silently brooding. Three days had passed, and she still found herself barely able to eat, sleep, or think properly. She lay around the apartment sulking over the terrible misfortunes she had to endure over time. She once again entertained the thoughts of suicide.

By the fourth day, Kate was still not answering phone calls or trying to accept all that had happened to her. Her sullen mood kept her from any motivation to try to put her life back together. She just continued to think about the same things and ask herself the same questions over and over again. She found herself unable to move forward, not even to search for other answers she hadn't yet allowed herself to think about.

Kate contemplated. What is the purpose for my being? I mean, why should I go on? I have no one here for me; I'm all alone. I don't really have a family. I have a good and caring friend that wouldn't understand me or what has happened, even if I tried to explain. Just like before, when I went back in time, I can't tell anyone. If I do, they'll think I'm crazy. This time around I can't say or do anything to prove it to anyone. Leala is no longer capable of dealing with anything of this magnitude, and Stephan—

For the first time in days, Kate found herself really able to feel. She began crying and wishing desperately for Stephan's comforting arms to be wrapped around her.

I wonder if Stephan is even alive, she thought to herself in misery. I wonder if he would even care about me now, almost forty years later in his life. I know he loved me, but he's had a lifetime pass. I'm sure if he is alive, he has long forgotten me, especially since he would have believed I had died 36 years ago.

Suddenly, Kate found herself gaining interest in her life again. Just as before, it was Stephan who sparked her desire to continue on with her life. She now had a burning desire to find out what happened to Stephan over the last thirty-six years. She needed to know if he was still alive.

What Kate didn't know was that she was to renew herself over the next few months while she searched for Stephan. She drew strength from herself and the experiences she had in 1955 and 1956. She would find answers, within herself, to the many questions she had.

By early Spring, Kate was settling into a comfortable routine in her life. She had gotten a new job she enjoyed as a manager in a flower shop. She had made several new friends and felt closer than ever to her long-time friend, Sara. She volunteered two nights a week at a shelter for the homeless, and went to visit her Mother at least once a week at her new home, which she shared with her sister Vera.

Her relationship with her Mother remained very much the same as it was before Kate had went back in time, although she now had a new respect and insight into her Mother's being. Kate never tried to tell her Mother what had happened and who she was. She decided it would be pointless to upset and confuse her Mother by trying to tell her the truth. Kate herself still had difficulty at times trying to accept her friend Leala and her Mother as one in the same. Silently, Kate gave in to the loss of a long-lost friend and renewed her relationship with her Mother for the better.

Kate once again appreciated the quality of life and seemed to better understand her place in it, despite the long and often cruel road in getting there. She realized that happiness was not in what life gives to you, but in what you give to yourself and others in your life. She knew that life wasn't always fair, but she had accepted it and herself. However, there was still a small part of her that had resentment for time and its power over her.

By mid April, Kate knew that it was time for her to find Stephan once and for all. She had known for a couple of months where she might find him, but had been reluctant to examine that part of her past, fearful of what she would find. The possibility of having to close that chapter of her life was something she hadn't wanted to do. He is the love of her life, or was as she feared might be the case, but she knew that she was now ready to deal with what she needed to do.

Kate got in her car and drove to the University. She knew he would no longer work there, but had hoped they would be able to tell her where he is and what has become of him. She winced at the idea that Stephan may be dead. Yet, she felt just as apprehensive about learning that he may be alive.

What if he is married and living with his wife? He could have grown children and grandchildren by now. How could I come back into his life and disrupt his serenity? He thinks I'm dead. I could cause him to have a heart attack or something if I were to just pop up at his house. He might even think that I'm an imposter; and, for goodness sakes, what would he tell his wife about who I am?

Although the idea sounded cruel and heartless, there was a part of her that almost wished Stephan were dead. She couldn't bear to think of him being with another woman, even though she logically knew he was entitled to have had a happy life filled with love.

She began to talk to Stephan in her mind as if she were meeting him again, now.

"Oh, Stephan, if you only knew how much I love you. I truly hope you've had a fulfilling life, but I still resent not being part of it. I don't understand why it was not meant for us to be together, but I'm grateful for the time we did have. There will never be anyone else who could ever compare to you or the love we shared. I know to you, I've been dead for thirty-six years; but for me, you've only been gone for months . . . ."

"Miss, Miss, may I help you?" a young, handsome student asked Kate, who stood in a daze in the school hallway.

"What? I'm sorry," she apologized. "I was just lost in my thoughts."

"I asked if you needed some directions or something. You seemed a little lost."

"I'm sure I'll find my way." She stated through a smile as she walked confidently away.

Kate located an information desk nearby and inquired about Stephan.

"I don't see his name here on the list of staff members. I'm sure he is probably retired." The girl looked at Kate over her glasses that were sliding off her nose.

"Because of his age, I would be inclined to think he had retired several years ago."

"I'm sorry, I can't help you then." The girl turned away.

"Wait a minute. Isn't there some way you could find out where he might be living?"

"Even if I could, I wouldn't be able to give you information like that. We're not allowed to give out the teachers' phone numbers and addresses."

Kate became very discouraged. She may never be able to know what happened to Stephan.

"Are you absolutely sure there isn't some way I can get some information on him? I really need to know—"

The girl interrupted, "I just had an idea. I think one of my teachers would know about him. I think I've heard him talk about a Professor Adler. My teacher talked about some research studies that this Adler guy conducted or something." She seemed impressed with herself.

"Great! What's your teacher's name and where can I find him?"

"You can find him on the third floor in the east wing. His name is Professor Wyler. He might be in his office right now. It's right down this hall on your left. Look for the nameplate on the door"

"Thank you very much." Kate rushed away feeling a rush of adrenaline go through her body.

After having to stop twice again for directions, she finally located room 3311. She hesitated a few seconds before knocking on the door and opening it.

Startled by her sudden entrance, Professor Wyler looked surprised as Kate quickly introduced herself.

"I'm sorry to burst in on you like this. I didn't realize . . . . I thought this room would be an outer office that yours would adjoin to." She looked a bit embarrassed.

"That's quite alright. Is there something that I can help you with, Miss Taylor?" He came to the door to greet her.

"I understand that you and I have a mutual friend, Stephan Adler. I lost contact with him many years ago and would sincerely appreciate any information on his whereabouts today."

"You knew Professor Adler? He was one helluva man! Pardon my exuberance."

After a few minutes of what seemed casual questions, Professor Wyler assured himself that Kate was indeed a friend of Stephan's. He then invited her in and proceeded to tell Kate what she came there to find out.

"You want to know about Professor Adler? I'd be glad to tell you about him. He was a well-liked man around this University. He was one of my favorite professors."

Unsettling as it may be to know the truth, Kate entered, closing the door behind her.

****

The clouds gathered quickly, covering the April sun. The fresh scent of Spring filled the air. The trees sprang forth with new leaves and the flowers with new blossoms. Time, with its infinite power, once again rejuvenated life.

Kate no longer feared her own mortality. Her insecurities and restlessness gave way to a new-found strength and contentment she had discovered within herself. Yet, she still resented time as if it were her enemy.

As the white stucco house on Crawford Street came into sight, she clutched her hand to her heart. When she pulled into the long and winding stone-pebbled driveway, she no longer could prevent her hands from trembling. Stepping out of the car, she looked at her surroundings briefly. The landscaping on the grounds were well groomed. Moving closer to the front door, Kate reached for the bell and pushed it twice. Her anticipation was building.

A distinguished looking man opened the door and greeted her.

"Hello, may I help you?" he asked in a gentle voice.

"Is this the home of Professor Adler? Stephan Adler?"

"Yes, whom should I say wishes to speak with him?"

"Well, I'm not sure . . . . That is . . . . My name is Kate Taylor."

Without hesitation, but with a compelling stare, he immediately ushered her in. He turned about and left Kate in the foyer as he disappeared from her sight into another room.

The foyer appeared so majestic with its lofty ceilings and stately décor. Its immense size alone impressed Kate. Stephan must be a successful and respected man.

Moments later he returned. "Please follow me this way," he stated mannerly.

233

Swelling with countless emotions, she followed him while trying to contain herself. As he opened the door, Kate's thoughts raced. How wonderful were the times she had been with Stephan, and how much love they had shared. Will he recognize me, she thought.

The room was dim and smelled of a musty odor. Her attention was quickly drawn to an antique oak floor lamp. The yellowed light it gave was anything but profuse. A few more steps forward brought Kate to a halt.

Stephan, now a man of 80 years old, sat before her. His hair, now white, had thinned, showing much of his scalp beneath. His face was pale and worn, and his cheeks appeared hollow. Not only had time been Kate's enemy, it had also been Stephan's. Her heart pained as she stood in a moment of silence.

Without saying a word, Stephan extended his trembling hand. He slowly unfolded his clutched fingers to reveal the missing half of Kate's locket nestled in his hand. Her locket he had retrieved from the site of Kate's plane crash so many years ago.

His eyes, looking sad and distant, filled with tears.

"I wanted to find you and contact you so many times over the years, but I knew it could disrupt the time continuum. I wanted to make sure you made your way back to me in 1955. Time can play cruel tricks," he continued, his voice quivering with every syllable. "I've waited for you and your return for so long. I've been expecting you . . . "

About the Author

Mary Marshall

Educator - Mary helped institute and develop one of the first Paranormal Studies Program in the country that is taught at a college. As a paranormal educator and innovator she now teaches various metaphysical, science, and cultural based paranormal studies courses, and workshops at various colleges, and institutions in the Chicagoland area. She also lectures at events, libraries, and conferences on how the sciences, including physics, neuroscience, and cultural anthropology relates to paranormal phenomenon.

Investigator & Researcher - As a paranormal investigator and researcher with over 20 years' experience, Mary is the founder and director of The Paranormal MD Investigations a scientific and technology based organization located in northern Illinois. The Paranormal MD is not limited to ghosts and hauntings, and delves into all fields, and aspects of phenomenon. The Paranormal MD experiments, observes, and looks for correlations. TheParanormalMD.com is an investigative and research science orientated website that contains many answers and explanations about paranormal phenomenon.

Radio Host/Personality - As a radio personality, Mary produces and hosts her own talk radio show podcast titled, The Paranormal MD. In the past, Mary has guest hosted and co-hosted a few different radio shows other than her own. Her break into radio was as a co-host on a paranormal talk show at an AM/FM radio land station in WI. She's frequently a guest on others radio shows too. To listen to her show and for more information go to theparanormalmdradio.com

TV & Film – Mary has appeared as a guest and been featured on several shows and TV news stations. She is currently working on a documentary, and the title and release date is pending.

Author – Did you think this story, Continuum, has ended? It hasn't. There will be a second book in this series which continues to follow Kate in her journeys, titled *Forever After*. Also, be on the lookout for Mary's nonfiction book, *Paranormal Entanglement*.

www.ingramcontent.com/pod-product-compliance
Lightning Source LLC
Chambersburg PA
CBHW050514260626
47157CB00004B/1318